BONES to PICK

4 50

BONES to PICK

A PHOEBE FAIRFAX MYSTERY

SUZANNE NORTH

M&S

National Library of Canada Cataloguing in Publication

North, Suzanne, 1945-
Bones to pick / Suzanne North.

"A Phoebe Fairfax mystery".
ISBN 0-7710-6804-2

I. Title.

PS8577.O68B66 2003   C813'.54   C2002-906107-5
PR9199.3.H39N34 2002

We acknowledge the financial support of the Government of
Canada through the Book Publishing Industry Development
Program and that of the Government of Ontario through
the Ontario Media Development Corporation's Ontario
Book Initiative. We further acknowledge the support of
the Canada Council for the Arts and the Ontario Arts Council
for our publishing program.

Typeset in Minion by M&S, Toronto
Printed and bound in Canada

McClelland & Stewart Ltd.
The Canadian Publishers
481 University Avenue
Toronto, Ontario
M5G 2E9
www.mcclelland.com

1   2   3   4   5   07   06   05   04   03

To
Ian Cushon and Gabriel Regnier
gentle men

BONES to PICK

"COME ON, DRIVE. We're going to be late. Let's go." Ella pointed straight ahead over the young woman stretched out in front of our van.

"But I can't just run over her," I protested.

The woman lay face up on the pavement in a shallow puddle of water left by the recent storm. She clutched the wooden end of a picket sign under her arm, positioning it vertically so that it looked almost as if someone had driven the stake through her heart. Above her body, the sign on the picket's other end proclaimed CREATION YES, EVOLUTION NO in large black letters. I had tried to drive around her in the other lane, but as soon as I backed the van into position, she anticipated the move and scrambled over to block me. She looked up at us, gave her sign a belligerent little shake, and smiled triumphantly.

A dozen other demonstrators marched quietly by the side of the road. Although less flamboyant than their supine colleague, they all carried picket signs expressing similar sentiments: GOD IS THE ONLY CREATOR; LOVE THE TRUE GOD, NOT FALSE SCIENCE; I'M ON THE SIDE OF THE ANGELS. The best one had a photo of a winsome young orangutan under which was written IN HIS OWN IMAGE? followed by a string of question marks.

"Don't worry, you won't run over her," Ella stated with a confidence I didn't share. "If the woman has any sense at all, she'll get out of the way as soon as she sees the van start to move."

"How many sensible religious fanatics do you know? I am not going to run over her and that's final."

"Don't be so unreasonable, Phoebe. No one could possibly be that dumb."

"She's dumb enough to lie down in front of a television van."

"Just drive ahead very slowly. You'll see, she'll get out of the way before we hit her."

"But what if she doesn't?" Candi chimed in from the back seat. "Suppose we do run over her. I guarantee you that will waste a lot more time than stopping to get her out of the way now. We squash that woman and we'll never get to the museum."

"I didn't think of that," Ella admitted. "You could be right."

There's no doubt that Candi knows how to reason with Ella better than I do, probably because, even after four years of working with the pair of them, I'm still fairly sane. When I think of some of the conversations we've had, this seems nothing short of miraculous. Today's discussion was only middling lunatic by *A Day in the Lifestyle* standards, but it was still in its infancy, a mere chat.

"What's he doing?" Candi pointed to one of the protestors, a short, bald man dressed in a green coverall, who had left the group and was now standing beside our human roadblock. The two of them began a very animated discussion. He pointed to the side of the road. She shook her head and stamped her foot. It's a challenge to stamp your feet while you're lying down so the gesture lost something in the way of vehemence, but still, its meaning was clear. "Looks like he's trying to convince her to move," Candi answered her own question.

Mist from the drying pavement curled around the woman's body. In the ditches on either side of the road, small drifts of hail lay melting in the August sun. In typical prairie fashion, a late-afternoon thunderstorm had blasted through the area with such violence that we'd had to pull off the highway a few kilometres back until the worst of the lightning and hail passed and I could see to drive again. Now, fifteen minutes later, the slush and the steaming asphalt were the only evidence that there had ever been a storm. And, of course, the double rainbow that arched over the hills to the east.

"It's five-thirty," Ella checked her watch for the nine hundredth time. "So now it's official – we're late for the interview."

"The people we're going to see have been waiting around for a few million years," Candi said. "I guess they won't mind an extra fifteen minutes."

"Unless we can get this idiot off the road you probably will end up talking to the fossils." Ella rolled down the window and stuck out her head. "Get out of the way, you moron!"

Perhaps this was not the most helpful contribution to the moment, but it was an understandable one. Ella had every right to be angry. She had worked very hard to set up this interview and to be stopped first by a storm and then by protestors was more than our perfectionist producer could take. The woman on the asphalt responded with another defiant shake of her sign as Ella subsided back into the van. "Why can't he get her to move?" The two protestors had resumed their argument. "We've only got an hour with Dr. Maxwell, as it is." She looked at her watch again. "Make that fifty-eight and a half minutes."

Ella, Candi, and I all work for a Calgary television program called *A Day in the Lifestyle*. As the name so subtly hints, it's a lifestyles program, a weekly half-hour devoted to documenting what's going on around southern Alberta and who's making it go. Ella is our producer, Candi is our on-camera host and interviewer, and I'm the photographer. We've worked together since the program's beginning, four years ago.

Today, we were on our way to the Royal Tyrrell Museum in the town of Drumheller, one hundred and forty-five kilometres east of Calgary, to interview Dr. Graham Maxwell, a visiting paleoanthropologist. Although the public generally associates the Royal Tyrrell with dinosaurs, the museum is dedicated to all branches of paleontology, including Dr. Maxwell's area of expertise, the study of the human fossil record.

The doctor was a world leader in the field. He had spent most of his working life in Africa searching for the remains of the ancestors of modern humans. His ability to find these rare fossils had contributed to his international reputation in scientific circles. However, it was his spectacular discovery of a group of three near-perfect specimens of what he claimed was not just the earliest ancestor of humanity but a whole new hominid species that had made Graham Maxwell front-page news all over the world.

Like their modern descendants, the creatures Dr. Maxwell had found lived and raised their young and died, but they had done so three and a half million years ago. His discovery of their remains added a million years to human history and generated a storm of controversy. Most anthropologists flatly disagreed with Maxwell's assertion that the fossils represented a new species and many disputed his age-dating. At the same time, certain members of the religious community, those still fighting Darwin's theory of evolution, denied the very existence not only of Maxwell's finds but of the whole human fossil record. It seems that just when you think evolution is a done deal, the battle heats up again. Perhaps because of all the publicity surrounding them, Dr. Maxwell's fossils had lit new fires in the anti-Darwinist forces. I sometimes wonder if we're about to have a resurgence of the flat earth theory or maybe the geocentric universe. It's discouraging.

Usually, *A Day in the Lifestyle* doesn't tackle such weighty subjects as human evolution, but Graham Maxwell, besides being world famous, was also a native Albertan, raised in Nanton and educated at the University of Alberta. It was largely because of this Alberta connection that Ella had been able to coax our station's management into letting her do a feature program on him. She had even managed to convince them that Dr. Maxwell was such a big deal we would need a whole hour, not just our usual half, to do him justice. I don't think she would have been able to persuade them of his importance without the help of a full-page feature on him and the celebrated bones that had appeared recently in the *New York Times*. That article was the clincher. If a big American newspaper thought Maxwell was important enough to deserve a whole page, then he just might rate an hour on *A Day in the Lifestyle*.

An exhibition of the famous fossils was slated to open later that evening at the museum, and Dr. Maxwell had promised he would announce the official scientific name of his new species at the ceremony. Our station's news department planned to cover the opening, but it was our five-thirty interview with the great man himself that had made us the first vehicle to meet the protestors at the turnoff from the main highway to the museum.

"Since we're stuck here anyway, I think I should get some shots of the protestors for News," I said. The news department regards *A Day in the Lifestyle* as a joke, but they're not above using any good footage we manage to get.

"Absolutely not," Ella snapped. "That's exactly what these jerks want – publicity. We'd be playing right into their deranged little hands. Besides, this is Alberta. Religious loonies aren't news."

"But why shouldn't we give them what they want?" Candi asked. "I mean, if what they're after is publicity and Phoebe takes a few shots of them marching around with their signs, then maybe they'll figure they've made their point and let us through. You know, like a trade."

"Well, I guess we could try it," Ella relented glumly. "We don't have a lot to lose." As I said, Candi is much better at reasoning with her than I am. "Okay, Phoebe, go take a few quick shots and then get that idiot out of our way."

"Me? What makes you think I can get her to move?"

"You're the one who won't drive ahead like I suggested, so you're the one who gets to make this idea work."

I climbed into the back of the van, got the camera, and put a tape in it. Then I slid open the big side door and prepared to go to work.

"Phoebe, wait! You can't go out there in those." Candi looked down at my flimsy evening sandals. "The water will ruin them."

Although it was early, the three of us were already in evening clothes, dressed in our finest and ready to knock 'em dead at the museum's black-tie reception and dinner that were to follow immediately after our interview with Dr. Maxwell and the opening of his display. I had on a deep blue Vionnet satin that dated from the 1930s, one of the antique dresses that Cyrrie sometimes finds for me on his trips to England. I'd sprung for the shoes, airy concoctions of narrow patent leather straps that even on sale seemed more like an investment than footwear.

I rummaged under the back seat and fished out the old pair of gumboots stored there for just such emergencies. I leaned out the van door and, holding a boot in each hand, whacked them together a couple of times, knocking clumps of dried mud off their bottoms. Even cleaned up, the red-toed rubbers looked a little odd poking out from under my dress. They were also about five sizes too big.

I slopped over to the opposite side of the road to get an establishing shot. The air was chilly from the hail, far too cold for satin and bare shoulders. I moved in for a closer look at the protestors and their signs. I finished the sequence with a shot of Ella's nemesis, still languishing in her puddle. In close-up, she looked overweight, under-clean, and radiated ill-temper. Dirty water had soaked the back of her blue jeans and T-shirt, and her podgy arms were covered in pale gooseflesh. The man in the green coverall had given up trying to make her move but remained by her side. At close range he looked much older than the rest of his group, in his mid-sixties at least. The woman was somewhere in her twenties.

"Will this be on tonight's news?" the man asked.

"Sorry, I don't know," I said.

"But when are they coming to interview us?"

"When is who coming?"

"Your reporters," he said. "I sent a press release about our demonstration to every television and radio station in Calgary. Newspapers too."

"I'm not with News. I don't know what they have planned."

This wasn't quite true. I knew that our news department, like those of other Calgary stations, was sending someone out to cover the opening of Dr. Maxwell's exhibit. However, I'd have bet my house that not a single one of the reporters had read past the first sentence of this guy's press release.

"But we're the Geologists for Jesus," he said as if it explained something. All it told me was that the reporters probably hadn't even opened the envelope.

"We're highly trained scientists who've given our hearts and lives to Jesus," he continued earnestly. "Geologists who believe that God created the earth and all that's in it and that so-called evolution as preached by Graham Maxwell and his kind is a lie." I think he had begun to recite from his own press release. "Geologists for Jesus has scientific proof that God created ..."

"Can it, Stan. She's never heard of us." The words floated up from the pavement.

"But, Myrna, I sent press releases." He made them sound like a form of Holy Writ.

"Yeah, and I'll bet they went straight into the garbage." For all that she was speaking from a puddle, Myrna did seem to have a firmer grasp of reality than Stan. "We don't need press releases, we need direct action. We should form a human chain across the road."

"I think you should get up now and let us past," I suggested in a less than dynamic launch of our move Myrna campaign. Not surprisingly, neither Myrna nor Stan seemed to care what I thought. They both ignored me.

"But all of us agreed that this would be a peaceful demonstration," Stan said.

"And it will be unless they start something." Myrna looked up at Ella, who glared back at her through the windshield with an intensity that practically melted the glass.

"But, Myrna," Stan pleaded, his voice rising and his bald head flushed with frustration. "There could be trouble."

By this time Candi had opened the van's side door and stood leaning out of it in order to get a better view of the little drama being played out in front of her. All of the male protestors stopped marching. They stood and stared at her from the side of the road. Candi often has this effect on men. To say our interviewer is beautiful is like saying that Mozart wrote some nice tunes. That afternoon, in her off-the-shoulder white gown with her halo of spun-gold curls shining in the sunlight and her eyes bluer than the antique lapis lazuli pendant that was her only jewellery, she rated somewhere between a movie star and a minor goddess. Even Stan seemed momentarily struck dumb. Candi took no notice. She's used to stopping traffic.

"Stan's right, you could get into some real trouble," I plodded on. "A lot of media crews will be along here soon and not all of them are as reasonable as we are. You're lucky we got here first."

"Yeah," Candi agreed from her perch. "Some of those network guys and you'd be roadkill." This wasn't quite the kind of trouble I had in mind, but, while it may have been exaggerated, I couldn't honestly say that her assessment of our colleagues was altogether inaccurate.

"Myrna, there's a police car coming," Stan said urgently. "Either you get up right this minute or so help me I'll get Carl and Jason to come over here and carry you off."

When she didn't move, Stan made good on his threat and called to the two burliest demonstrators who managed to tear their eyes off Candi long enough to hustle across the pavement to where Myrna lay. Even for them she was a load, but I think Stan must have done a little pre-protest coaching for just this eventuality because neither man hesitated. One grabbed her legs, the other her arms, and together, on the count of three, they heaved her limp body off the highway. Her bottom sagged perilously close to the pavement and dirty water streamed off her jeans as they hauled her away and dumped her in the loose gravel at the side of the road. She shook off their attempts to help her to her feet. She sat, a sullen heap of resentment and wet clothes, and aimed an unmistakable gesture in Stan's direction, a gesture unworthy of a Geologist for Jesus.

While Myrna made her unwilling exit, the police car had pulled up behind the van. An RCMP officer got out and walked toward Stan and me. Tall and imposing in his immaculate scarlet dress uniform, he was obviously on his way to take a decorative part in the evening's events at the museum. Ornamental value aside, he was still very much a cop. He looked at us and then at Myrna, who by now was on her feet glowering at us from the side of the road. The other demonstrators had resumed their marching.

"What's the problem here?" he asked.

"We're the Geologists for Jesus," Stan launched into his press release. "We're highly trained scientists . . ."

"There's no problem, officer," I interrupted.

"What's this van doing in the middle of the road?"

"I stopped to take a few shots of the demonstration for our News department."

"We're scientists who've given our hearts and lives to . . ."

"You know you can't stop here." This time it was the Mountie who cut Stan off. "Your vehicle is blocking the road. Move it."

"We've given our hearts to . . ."

"And you." At last he focused his attention on Stan. "Keep your people off the highway. Any more of this nonsense and you'll be doing your picketing back at the detachment."

"We've given our lives to . . ."

The Mountie turned and strode back to his car, leaving Stan talking to the air.

"Jesus."

2

I DROVE THE REST OF THE WAY to the museum very decorously. So did the Mountie who followed directly behind us. Ella sat with her eyes fixed on her watch, counting the seconds of her precious interview time tick by. Candi lounged in the back, her silk dress incongruously elegant against the van's cracked and grubby vinyl seat. She gazed out at the muted browns of the hills that surrounded us.

Typical of badlands, the Drumheller hills are mostly bare and such vegetation as can be seen from a passing car is limited to the low brush and clumps of prairie grass clinging to their tops. This makes it easy for even amateur eyes to pick out the hills' clearly defined strata, deposits of sediment laid down layer by layer through the ages. The hills, themselves, are unexpected. For the most part, the prairies hide their geological secrets beneath the flatness of grain fields and pastures, a monotony that stretches to the horizon. But here, water and wind and time have cut deep into the earth, sculpting the badlands and laying bare the bones of creatures that vanished from the planet millions of years ago.

The Red Deer River valley is the site of one of the world's great accumulations of dinosaur fossils. After every rain, crumbled fragments of their skeletons wash down from the hills along with small pieces of petrified wood, remnants of their lush forest home. The sheer profusion of material that weathers out into the gullies is both evidence of the richness of the ancient environment and harbinger of the abundance still buried in the hills. How many albertosaurs and chasmosaurs, ankylosaurs and hadrosaurs, are still waiting to be excavated, reconstructed, studied and stared at in museums, or perhaps, and this is more likely, to be eroded into dust?

"Does Dr. Maxwell look like his publicity photos?" Candi broke the silence with a question that was not as silly as it sounded. We have plenty of guests on *A Day in the Lifestyle* whose publicity photos and reality parted company at least ten years and twenty pounds ago. For some reason, writers seem especially fond of this form of fiction.

"Maybe a few years on the optimistic side," I said. "But otherwise not bad." Unlike Candi and Ella, I had actually seen Graham Maxwell the day he arrived in Alberta. A few hours before his plane landed, one of our station's news photographers had called in sick. I happened to be in the office collecting a paycheque at the time, so I got drafted into going to the airport to tape the event. Every station in Calgary sent a news crew and there were reporters from both dailies and most of the radio stations too. A few religious protestors milled around carrying signs, although I hadn't noticed Stan and the Geologists for Jesus among them.

"Too bad you didn't get a chance to watch some of the tape I shot for News," I said. "Dr. Maxwell held a press conference at the airport. I got some good close-ups."

"It was after lunch when I got back to Calgary and I only had time to pack and meet you guys." Candi had been out of town researching a piece on a performance artist who planned to spend the next two weeks atop a hoodoo near Canmore in homage to St. Simeon Stylites. "I read in the press kit that Dr. Maxwell has a couple of assistants with him. Were they at the press conference?"

"No, just him. There was only one star at that show."

Dr. Maxwell's press conference had been an impressive solo performance. He was informative, witty, charming, and a total egomaniac. Without a blush, he had lectured the group of reporters in front of him about the monumental significance – his words – of his contributions to science. Maybe having an ego like an army tank had been an advantage over the years because now, at least in the public eye as well as his own estimation, Graham Maxwell was far and away the world's most important paleoanthropologist. No doubt some of his less-celebrated colleagues did not share Dr. Maxwell's own assessment of his achievements, but even they had to admit that, by anyone's standards, he was the most famous of their tribe.

It quickly became evident at the press conference that Dr. Maxwell planned to take full financial advantage of his fame to raise money for future digs. His African expeditions, with their huge complement of scientists and support staff plus all the vehicles, equipment, and supplies necessary to transport and maintain them in the field, cost immense amounts of money. In order to top up the treasury, the celebrated fossils and their finder had taken their show on the road. The exhibit at the Royal Tyrrell was only the first stop on a lengthy North American tour that would include the

Royal Ontario Museum, the Smithsonian, and the American Museum of Natural History.

"How old do you think he really is?" Candi asked. "The press kit tells you the age of those fossils about ten times a page, but it doesn't mention once how old Dr. Maxwell is."

"He was pretty coy about it at the conference too," I said. A reporter from the *Sun* had asked him his age, but Dr. Maxwell pretended he hadn't heard the question. "But Professor Woodward told me that he's sixty-five. They were classmates at the University of Alberta and they're the same age."

"You mean Graham Maxwell went to university with that old pervert who lives on your land every summer?" Ella looked up from her watch.

"Adam Woodward is not a pervert," I said. "He's a university professor. He teaches geology at the University of Calgary and he doesn't live on my land. He only comes over to take a bath in the stream now and then. He mostly stays on the forest reserve."

I live on an acreage in the Rocky Mountain foothills about an hour's drive southwest of Calgary. My land borders on the provincial forest reserve where Professor Woodward does his fieldwork during the university's summer break.

"In the stream? That water is freezing. It's right off the mountains. Why doesn't he go inside and use a bathtub like everybody else?" Ella asked, not unreasonably.

"Because he's an integral part of his research and it would ruin the project if he came in contact with civilization."

"So he's still working on that de-evolving thing, is he?" Candi asked.

"Yeah. And I'm actually kind of worried about him. He's had a terrible cold this summer. I was afraid it might be pneumonia."

"Do you think maybe he gave up fire or something?" Candi asked.

"De-evolving?" Ella was sufficiently curious to forget for a moment how late we were. "What's de-evolving?"

"The opposite of evolving," I said. "Professor Woodward is going backwards. He's trying to see how far back along the evolutionary path a modern man can go and still survive."

"That's crazy," Ella said and I had to agree, although I'd never admit it to her. I sometimes wonder how Professor Woodward manages to justify his current research to the university administration. Presumably someone there knows what he does with his summers. Maybe they don't care or maybe they've simply given up on him, figuring that a tenured professor near retirement is a hopeless cause.

"Before you go calling him crazy, you should take a look at some of the flint napping he did when he started into his paleolithic period," Candi said. "He gave Phoebe a couple of really beautiful hand axes, didn't he, Phoebe? You know, he'd make a great guest on *Lifestyle*."

"Now there's an idea." Ella was at her sarcastic best. "You could ask him all about the time he was arrested for indecent exposure."

"Come on, that's not fair. It wasn't Professor Woodward's fault," I protested. "Everyone knows that was an accident."

"So they called him the Foothills Flasher for nothing?"

"Look," I said, considerably annoyed by her attitude, "Professor Woodward is a very decent human being, as you will find out for yourself tonight. He's going to be at the opening. I'll introduce you."

"If we ever get there." Ella went back to worrying her watch.

We rounded the last hill and pulled up in front of the museum, a low, wide building that gives the illusion that like the surrounding hills it is built in many layers. Long runs of polished rose granite separated by thin horizontal bands of concrete make it an architectural metaphor for the strata of the badlands. When it was first built, the Royal Tyrrell seemed an almost integral part of the landscape. However, prairie people have an irrepressible urge to plant greenery. Given the chance, they'd do their best to make petunias grow on the moon. Now, a profusion of well-watered shrubs and trees surround the museum, obscuring its austere lines.

Ella was out the door and on the pavement almost before the van had stopped. She hovered anxiously while I began to unload the equipment. "All right, Phoebe, let's pick up the pace here. Go, go, go!" She slapped her clipboard with her free hand.

I think I'm a pacifist at heart, but some days working with Ella could shift the Mahatma's views on physical violence. Fortunately, before I could brain Ella with the tripod, Candi stepped between us. She yanked a microphone case from the mound of gear at the curb, tucked it under our producer's arm, and pointed her toward the museum. Ella dashed into the building, living to nag another day and leaving us to haul the rest of the stuff.

"Phoebe, you've still got those gumboots on," Candi pointed out as she loaded up with the tripod and extension cords and headed to the front door. I changed into my shoes, tossed the gumboots back in the van, and slung my workbag over my shoulder. A capacious old canvas carry-all, it holds extra tapes and batteries and all sorts of other miscellaneous junk like plastic bags and gaffer tape and lens cloths and whatever else comes in handy on a shoot. It also weighs a ton. Camera in one hand, light kit in the other, I caught up to Candi near a group of sculpted pachyrhinosaurs ambling their peaceable ceratopsian way across the building's forecourt. We hurried past them and on into the museum. Our high heels tapped their feminine tattoo across the lobby's granite floors, past the gift shop, and through the entrance to the display area.

Candi led the way. I assumed she knew where we were going. She usually does, which is fortunate because I was already lost. The Royal Tyrrell has that effect on me. I get disoriented the minute I go through the doors. Perhaps this is because the public areas of the museum are built to accommodate changing exhibits as well as the permanent displays, and the spaces shift between my infrequent visits. The interior is like a vast theatrical set. The walls separating the exhibits are movable, as are the banks of lights that hang from bars overhead and the ramps and platforms that vary the levels in each show. Even the permanent displays can be altered to accommodate special events.

One left turn later and we arrived at the area devoted to Dr. Maxwell's exhibit. It was divided into two rooms. The first and larger was filled with maps and huge aerial photos of the excavation site, as well as a series of smaller photos that showed each stage of the fossils' recovery and restoration. A half-dozen monitors played videos shot at the dig. From one corner, a curving passage led to the second room, the one with the fossils. The passage's walls and ceiling were painted black and the only illumination came from strips of track lighting on the floor and handrails. We rounded its last dark bend and emerged into a blaze of light.

"My God," Candi exclaimed. "This is fantastic." And she was right. Even under the harsh beams of the work lights the display was impressive. In a twenty-by-thirty-foot space, the museum's artists had recreated a section of the gorge where Dr. Maxwell had discovered his group of hominids. One wall of a small gully ran the length of the space and, at its highest point, rose more than fifteen feet above the museum floor. The buff-coloured rock and dusty thorn bushes looked so real I could hardly believe they were creations of the Royal Tyrrell workshops. It was only when my gentle knock produced a hollow sound that I knew it was fibreglass under my knuckles and not solid stone. Nothing in the exhibit was real but the fossils themselves. The press release had made much of this because it was so unusual. Museums are loath to expose real fossils, especially rare and important specimens like Dr. Maxwell's, to the depredations of the viewing public. Many of the large vertebrate fossils on display in museums today, including a good few of the Royal Tyrrell's own dinosaurs, are fibreglass reproductions, meticulous in their detail and indistinguishable from their precious originals. They are light, easy to mount in displays, and much sturdier than real fossils, which tend to be very fragile and crumbly.

In this exhibit, however, Dr. Maxwell's three genuine fossil skeletons had been embedded in the fake gully. They lay partially exposed, creating the illusion that they were eroding from the side of the hill. In reality, the fine detail observable in the bones, their wholeness and their far too perfect positioning, bore witness to the many hours of patient reconstruction and deliberate design that had gone into preparing them for display. The few chunks of bone and thousands of jumbled fragments that Maxwell's team of excavators had unearthed were, once again, complete skeletons, or at least as complete as skilled technicians could make them. I suppose a case could be made against the sacrifice of accuracy on the altar of theatrical impression, but who would quibble when that impression was so overwhelming?

At first, Candi simply stood and stared. Then, hardly noticing what she was doing, she put down her load of camera gear and walked toward the first of the fossils. It was the largest of the three and the most complete. It lay with its left leg straight and its right drawn up to the body. Its torso was twisted so that the right arm seemed to be reaching back toward the smaller skeleton behind it. Shadowed indentations in the fibreglass indicated where bones were missing or incomplete.

"They're so little," Candi said, amazed. The skeletons were much smaller than those of modern humans. She moved on to the second fossil, which lay curled in the fetal position about ten feet away. "Where's the third one?" she asked. "There are supposed to be three."

I stood beside her and pointed to another very small skull in front of the second skeleton's chest, nestled in its arms. Except for part of the cranium and a few of the upper vertebrae, the remainder of the third fossil's tiny bones were missing.

"Oh no," Candi was horrified. "It's a baby." She is the only person I know who could be genuinely grief-stricken over something that died three million years ago. "Oh, Phoebe, what can have happened to them? The poor little things."

As she spoke, the work lights went out and we were left in total darkness except for the red glow of the Exit sign over the double doors in the back wall. In the next second the banks of display lights blazed to life like lights in a theatre at the start of a play. Their focused beams and gelled lenses added the last touch of perfection to the display's illusion. We stood at the bottom of an African gully, under a cloudless African sky, staring at stones that were once alive.

"Wonderful, isn't it?" A deep male voice that I recognized as Graham Maxwell's boomed from the darkness behind us. "Of course we came in through the emergency exit, but the public enters through a darkened passage from the outer room and so they get the real drama of the lighting full force."

"And the whole thing was built here at the Royal Tyrrell?" I heard Ella ask.

"Right down to the last thorn bush," Dr. Maxwell confirmed. "And you can take the whole thing apart in an afternoon, toss it in a shipping container, and truck it to the next exhibition site."

"Even the fossils?"

"No no, not the fossils. They travel separately. I don't know if you can see from here, but each bone is mounted individually in the exhibit," he explained. "They rest in lined cradles that are built right into the fibreglass. When it comes time to move, Gillian takes them out of their cradles and packs them in crates in hunks of moulded foam. She's got it down to an art. Turn the working lights up again, would you please, Gill?" He called to someone outside the room.

The display lights faded and the work lights came back on, revealing Ella and Dr. Maxwell standing behind us, near the exit doors at the back of the room. Dressed in his Savile Row evening clothes, he exuded the same vitality and confidence that I'd seen at the press conference. A young woman in a white lab coat came in through the exit doors and joined them. A weary Laura Ashley print skirt drooped below the coat.

Although I could tell Ella begrudged the time and would far sooner have charged ahead with the interview, she did introduce us to the scientists. For all the notice he took of me, Dr. Maxwell might as well have shaken hands with the tripod. Candi possessed his attention totally. He stood transfixed, her hand in his. Candi and I have worked together for so long that I forget how overwhelming her beauty can be at close range, particularly to men appearing on *A Day in the Lifestyle* for the first time. I've seen her poleaxe some of the young ones into such stunned silence that they forget to breathe. On the other hand, older men seem to need extra oxygen. Candi is always very polite and waits until their panting settles down to mere heavy breathing before she starts the interview. However, Dr. Maxwell didn't seem to be suffering any respiratory irregularities perhaps because, unlike many of our male guests, he didn't try to suppress his growing feelings for her. On the contrary, I wouldn't have been altogether surprised to see him lick his chops and rub his hands together.

"I understand you ran into a lot of rain and a little protest on your way to the museum." Dr. Maxwell reluctantly relinquished Candi's hand. "I'm so sorry. I should have warned you." He flicked an unruly lock of hair from his eyes, and gave her his best boyish smile. The hair had just enough grey to be believable. Beautifully capped teeth gleamed from the dark tan of his face. "They're usually pretty simple to get around if you know what you're doing."

"Well, it sure was spectacular." Candi returned his smile with her own toothy dazzler. "Not just rain, either. There was a ton of hail and lightning flashing all over the place."

"No, not the thunderstorm," Dr. Maxwell laughed gallantly. "Even I can't control the weather. I meant the protestors."

The years of exposure to the harsh tropical sun that had bronzed his skin had deepened the creases around his eyes as well. It almost seemed as if the sun had been at work on the eyes themselves, bleaching them to a pale, Nordic blue. It was very easy to imagine Graham Maxwell in khakis and a bush hat squinting at a fragment of fossil bone amid the parched hills of his African field sites.

"No matter where I go there's always a contingent of the anti-evolution brigade out marching with their signs. I'm so used to it I'd probably feel lost without them, but they can be a damned nuisance at times."

The young woman in the lab coat gave my hand a limp shake, then went back to the doorway where she stood staring at Candi and Dr. Maxwell. The single sentence allocated to Gillian Collins in the press release described her as a British anthropologist, with a doctorate from Cambridge and a job as Dr. Maxwell's personal assistant. The fossil-packing Gill was pretty enough in an English rose sort of way, except for the peevish frown that seemed to be her only expression. I wondered if the frown was a reaction to Candi. When Candi is in the room, mere pretty, no matter how rosily English, can't compete.

Simon Visser arrived just in time for the last of the handshaking. His sentence said he was South African, had worked for Maxwell for almost twenty years, and had been with him at all his major finds. But, where Dr. Maxwell glowed with vitality and self-assurance, Simon seemed faded, as if some interior light had been extinguished. He was middle-aged, of middle height, and pretty much middle everything else. Even his eyes and hair were mid-brown. Still, he was the only one of the three who looked at me when we shook hands.

"Time to get started, everyone," Ella ordered in her best take-charge voice. "You can set the camera up there, Phoebe." She pointed to a spot in front of the display now presently occupied by Simon. He smiled as he politely stepped aside and strolled over to lean against the door jamb next to Gillian. Only that smile, with its flicker of irony, hinted at something more beyond the blandness.

"And, Candi," Sergeant Ella snapped off another command, "maybe you'd like to go over some of this with Dr. Maxwell." She handed Candi a clipboard with a copy of her script for today's interview. Really, Ella is an optimist at heart. In all the programs we've taped for *A Day in the Lifestyle,* Candi has not once managed an entire interview that sticks to Ella's meticulously prepared script with its list of appropriate questions. Still, Ella never gives up and Candi always starts with the best of intentions, all of which makes it fun for me to see how far we get before they part company.

"I guess I'd better get a couple of chairs in here." Ella fussed in front of the camera.

"Simon, you heard the lady," Dr. Maxwell said. "Be a good fellow and find us some chairs, would you please?" He asked pleasantly enough, but there was no doubt that Simon had been given an order. He ambled off to do as he was told.

Gillian didn't notice him leave. Gillian wasn't noticing anything except Dr. Maxwell and Candi. I'm not sure she even remembered there was anyone else in the room, and if she did, she didn't care. She simply stood and stared, totally absorbed in her boss's reaction to our interviewer. Poor Gill had plenty to watch.

Dr. Maxwell and Candi had deserted Ella's script for a private tour of the fossils. I heard him explaining how he had designed the display himself. He stood close behind her and pointed out details over her shoulder.

"Now that bone is what we call a cranium." Dr. Maxwell put an arm around Candi's shoulders as he leaned forward and pointed to the first skeleton's skull. "Cranium is the technical word for the top part of the skull that fits over the brain. And this one is a very special cranium because it is almost complete even though it was hidden in the ground for three and a half million years before I found it."

Dr. Maxwell used simple words as if he thought that Candi might be a little simple herself. Quite a number of *A Day in the Lifestyle* guests make this mistake. They are mostly men, usually over fifty, and always the possessors of hypertrophied egos. Dr. Maxwell fit the bill on all three counts and added a sizable dollop of sexual vanity to the mix, all of which made it impossible for him to grasp the notion that a woman as blonde and beautiful as Candi could still have a brain. Then again, Candi's brain was not the part of her anatomy that interested him.

"Golly, just look at this one." Candi slipped out of his grasp and went to stand in front of the smallest skull. Being taken for a dumb blonde used to annoy her. Now she simply plays up the image and waits to get her revenge when the camera is running. "This is a very tiny cranium, isn't it?" She hesitated before the big word as if she were trying it out for the first time and needed a little run-up.

Dr. Maxwell moved to stand beside her. "Do you realize, Candi, that you could be looking at the skeletons of your own great-grandparents, a hundred and fifty thousand generations removed."

"Wow! I'll have to make sure my Aunt Cynthia sees this exhibit. She's a real genealogy nut, but so far she's only got our family back to 1790."

By the time I had finished setting up the lights, Simon reappeared carrying a couple of chairs that he placed in front of the camera. Dr. Maxwell and Candi sat down. Under the guise of getting comfortable, he edged his chair a little closer to hers so that their thighs were touching. Then he began to fumble with the microphone that Candi had clipped to his lapel. As she leaned over to help him adjust it, the back of his hand brushed against her breast, lingering a moment too long to be accidental. I glanced over at the English rose. She had turned several shades redder.

I adjusted the lights and loaded a fresh tape in the camera. Gillian continued her vigil in the doorway while Simon lounged against the back wall. He stood, detached from the proceedings, but watching everything. I could have sworn he winked at me as I moved into place behind the camera. I checked the sound levels and then my watch. It was almost six, not nearly enough time to get the footage we'd need.

"Everyone ready?" Ella asked as she took her usual interview place, a couple of feet behind my left elbow. I started the tape rolling. Dr. Maxwell took a deep breath and sat a little straighter in his chair. Candi glanced quickly at her clipboard with its list of questions and then looked up and nodded. Ella pushed the button on her stopwatch. We were off.

"Our guest on this week's edition of *A Day in the Lifestyle* is the world-renowned paleoanthropologist Dr. Graham Maxwell." Candi usually makes it all the way through the scripted introduction without embellishments or departures, and she delivered Ella's economical outline of Dr. Maxwell's recent accomplishments exactly as written. I waited until she began the last sentence before I pulled back to include him in the shot.

"For the next few months, Dr. Maxwell and his research team, along with their famous fossils, will be based here at the Royal Tyrrell Museum of Palaeontology in Drumheller."

She turned to her guest. "Welcome to Alberta, Dr. Maxwell."

"Thank you, Candi. It's wonderful to be home," Dr. Maxwell said, stressing the word "home."

"But isn't your home in Africa?" Candi made her first departure from Ella's script. This was much earlier than usual, probably a record. I heard our producer's teeth begin to grind very softly in the background.

"Well, Candi, it's true that I now work mainly in Africa. But I was born in Alberta. I grew up here. I was educated here. And I like to think I still have many good friends here," Dr. Maxwell answered with a politician's suaveness. "So no matter where I work or how long I've been away I can honestly say that for me, Alberta will always be home."

It was pretty obvious that the man had something to sell and was soaping the way before he launched his pitch, but this isn't unusual on our program. People don't appear on shows like ours unless they are after publicity, and an hour's worth of what amounted to free promotion broadcast all over southern Alberta would be even more valuable to Dr. Maxwell's fundraising campaign than yesterday's press conference or tonight's celebration at the museum. And, since local purses tend to open for local causes, it was no surprise that he had conveniently regrown some very old, very deep Alberta roots. It was a sound strategy, and Candi might have let him get away with it if he hadn't been so patronizing before the tape started rolling.

"Exactly how long have you lived away from Alberta, Dr. Maxwell?" Candi asked.

"Since I left the University of Alberta to study for my doctorate in the United States. And please, Candi, my name is Graham." He deftly avoided dates and years.

"Gosh, Graham, I seem to have forgotten what year that was." Candi sounded a touch annoyed at her own forgetfulness. She's so good at this faux naïve stuff that sometimes she almost convinces me. "But I'm sure I've seen it written down here somewhere." She began to leaf through the papers on her clipboard while, behind me, Ella shaved another layer of enamel off her molars.

"I left for graduate school in 1955," Dr. Maxwell finally admitted when the pause became too uncomfortable.

"You know, I think it's really wonderful that after all those years away you still consider Alberta your home." Candi beamed at him and shook her head in amazement. "In 1955," she repeated mercilessly. "That's the year my mother was born."

This time I thought Ella might gnash her way down to the pulp. Nevertheless, the brief exchange did seem to be a kind of wake-up call for Dr. Maxwell, who, for all his ego, was definitely not stupid. He looked at Candi in a whole new way and for the rest of the interview there wasn't a hint of condescension in his replies. As a matter of fact, for my money, Graham Maxwell proved to be one of the most interesting guests we've ever had. He possessed the rare ability to explain complicated scientific concepts in terms understandable to the general public. He also managed to communicate his own love of anthropology, speaking of his work with such passion that ten minutes into the interview he had me hooked. I wanted to be a paleoanthropologist too, and join him on his next African dig.

It was almost six-thirty when I remembered to check my watch and load another tape in the camera. The interview was going very smoothly. Even Ella had relaxed a little, although I could still hear some tiny dental disturbances from her direction every now and then. Perhaps she was on edge because she knew we were running out of time. So did Candi. She had hurried the questions on Maxwell's background and, for the past fifteen minutes, concentrated on the digs and the fossils.

"But how do you decide where to dig?" she continued at my signal that the new tape was rolling. "For instance, how did you know where you would find these fossils?"

"Over the years I seem to have acquired a reputation for having a sixth sense where fossils are concerned. People say that somehow I know instinctively where to dig, that I have a nose for hominids. I only wish it were true. I'm afraid the answer to your question is much more mundane, Candi. Knowing where to dig is the result of years of study and experience and a lot of very hard work. And, to be honest, I have to admit that a little luck never hurts either. I certainly had more than my fair share of it with this lot." He glanced over his shoulder at the display. "Just one of these bones would constitute a very important find. But three skeletons – and such complete ones? That's like winning the lottery ten times in a row. It's simply astounding good luck."

"Well, I guess your luck's a whole lot better than theirs was and that's for sure," Candi said. "What do you think happened to them?"

It took Dr. Maxwell a moment to realize that Candi was referring to the fossils. "We can only speculate, but I think it's likely they took shelter under an overhang, perhaps under the cut-away bank of a stream. Then, for some reason, maybe an earthquake or some such disturbance, the overhang collapsed and preserved them for me to find all these millions of years later."

"You mean they were buried alive?" Candi asked, aghast at this new development. "The whole family?"

"We mustn't jump the gun here, Candi," Dr. Maxwell cautioned. "We can't say with any certainty that they were a family. As yet we have no concrete evidence of any familial relationship."

"The poor little souls. They smothered to death," Candi continued as if Dr. Maxwell hadn't spoken, so lost in the drama of her ancestors' tragic demise that I really don't think she had heard him. "All three of them suffocated in dirt."

"That's not to say that we haven't made some truly amazing discoveries about these creatures, discoveries that we can back up with concrete evidence." Dr. Maxwell returned the compliment by ignoring Candi and blithely carrying on with his own line of thought.

"Or maybe they were crushed by the weight of the overhang and died instantly and didn't really suffer?" Candi's worries about the fossils' last moments continued.

Now, instead of an interview, we had two monologues going. This was a first for *A Day in the Lifestyle*, as was the fact that Ella had stopped grinding her teeth and begun to emit high-pitched whimpers, like an overwrought bat.

"I've waited until tonight and the opening of my exhibit here at the Royal Tyrrell to announce the most important of these discoveries – a discovery that is going to take accepted thoughts about our earliest ancestors and stand them right on their heads." Dr. Maxwell reached into the inner pocket of his jacket and produced what looked to be some small creature's leg bone with one of the joint ends broken off straight across.

"Not this crap," I heard Simon mutter under his breath. "Not again." More of Ella's agitated wee squeaks punctuated his words. The interview had now become a work for two solo voices with choral accompaniment.

Dr. Maxwell held the bone up to the camera like an offering. "This is my way of thanking the Royal Tyrrell Museum and the people of Alberta for their continued support of my work."

At last Gillian joined the choir. "Sorry to interrupt, Graham," she called loudly from her place in the doorway, sounding not sorry at all. "You told me to let you know when it was half-past six. It's nearly twenty-five to seven now. We have to get set up for the opening ceremonies."

I think Candi must have heard Gillian. Either that or one of Ella's sonar signals managed to penetrate and call her back from ancient calamity to the present.

"What is that?" she asked Dr. Maxwell. "It looks like some sort of leg bone."

"This is an exact reproduction of a prehistoric gazelle femur that I found buried very near the skeletons. The original bone is so precious that it stays in a climate-controlled vault and will probably never be put on display. This replica is made of a synthetic resin and is, in every detail, like the bone would have been on the day it was buried with these fossils, right down to its hollow centre and the holes you can see here in its front." Dr. Maxwell pointed to three small, roughly round holes running in a line down the length of the bone. "But that's not what's so remarkable. Here's what makes this bone truly miraculous." He covered the holes with his fingers, put the broken end of the bone to his lips, and blew across the opening, like children do with pop bottles. The bone produced a small, flutey whistle that he varied in pitch by opening and closing the holes with his fingers.

"You bloody fool," I heard Simon say quite clearly in the background.

I know he must have heard Simon, but Dr. Maxwell continued to play more hooty notes on the fake gazelle bone, this time producing what sounded like an off-key try at "Three Blind Mice."

"What you are now hearing," he announced with the fervour of someone who has undergone a mystical experience, "is the sound of the first music ever played on earth." He blew into the bone again and the mice wobbled along for another bar or two. "This is mankind's earliest song – our primal melody. And that is why I have chosen the name *Homo musicus* for my new species. *Homo musicus* – man the musician."

Then the lights went out.

3

GILLIAN HAD DOUSED THE LIGHTS. We all went along with the polite pretence that my two little floods had overloaded the circuits and tripped the breakers, but that was nonsense. The Royal Tyrrell's electrical system is more than up to anything I could throw its way. It was Gillian. She'd flipped the switches not just on the overheads but on the circuits that controlled the outlets for my lights. At least I'm pretty certain it was Gillian, and for my money she'd done us all a favour by putting the interview out of its misery. What with Ella's squeaks and Simon's expletives, Candi's morbid maundering and Dr. Maxwell's little recital, the last five minutes of the tape were such a mess that they were useless. Even Ella looked relieved. Actually, the only one who minded much was Dr. Maxwell.

"When can we continue this?" he asked after Gillian had reset the breakers and turned the work lights on again. "We can't stop here. I have to finish what I was saying about the flute."

"No time now, Graham," Gillian said happily. "The men are waiting to put the barriers back up."

"You could finish the interview tomorrow." Ella jumped at the opportunity to save her program. "At your convenience – we can make it any time. I have to get back to Calgary tonight, but Candi and Phoebe can be here all day. Phoebe has some cover shots to get tomorrow anyway."

The museum shots would take me an hour or two in the morning, tops, but if Ella wanted another full day of my time I wouldn't complain. The Royal Tyrrell is a splendid place to spend a day, especially one you're getting paid for.

"I'm so sorry, but tomorrow is all booked." Gillian couldn't resist a smug little smile. "Graham starts with a breakfast meeting at seven-thirty and his schedule is solid from then to midnight."

"Meet me here at six A.M. sharp," Dr. Maxwell said to Candi, completely ignoring Gillian. "I'll make sure the night security guard knows he's to let you and your photographer in tomorrow morning right before six. And now I suppose I'd better get this show on the road." He rose and dropped the replica gazelle femur back in the inner pocket of his jacket.

"Here, Graham," Simon wandered over. "Maybe I'd better take care of that. There's going to be a real crush out there. Wouldn't want anything to happen to it."

"Don't be ridiculous." Dr. Maxwell patted his pocket. "What could possibly happen? That resin is hard as iron." Dismissing Simon, he turned to Candi and took her hand in both of his. "I'm looking forward to tomorrow morning, but I think you might want to come with me this evening too. If you're doing a program about me and my work, you ought to get the whole picture." He tucked her arm firmly under his and began to walk her to the exit. "You see it's simply not enough to be a good scientist these days. You have to be an administrator and a fundraiser and a public-relations expert too. Evenings like this are as much a part of my job as organizing digs. So, come with me and observe a paleoanthropologist hard at work." He swept Candi out the door, leaving a stunned Gillian staring after them. Ella and her clipboard followed.

The door hadn't closed behind them before the RCMP officer we met on the highway strode through it, followed by two members of the museum staff wheeling a large dolly stacked with Plexiglas panels about five feet wide by eight feet high. The panels fit into slots in the floor of the display forming a transparent wall in front of the fossils. Gillian supervised their placement, making sure each panel was solidly fastened. The Mountie followed behind her checking that every edge was flush with its neighbour. In order to prevent the unwary from attempting to walk through the glass, two thin lines of red tape ran the length of the barrier at knee and shoulder height.

Simon must have seen the look on my face. "It's a pity, I know, but the wall does have to be here." He helped me to gather up the extension cords and pack the lights back in the kit. "It was either that or use fibreglass reproductions. There's no way we could let people get close enough to touch them. We only had it down for you to tape the interview." I knew he was right, but, even so, the Plexiglas barrier did dim the fossils' magic.

"What's going to happen when the Mountie leaves?" I asked. I couldn't see the RCMP supplying an officer to guard the display for more than tonight's ceremonial evening and even for that the constable had probably volunteered his time.

"The regular museum staff will take over. There will be someone here watching whenever the exhibit is open to the public. Now what are we going to do with all of this?" He pointed to the mound of camera equipment.

"Leave it here until after the opening ceremony?" I suggested. "I only need the camera and tripod for that."

He shook his head. "As soon as that's over the exhibit is open to the museum's guests for an hour, so you can't leave anything here. But you could store what you don't need upstairs in our office and collect it later," he suggested. "I'd be happy to help you carry."

Simon was as good as his word. Laden with equipment he led the way through the exhibit's back door and along the corridor to an elevator that took us up a floor to the section of the museum that houses the research offices and library. The visiting anthropologists' office consisted of two rooms, the first a small laboratory with a lab bench, a row of free-standing metal shelves, and no windows, and the second a comfortable inner office with a large desk, a well-upholstered chair, and a panoramic view of the hills behind the museum.

"The inner sanctum is Graham's." Simon put the light kit down in front of the shelves and shifted his load of cables onto the scarred surface of the lab bench. "Gill and I occupy the hatchery." He nodded toward the shelves filled to overflowing with what looked like large oval rocks but were, in fact, fossilized dinosaur eggs. "The regular occupant is off somewhere in China digging up more of these things so we're camping here while he's away."

"I'd hate to meet their mother on a dark night." A half-dozen of the largest fossil eggs balanced in a precarious row on the top shelf. A couple of them must have weighed at least twenty pounds. "What laid eggs that big?"

"Could've been a jumbo jet, for all I know," Simon said. "Unless it's human, it's not my line." He opened a cupboard door under the lab bench and pulled out a bottle of bourbon. "Would you like a drink?"

"Not enough time. I have to get back for the opening ceremony. Aren't you coming?"

"Not me, thanks. I've been to too many of these things. I'll drop in later after the speeches are done – skip the politicians and bull and go directly to the champagne." Simon took a coffee mug out of the cupboard and tipped a shot of the whisky into it. "Sure you won't have one?" I shook my head. "Then here's to the lovely Phoebe Fairfax in her beautiful Vionnet frock."

I must have looked as amazed as I felt because Simon began to laugh, a full, rich booming laugh very much at odds with his subdued looks.

"I've waited nearly twenty-five years to drop that name. Thank you." He raised the mug, downed the bourbon, and promptly poured himself another generous tot.

"How on earth did you know it was made by Vionnet?"

"Phoebe, are you implying that I'm not the kind of man who knows his antique haute couture frocks?" He laughed again. It animated his whole being and, at that moment, I liked Simon very much.

"Well, I don't want to insult your hidden depths," I said, "but it does seem a little unlikely."

"You're right, it does. But I'd bet the farm that your frock was made by Madeleine Vionnet in Paris, probably in the late 1930s. Either that or it's an amazingly good copy."

"You'd win your bet. It is a Vionnet and it's real," I said. "A friend of mine sometimes brings home antique dresses for me from England."

"Then here's to your friend and to Professor Krieger." The second shot disappeared. He poured a third.

"Professor Krieger?"

"In my first year at university, before I transferred into anthropology, I studied engineering. Professor Krieger lectured on strength of materials. He was famous for being as tough as he was boring and he lived up to his reputation. Except for one day when he brought a white frock to our lecture. We all thought it must be some sort of joke except that Professor Krieger never joked. He hung the dress at the front of the lecture theatre and told us that the woman who made it was an engineering genius. Then he explained why. For the next hour he lectured us on Vionnet and how she engineered her frocks – the drapes, the bias cuts, the whole business. Then he set us some problems. What an afternoon. I think it was one of the funniest sights I've ever seen – a roomful of footballing, beer-swilling engineering boys, fussing and tugging and measuring that frock every which way. We sweated blood calculating the relative strengths of bias-cut satin versus straight-cut silk and whatever else old Krieger had dreamed up for us. I'll never forget it. And, by God, I'll never forget Vionnet either. So here's to Professor Krieger, should he still be among us, to Madeleine Vionnet, and to you." He polished off the bourbon.

"No toast to *Homo musicus*?" I asked. He shrugged and tipped more whisky into his mug. This was Simon's fourth shot in under five minutes. Maybe no one had explained to him that in drinking it's endurance, not speed, that gets the big scores. "Why did you decide to wait until tonight to announce the fossils' name?"

"I didn't decide," he said. "I don't do decisions. Graham does." The animation vanished.

"You sound like you take exception to this one."

"The timing's fine. The name's not."

"So you don't agree with Dr. Maxwell about the flute?"

"You mean do I agree that we should take a broken gazelle bone that happened to be lying near the fossils and name the greatest anthropological find of all time *Homo musicus* simply because Graham can make noises on it? No, I do not. I think you can say that Graham and I have a divergence of professional opinion on this one."

"Then you don't think it's a musical instrument?"

"I know it isn't."

"But what about the holes and the break across the top?"

"What about them?" The level of the whisky in Simon's mug dropped a little more, but the only effect the alcohol seemed to be having was to make him talkative. Clearly, Simon and the bourbon bottle were old friends.

"Some large carnivore probably ate the gazelle for dinner and punched a few holes in the bone with its teeth during the process," he continued. "Believe me, Graham's femur is no more a musical instrument than the bone from a roast of beef. If that thing is a flute, then I'll stand you to a prime rib dinner and we'll play concertos on the leftovers."

"Is a name all that important?"

"I guarantee you this one will turn us into a scientific laughingstock." Simon stared into his coffee mug and began to talk almost as if he had forgotten I was there and, considering the amount he'd had to drink, maybe he had. "A name should describe the fossil and its place in the evolutionary record – it should describe how the creature fits into the pattern of life, how it relates to other animals. A name should not be a monument to one man's ego. *Homo* bloody *musicus*." The level of the bourbon fell another gulp.

"What do you think they should be called?" I asked.

Simon looked up sharply from his mug, as if he suddenly realized that he might have said too much.

"Ah, Phoebe, the naming of cats is a difficult matter. And fossils are even more of a problem." He smiled and tossed back the last of the whisky. "We'd better get you to those speeches. I hope they pay you well for evenings like this. What can I carry?"

Simon carried the tripod. I wasn't letting someone who had downed four bourbons in five minutes anywhere near the camera, although I had to admit that he showed no signs of being drunk. He walked and talked in a perfectly normal manner in spite of a load of booze that would have had me crawling the corridor. This time we didn't bother with the elevator. Simon took me down a flight of stairs, through what looked like a staff lounge, down more stairs, and through more doors until I was thoroughly lost. Finally we came to a corridor that led to the main entrance hall where the speeches were almost due to begin.

The news reporter from our station waved to me over the heads of the museum's guests who had gathered in a close-packed crowd behind a line of reporters and photographers. She beckoned us to the place she'd snagged directly in front of a raised platform that stood near the main entrance to the dinosaur exhibits. Simon managed the tripod with great skill and, with an occasional nicely timed prod, cleared us a way through the crowd. In the minute or two it took us to work our way to the front, that tripod nudged some of the richest rumps in Alberta. I saw the presidents of two oil companies, a senior partner in one of Calgary's biggest law firms, a couple of property developers, and a man who spent his working days managing the money of a zillion-dollar charitable foundation established by his grandfather. And those were just the ones I recognized. Although money reigned that evening at the Royal Tyrrell, there were a few senior academics from the University of Calgary scattered through the crowd – a history prof I'd once taken a class from, a couple of anthropologists, and, of course, Professor Woodward. Doubtless due to Mrs. Woodward's efforts, he was cleaned up and dressed in a surprisingly well-cut tuxedo. Even his usually wild grey hair and full beard looked to have been tamed for the occasion. At least I didn't expect to see small creatures peering out. Simon nudged him gently with the tripod, but Professor Woodward didn't move except to turn his head and look at me.

"Why, Phoebe, how good to see you." He smiled benignly if somewhat vaguely. "What on earth are you doing here?" Simon and the tripod gave the professor's nether regions a second, less gentle, poke, which he also managed to ignore.

"Adam, can't you see that Phoebe's working? Look, she's carrying her camera," Mrs. Woodward said. Mrs. Woodward spends a lot of time explaining everyday life to her husband. "Good evening, Phoebe," she added as an after-thought, inclining her head with its perfectly cut grey hair in my direction.

Mrs. Woodward is tall and elegant and still very beauti-ful. She wears her slightly unconventional clothes with great panache. Tonight, a Navajo-patterned shawl topped her very plain and plainly expensive black dress. In keeping with the Navajo theme, a large silver-and-turquoise spider hung from her left ear. Its accompanying silver web dangled from the right. Mrs. Woodward must have been a real stunner when she was young, but, even so, I can't figure out how she and the professor ever managed to get together. Talk about opposites. While he roams the forest reserve dressed in rough-cured animal skins searching for edible roots and berries, she drags her full-length mink into La Chaumière foraging for escargots. For Mrs. Woodward, a primitive society is one in which they don't chill the martini glasses. Still, the pair of them have been married forever so they must have something that keeps them together.

"If you're going to be around after the speechifying is over, I hope you can join us for a drink," Professor Woodward said to me. "My son is here on a visit. He lives in Halifax. You haven't met Trevor, have you?" He smiled at a tall man standing behind Mrs. Woodward. Trevor looked to be in his mid-forties and, like his father, he sported a beard, only his was a neatly trimmed Vandyke. "Trevor, I'd like you to meet Phoebe Fairfax. She's the young woman I told you about who helps me when I'm out doing my research."

"Good to meet you, Phoebe." Trevor reached an arm over his mother's shoulder. I managed to shift the camera and shake his hand. He looked so familiar that I wondered if we'd met before. Even his voice sounded familiar. "And thanks for taking care of my dad. He's told me about your place and all that you do for him."

Before I could reply, an impatient Simon gave the professor's behind a third bop with the tripod. Professor Woodward looked down over his shoulder and then back at me with a puzzled expression. "Why does your friend keep hitting me with that thing?" he asked in genuine bewilderment.

"For heaven's sake, Adam, they want to get by us." Mrs. Woodward pulled her husband closer to her. "Can you make it?" she asked as we squeezed past. With a promise to join the three of them later, I followed Simon to the front.

I set up the camera and went to work. Poor Simon, trapped by the crowd, found himself doomed to twenty minutes of politicians. He sighed a resigned waft of bourbon and boredom. Unfortunately, the man knew his opening ceremonies and this one more than lived up to his predictions. Elected representatives from two levels of government droned on, each claiming responsibility for the considerable accomplishments of the Royal Tyrrell, conveniently forgetting the brutal budget cutbacks and belt tightening they and their colleagues had imposed on every research institution in the country. Members of the legislature who couldn't pronounce paleoanthropologist, let alone explain what one did, were suddenly on a first-name basis with their close personal friend Graham, the Alberta boy made good.

Finally, Dr. Maxwell himself took the podium, which was a relief. Unlike the politicians, he managed to camouflage the more blatant aspects of his self-promotion by talking up the fossils. His speech was a fundraiser's dream, flattering to his audience while at the same time enticing their interest in his work. Somehow, he managed to make his listeners feel that by donating money they, too, would be participating in his grand scientific adventure. You could practically feel him charming the cheque books out of their pockets. Dr. Maxwell only stumbled once and that was near the end when he announced the name of the fossils. Just as he'd done earlier, during Candi's interview, he pulled the gazelle bone from his pocket and told the story of finding what he called the world's first musical instrument. Then he blew across the resin replica's top, but in the cavernous entrance hall, even with the help of a microphone, the tiny sound barely breathed its way past the front row of listeners.

"I have waited until the opening of this exhibit at the Royal Tyrrell Museum of Palaeontology, waited until I was here in Alberta, at home and amongst friends, to announce the official name of my fossils," Maxwell said. "This name not only marks them as a new species but also as the first musicians on earth. Ladies and gentlemen, here is my gift to you and to all of humanity, our ancestor . . . ," pause for effect, ". . . *Homo musicus*. Man the musician."

Perhaps the audience didn't understand the name's scientific significance or maybe the bone's small sound proved anticlimactic, because the proclamation of *Homo musicus* did not create the stir that Dr. Maxwell so obviously expected. Simon muttered something under his breath. I heard a loud "holy shit" followed by a muffled snort of laughter from the direction of the university anthropologists. The rest of the crowd applauded politely, if briefly. And that was it. The lack of reaction puzzled Dr. Maxwell, but, like all good showmen, he cut his losses and moved on.

"And now it gives me great pleasure to declare my exhibit officially open and to invite you to visit with your musical ancestors for the next hour. When you've said your hellos to them I hope you'll come and do the same to me. You'll find me and my staff right through those doors, in the Dinosaur Hall. We're looking forward to the opportunity to talk with you. Thank you for coming to our celebration." Dr. Maxwell moved away from the podium to the sound of enthusiastic applause, but before it had quite died down, he stepped back to the microphone. "And, just to make certain that you will come visit us, we've put the champagne in there too." He grinned and this time the applause was warmed by laughter. Even Simon perked up, though I suspect it was the promise of more alcohol that cheered him.

After Maxwell left centre stage, the audience broke up quickly. Simon followed his boss into the reception. The entrance hall was nearly empty when I taped our reporter doing her stand-ups. I gave her the tape and she wandered off to find Ella, who was catching a ride back to Calgary with her later in the evening. Ella is the mother of an infant daughter and, as the food source, refuses to be away from home for more than ten hours at a stretch. Officially she is still on maternity leave, but the chance to do a program on Dr. Maxwell had proved too much of a temptation. So after storing who knows how many bottles of breast milk against her absence, and leaving their daughter, along with seven pages of instructions, in the care of her husband, Ella packed her breast pump and fretted her way out to Drumheller to supervise Candi and me.

I hadn't seen either of them at the opening ceremony but, considering the crowd, that wasn't a surprise. Candi appeared just as I finished loading the camera with a new tape and battery.

"Need some help with this stuff?" she asked.

"Given up studying a paleoanthropologist at work?"

"God, I thought I'd never get away from him. I snuck off while he was making his speech. Is he some kind of classic old lech, or what?"

"Probably the type specimen," I said. "You could dump the tripod back in the van. I won't need it for the reception."

"Where's the rest of the gear?" Candi asked. I explained about Simon and the equipment stash in the office. "Then go ahead," she said and picked up the tripod. "I'll get this to the van while you start taping. See you in there."

I hoisted the camera onto my shoulder and followed the champagne crowd into the main dinosaur gallery, where the caterers were dispensing chilled California bubbly. The crowd that had felt like a crush at the opening ceremony was now spread into comfortable groups scattered here and there along the walkways that wind past the exhibits in the vast space. Canapes and drinks in hand, people strolled amid the giant skeletons, sipping and nibbling their way past the bones of the thunder lizards, largely oblivious to the drama of the dioramas surrounding them. The sharp-toothed jaws of an allosaur crushed the bones of poor camptosaur, a hapless vegetarian. Armour-plated *Edmontonia*, his mouth full of ferns, pondered the fate of his fellow herbivore. A herd of chasmosaurs grazed peaceably, huge protective frills rising like sails above their heads. But all to no avail. The most magnificent creatures to walk the earth were now background decoration for gossip and champagne and money.

I wandered along the paths, taping groups of people as they stood talking. Ella would decide later which ones were sufficiently important by *A Day in the Lifestyle* standards to make the final cut. I tried to include as many of the dinosaurs in the background as I could. I was finishing a shot of one of the oil presidents and his companion velociraptor when Simon caught up to me.

"Graham wonders if you'd lend him your services for a minute or two, Phoebe?" He led me over to where Dr. Maxwell stood talking with the Woodwards and their son.

"Good of you to interrupt your work for us, Phoebe." I expect that Simon had also supplied Dr. Maxwell with my name. "I wonder if you would be so kind as to take a shot of the three of us." Dr. Maxwell and the professor stood on either side of Mrs. Woodward. "Adam and Diana and I went to university together and tonight is the first time we've seen each other since graduation. And you might tell your producer that I'd like this shot to appear in her program about me. Come on, Trevor, let's get you in here too."

I began to frame a shot as the Woodward's son moved into the picture. I nearly dropped the camera. Trevor Woodward looked exactly like Graham Maxwell. And I do mean exactly. Except for the beard, he was simply a younger version of the same man.

"Is something wrong, Phoebe?" Mrs. Woodward asked. I realized I'd been standing gaping at Trevor and Dr. Maxwell. "Should we move closer together or something?"

"No, no. That's fine."

As I began to tape I couldn't help wondering why no one else was staring at the two men. Couldn't they see that Trevor was practically Dr. Maxwell's clone? After I finished my shot, Professor Woodward pulled a small camera out of his pocket.

"Would you take a couple of pictures for me, Phoebe?" he asked.

"Adam, the poor girl is far too busy," Mrs. Woodward said quickly. "She's here working. We can't waste her time fussing with our little camera."

"That's okay. I have time. I'm almost finished what I have to do in here for now." I put the video camera on the floor in front of me, but before I could get a shot with Professor Woodward's camera, Mrs. Woodward broke rank and took a step forward. She stared over my shoulder, eyes wide with astonishment.

"My God, I don't believe it," she said. "After all these years. And here of all places."

"Is this a professional photography session or may amateurs join in?" A smiling Stan stood behind me, snapshot camera in hand. Dressed in a tuxedo, a dashing red cummerbund holding his little pot-belly in place, Stan looked very different from the harassed protester I'd encountered earlier. I wondered if he had been wearing the evening clothes under his coverall back out on the road. Obviously, his decision to attend the reception was not spur of the moment. And what would his fellow Geologists for Jesus, especially the militant Myrna, think of his turning up in the enemy camp?

Dr. Maxwell broke the stunned silence. "Good lord, it really is. Stan Darling, God's Right-Hand Man, himself." He opened his arms and enveloped the small fellow in a bear hug. "I didn't know if you'd come, but I'm glad you did. It's been too damn long, Stanley. Too damn long." I half-expected Stan to pull a protest sign out from under his jacket, but instead he returned Dr. Maxwell's embrace.

I stood back from the group, aimed Professor Woodward's camera, and got some shots of the hugging and handshaking that followed.

"Stan was in our graduating class. He's a paleontologist too," Professor Woodward explained to me. He had left the group and wandered over beside me and the cameras. "Well, he's sort of a paleontologist," he added after a thoughtful pause. "Worked in the oil business, you see." Before the professor could add any more qualifiers to his description of Stan's professional standing, Dr. Maxwell interrupted.

"This calls for a toast. Come on, Adam, get over here. Simon, let's find these people some champagne."

Simon obliged his boss by scoring a full tray of champagne glasses from a passing waiter, which he handed around the group. Then he retired, along with the five extras, to watch from a nearby bench.

"Shall we drink a toast to old friends?" Dr. Maxwell raised his glass.

"Surely not old. Anyone as beautiful as Diana can never be old," Stan said with unexpected gallantry and a little bow to Mrs. Woodward. "Perhaps a toast to happy memories?"

"Do we have any, Stan?" Professor Woodward smiled blandly. "I would have thought . . ."

"How about to friends of long standing?" Mrs. Woodward interrupted her husband.

"Well said, Diana, well said," Dr. Maxwell agreed. "To friends of long standing it is."

The four classmates raised their glasses. I snapped off some shots first with Professor Woodward's camera, then with Stan's. Trevor stood beside me blazing away with his own camera. It was a well-documented moment.

"I'd like prints of these photographs." Dr. Maxwell tossed off the last of his champagne. "And I'd also like you people to meet me later this evening for another glass of wine. We can have a proper class reunion then when all this business is over. It shouldn't last much later than ten. Simon will know where to find me. I'm sorry to leave you when we've just found each other again, but I have to get back to work. Simon, have you seen Candi Sinclair? Ah, there's Gill. Maybe she's seen her."

I picked up my camera and went back to work as well, leaving Stan and the senior Woodwards to reminisce about their college days while Trevor looked on, politely pretending to be interested. The room was much fuller now that those who had gone to look at the fossils had returned for refreshment. Candi joined me as I took my last shot.

"Maxwell left the room so I thought it was safe to come out from behind the tyrannosaur," she laughed. "What on earth was that old guy from the protest march doing here?"

"Stan? It turns out he's a classmate of the Woodwards and Dr. Maxwell and he really is a geologist, degree and all."

"He'd better hope Myrna doesn't catch him," Candi echoed my thoughts. "Who was the guy with the Woodwards? The middle-aged one with the beard."

"Their son," I explained. "Did you see him when he was standing next to Dr. Maxwell? Pretty amazing."

"What's amazing?"

"What do you mean, what's amazing? Candi, you had to notice. The man is practically Graham Maxwell's double. Add twenty years and he is Maxwell."

She thought for a moment. "I suppose there is some resemblance."

"Some?" Usually Candi is far more adept at seeing these things than I am. Why had she missed this one?

"By the way, we have to move the van. A commission-aire told me it's blocking the front entrance. Which, of course, it isn't," she added with uncharacteristic indigna-tion. For some reason Candi has it in for members of the Canadian Corps of Commissionaires. Claims they're nothing but a bunch of uniformed bullies cleverly dis-guised to look like your nice old grandpa.

"I'll move it after I give this tape to Ella," I said. "I have to get a battery from the van anyway. Have you seen her?"

"She's waiting for you in the lobby. Poor thing looks bushed. I think motherhood's taking it out of her. I'll go to the cafeteria and see where they've put us for dinner. Meet you there."

I found Ella, as Candi said, sitting in the lobby near the gift shop looking weary. I gave her the tape. In return, she presented me with a detailed list of the shots I was to get the next morning. I glanced at the list as we walked out of the building and past the half-dozen smokers scattered across the forecourt, some of them sitting on the steps, some lounging on a granite bench in the shadow of the pachyrhinosaurs, all of them busy topping up their nicotine levels before dinner.

"Come off it, Ella. Not another sunrise." It was the first item on her list. Ella is big on sunrise shots, especially when she's miles away in a warm bed.

"Taken from the top of that hill." She pointed to the hill directly in front of the museum. A long wooden staircase led to a lookout deck at its top. "Then you can turn around and get a shot of the museum. The quality of the light at dawn will be perfect for that reddish stone."

"Maybe it will rain." I didn't even try to keep the hope out of my voice.

"Don't be so negative, Phoebe." Ella's ride pulled up to the curb in front of us. She climbed into the passenger seat and fastened her seat belt, all the while issuing me a stream of last-minute instructions. She was still talking as the car drove off and I went to move the van out from under a parking ticket, the gift of Candi's commissionaire.

Candi was right, the van wasn't blocking anything. Even so, it was in a No Parking zone so I didn't have much in the way of grounds for argument. I put the camera on the floor, the shot list and the ticket in the glove compartment, and drove to the public parking area. The closest spot was in the lot reserved for buses and recreational vehicles. I pulled in next to an old camper, the kind that's a box mounted on a half-ton with a small door in the back and a couple of windows on either side. Out of the corner of my eye, I noticed a curtain in one of the side windows twitch. I turned to look and found myself staring straight into Myrna's face. She quickly jerked the curtain back into place and disappeared behind it. I looked around the parking lot, but there were no other Geologists for Jesus, at least none in sight.

I loaded the camera with another tape, changed the battery, and trudged back to the museum. Every tiny piece of gravel telegraphed its painful way through the thin soles of my fancy shoes. Things got even more dismal in the footwear department when I slipped on a patch of greasy clay that the hailstorm had washed across the road. My right foot sank into the mud. As I jerked it out, a blob of wet bentonite splatted onto my dress. By the time I made it back to the museum and the nearest washroom, the blob had oozed down to the hem, leaving a trail of grime behind it. I tried wiping off the remaining mud with some paper towel, but that only made the stain worse so I decided to give up on the dress. Instead, I took off my shoe and set about cleaning up my foot. That accomplished, I held the shoe under the tap and scrubbed. Drumheller bentonite, a top contender for the world's slipperiest clay, is probably the stickiest too so it took some work before I could see leather. I thought I was alone in the washroom until I heard a toilet flush in one of the stalls. The door opened and Gillian stepped up to the bank of sinks. She looked like she'd been crying.

"Hi," I said, holding up my shoe. "Slipped in some wet clay."

Gillian glanced at me but said nothing. She bent over the sink, splashed some cold water on her face and in her eyes, and then realized she didn't have a towel. Without lifting her head, she held out a hand. I obliged with some paper towels from the dispenser.

"Wet bentonite," I said, resuming my scrubbing. "It's like walking on grease. Be careful if you go out into the hills while you're here." The shoe was coming along nicely. Except for a little mound of muck on the insole and some in front of the heel it was almost ready to wear. "Especially if you're hiking in high-heeled sandals."

Gillian tossed the towels in the trash container and took a small makeup bag out of her purse. She proceeded to repair the damage caused by tears and a wash.

"Guess this will have to do." I dried the shoe as best I could, put it on, and walked around in a small test circle. It felt unpleasantly squishy but, other than that, seemed to have suffered no damage from its mud bath. Gillian glanced briefly at my foot, then returned her gaze to the mirror and began to apply mascara.

"Well, it certainly has been a pleasure talking with you, Gillian. Perhaps we'll have a chance to continue our conversation over dinner." I picked up the camera and squelched out the door.

Never be a snippy bitch. Sooner or later your nastiness comes back to haunt you. This time, mine came sooner. I got to eat dinner at Gillian's table. Not only that, I even got to sit next to her. As it turned out, each guest had been assigned to a numbered table. Originally, Candi and I were well below the salt at table fifteen. However, by the time I got back to the party, Dr. Maxwell had caught up to Candi and whisked her off to sit with him at the head table. This bumped Gillian down to Candi's officially assigned place, over beside me in the outer darkness of double digits. No wonder I'd found her washing away a tear or two in the ladies' room.

The cafeteria had been transformed from its everyday fast-food and stainless-steel self into a more than presentable banquet hall. Large red-and-white banners festooned the room. Suspended by wires from the ceiling and sporting a dramatic silhouette of the largest skeleton, they proclaimed the dates of the exhibition and lent a festive air to the utilitarian space. The caterers had done their best too. The Formica-topped tables were draped with heavy linen cloths, and the cafeteria crockery had been replaced by fine English china with a delicate border of wild roses, Alberta's floral emblem. Even nature seemed to be cooperating for the occasion as the soft gold light of the setting sun reflected off the hills and lit the room through the huge bank of windows that made up the east wall. There were half-a-dozen more tables outside the windows on the paved terrace that overlooked a decorative pond fringed with rushes. The outdoor tables weren't set for dinner, but some guests sat at them enjoying the last of the day's warmth and a final glass of champagne.

By eight, everyone had found a place indoors and the caterers began to serve the meal. I wandered from table to table, taping the diners before they had a chance to tuck in and make a mess of their plates. Congealing gravy and half-eaten vegetables are not pleasant photographic subjects. The museum had moved a model of the Royal Tyrrell's own mascot, Lillian the *Albertosaurus*, into a place of honour in the middle of the room. At two-thirds life-size,

Lillian was still an impressive sixteen-foot presence. She looked on as I worked, staring down at the guests' dinners like a very large, optimistic puppy waiting for treats from the table. Or was it the guests themselves she fancied as potential tidbits? I finished with a shot of the head table and, work over for the evening, returned to my assigned place to eat my own meal and do penance for being unkind to Gillian back in the washroom.

Gillian didn't seem to have grown any chattier during the interim, although she did speak when asked a direct question by any of the other people at our table. Me, she continued to ignore. Perhaps she regarded me as the friend of her enemy, Candi's henchwoman, and thus her enemy too. Even so, the dinner passed pleasantly enough thanks to the six other people at our table. One of the university anthropologists sat on my right. I asked her some questions about naming fossils and why I'd heard her laugh when Dr. Maxwell announced *Homo musicus*. Just my saying the name started her laughing all over again. She didn't settle down until her husband, seated on her other side, poked her in the ribs. Then she told me pretty much what Simon had about the subject, adding that this was one Maxwell couldn't possibly get away with, it was simply too silly. She called it an example of taxonomy by Monty Python.

After dinner Gillian left in a hurry, and a few minutes later, Candi came over carrying her coffee cup. It was only a little before ten, but most of the tables stood deserted. Although some guests remained to chat and finish their coffee, many had already left to make the drive back to Calgary.

"Graham had to go say goodbye to some of the rich kids so I'm a free woman," she said. "Until tomorrow at six, anyway. So how was dinner at table fifteen?"

I told her about Gillian's "don't speak until spoken to" silence during dinner and her tears in the washroom that preceded it.

"Poor Gillian, you gotta feel for her," Candi shook her head. "But that's what you get when you fall in love with a chronic lech, especially one who's old enough to be your grandpa. She's too far gone to know that nobody in their right mind would fall for a line like Maxwell's. It's older than Elvis. And deader."

"She must have fallen for it," I pointed out as I finished my coffee. "Have you seen Simon? I have to get the rest of the equipment out of his office."

"Last I saw, he was headed for the men's room, but that was a while ago. He didn't look very steady. A little too much champagne."

"Probably a lot too much and all of it resting on a bourbon base. Well, I can't go prowling the men's washrooms hunting for him so I'll just have to go to his office. He promised he'd leave the door unlocked."

"Need any help?" Candi asked.

"Why don't you take the camera to the van and then pick me up at the entrance? By the time you get there, I'll be waiting for you with the rest of the equipment. The van's in the RV lot." I gave her the camera and the keys.

"I can take your workbag too," Candi said.

I set off for the visiting anthropologists' office. One of the museum's security staff discovered me looking lost, and after I showed him my identification and explained my problem, he started me down the right corridor. I recognized where I was as soon as I saw the staircase that led to the mezzanine and the staff lounge. I heard singing as I climbed the stairs. The words floated down to me.

"She went upstairs to get undressed
When she came down she had no chest
It's magic."

Professor Woodward and Stan sat sprawled at either end of a big couch, singing at the tops of their lungs, an open bottle of single malt and two glasses on the coffee table in front of them. Actually, for a couple of drunks, they sounded pretty good. The song stopped abruptly when I entered the room. A grim-faced Mrs. Woodward stood surveying the scene.

"Hello, Phoebe," the professor said. "This is my friend Stanley and we're singing. We're singing songs we used to sing way back when we were students together. Well, I used to sing them. Stanley never joined in because it was against his religion to have fun. But I always knew that he knew the words, didn't you, Stan?"

"Adam, you're drunk," Mrs. Woodward stated the obvious. "And as for you, Stanley, you used to have a religious objection to alcohol, but I see that's a thing of the past. Just look at the pair of you. You're disgusting."

"But I had to drink a toast, Diana," Stan said with the overarticulated speech peculiar to drunks trying not to sound drunk. "I had to drink a toast because you're so beautiful. So beautiful. You know I've always loved you, Diana. Why didn't you ever love me?"

"Oh for God's sake, Stan, just hope you don't remember any of this in the morning." Mrs. Woodward's tone was much gentler than her words but that soon changed. "Adam, I'm leaving now. Trevor is waiting for us. Are you coming?"

"Can't." Professor Woodward shook his head solemnly. "We promised we'd meet Graham in here for a drink. Say, Stan, do you remember that one about the virgin sturgeon?"

Mrs. Woodward turned, said a polite good night to me, and stalked off down the stairs.

"Nope," Stan replied after giving the matter careful thought. "Don't remember it at all. But wasn't there another one about virgin wool or something?"

"I know the one you mean. I know it. It goes like this." Professor Woodward held up his hands for quiet in the audience and began to sing in a surprisingly full and pleasing baritone. "He was a sheepish virgin. She was a virgin sheep." I didn't stick around for the rest.

I made my way to the second floor and Simon's office. I heard him shouting as soon as I pushed open the heavy door that led from the stairs to the hallway. His words were slurred with alcohol. This was definitely my night for drunks, but Simon didn't sound nearly as jolly as Professor Woodward and Stan. His voice shook with rage. There were silent spaces between his outbursts and I realized he was having an argument with someone quiet. I reached the door but didn't have the guts to knock, especially when I heard the other voice.

"I swear to God, this time I'll blow the whistle. I've had it up to here," Simon bellowed.

"Please, not that old nonsense again." His soft-spoken adversary was Graham Maxwell. Compared to his drunken assistant, Maxwell sounded a little bored and very patronizing. "It's ridiculous. Besides, who'd believe you?"

"Want to risk it, you fifth-rate phony?" Simon had trouble with the f's.

"You're pathetic, Simon. You're a drunk and a failure and a liability." Simon must have hit a nerve because Maxwell no longer sounded patronizing nor quite so much in control. His voice began to rise. "So shut your trap and pull yourself together or you'll find yourself in the unemployment line. I don't need this and I don't need you."

"Oh, you need me, Graham. You and your famous nose for fossils need me." This time Simon spoke quietly, but the loathing in his voice was almost worse than the shouting. "You couldn't find a fossil in this museum unless I drew a map for you. I go and so does your career as the Great Man of Science." He had wanted to say the Great Man of Paleoanthropology, but after a couple of tries, both frustrated by his drunken tongue, he gave up and settled for science. Dr. Maxwell laughed at him.

"Poor old Simon. You don't understand, do you?" The doctor was back in command of himself and the fight. "I've just made one of the greatest fossil finds of all time. My reputation is safe if I never dig up another bone as long as I live."

"And without me you never will."

"And as for reputations, my faithful assistant, you don't have one. Except maybe as a drunk," Maxwell continued. "And, oh yes, I almost forgot, didn't I? You do have your reputation for faking data. That's still pretty secure, I think."

The argument raged on as I retreated back down the corridor. I couldn't see much hope of picking up my equipment until it ended and that didn't seem about to happen any time soon. Besides, all I needed until next morning's interview with Maxwell were the camera and the tripod, and those I already had. I'd collect the rest of the stuff tomorrow.

Candi was waiting for me at the curb, leaning against the side of the van, daring the commissionaire to give her another ticket.

"Where's the equipment?"

I told her.

"You mean you didn't stay to hear the rest?"

"No, I did not hang around eavesdropping on a private conversation." I sounded priggish even to my own ears.

"But you didn't find out what they were arguing about. Don't you care?" she asked in disbelief.

I had to admit that I didn't. I had hated the argument's noise and its rush of raw emotion and all I wanted was to get far away from it. I knew that Candi would never understand. She is passionately interested in people. Maybe that's why she's so good at her job. It's definitely why she's happy to be in the pictures and I'm happy taking them.

"I wonder what kind of data Simon faked? Do you think we could find out?" This had really got her going. "What do you think he has on Maxwell?"

Trevor Woodward saved me from any more of Candi's conjectures. He came out of the museum and stood looking around for a moment before he walked over to the van. I introduced him to Candi. He recovered from the experience relatively quickly, perhaps because he was preoccupied.

"Have you seen my parents?" he asked. "They were supposed to meet me in the lobby twenty minutes ago."

I told him where and when I had last seen them but refrained from mentioning that his father was pissed to the gills.

"I'm a little worried about Dad. For someone who hardly ever drinks he put away an awful lot of wine at dinner. I hope he isn't sick or something. Maybe I'd better go have another look for them." He hurried back to the building.

"Come on," I said before Candi could launch another round of speculation about Simon and Dr. Maxwell. "Let's go back to the bed and breakfast and watch junk on TV."

Personally, I'd had it with drunks and towering egos and wounded feelings. With all the nostril-flaring passions and smouldering resentments raging around the museum that evening, I figured the Royal Tyrrell could run an Italian opera some stiff competition. Or maybe I just had the wrong idea about paleontologists. How was I to know that given the slightest provocation they made *Tosca* look tame?

4

IT WAS DARK WHEN THE ALARM CLOCK WOKE ME at four-thirty. I looked out the window. No rain. Not even a hope. Nothing but the relentlessly cheerful twinkle of stars in a clear black sky, the kind of sky that guarantees a perfect prairie sunrise. Ella would be so pleased. I resisted the urge to phone and tell her the good news.

Because we only had one vehicle between us, Candi had to accompany me on Ella's sunrise shoot in order to be on hand for her early interview with Dr. Maxwell. Half-awake and feeling hard done by, I padded down the hall and knocked on her door.

"I'm awake," she called in a voice as cheerful as the stars. I showered and dressed, applied a swipe or two of makeup, and decided I was a done deal. Last night's Vionnet finery was back in my suitcase, replaced by more conventional work clothes – a sweatshirt over a black turtleneck and khakis. Candi was ready before me. She stood waiting at the van, her overnight bag at her feet. Despite the hour, she looked her usual fresh and impeccably turned-out self in a cream silk blouse, tweed cashmere blazer, and fawn slacks that fell in exactly the correct break over her matching suede boots. I swear you could set off a fire alarm under Candi's bed in the middle of the night and she'd run out the door looking perfect.

I'm not very good at conversation before I've had my first jolt of caffeine so we drove back to the museum in silence. Candi poured us each a big mug of coffee, strong and still hot enough to steam, from the Thermos that our hostess at the bed and breakfast had left for us. We were at the turnoff from the highway to the museum's driveway by the time I finished mine and began to feel almost human. No protestors blocked our way today. Even Myrna had the sense to be home in bed. This morning I'd have driven over her and enjoyed it.

I parked in the museum's public lot as the first hint of light began to change the world from black to grey. There were no other cars. Compared to the van's warm interior, the outside air felt cold and damp and I was glad of my sweatshirt. Candi helped me carry the camera and tripod up the hundred and some wooden steps to the lookout deck. We climbed up through geological time, over the cretaceous-tertiary boundary that marks the end of the Age of Dinosaurs and the beginning of the Age of Mammals, and on to the present. I set the camera up, lens to the east, ready for Ella's sunrise. Then we waited. Clever Candi had brought the Thermos along. We drank our second cups leaning on the guardrail in the dim light of the dawning hills. The aroma of the coffee mingled with the scent of sage that grew in small clumps near the lookout. A gopher poked his head out of a burrow near the top of the stairs, checking on the early-morning commotion. He sat staring at us for a few moments, then disappeared back down to his bed. Sensible creature.

"What are you and Tim doing this weekend?" Candi ended the morning silence. "Want to go to a movie with Nick and me Saturday night?"

"I'd like to but we can't. Tim's bringing his daughter out to my place for the weekend."

"You don't sound too thrilled."

"I'm not. I don't like Brooke and I feel guilty about it. It isn't fair to dislike an eleven-year-old child."

"Why not? Who says you're not allowed to dislike children? Where do you think unlikeable adults get their start?" As always, Candi's logic was irrefutable. "How are things with Tim?"

I shrugged.

"That bad, eh?"

Earlier in the summer, thanks to a combination of loneliness, lust, and opportunity, I'd rushed into an affair with Brooke's father, which, I suppose, is a polite way of saying we had great sex before we knew much about each other. But I'd come to realize that it was a relationship with no future. Tim was recently divorced and still carrying too much baggage from his marriage. I didn't want to help him with the load. For his part, I know he fantasized that Brooke and I would become great pals, that the three of us would be his new, made-to-order family, free of the acrimony and bitterness that plagued his first try at domesticity. I remember that after my own divorce I was a little prone to happiness fantasies, but I don't think I ever got that out of touch with reality.

"You're going to have to tell him," Candi said. "It will only get worse if you keep putting it off."

"It's just hard to find a time that seems right," I said. Even to me, it sounded pretty lame. "But I'm going to try to do it sometime this weekend. Really."

"Look, the sky is starting to colour a little," Candi tactfully changed the subject. "See, it's pinking up over there."

I swallowed the last of my coffee and went to work. I taped that sunrise in all its rococo glory from every angle and every focal length I could squeeze out of the camera. I panned, I zoomed, I damn near grew wings and shot aerials. Ella wanted a sunrise, Ella got a sunrise, right from the first pale wash of pink to the final brilliant shafts of light that beamed up from behind the hills like the ribs of a golden fan. I filled a whole tape.

"There," I flourished the finished product, "that ought to hold her for a week or two."

Candi laughed. "I think Ella's already written some copy that she wants to run with these shots. You know, stuff about the dawn of mankind."

"You're joking," I said, but I knew she wasn't. Motherhood has done strange things to Ella. "What time is it?"

Candi looked at her watch. "We're early. It's only five-thirty, but maybe we could go set up for the interview anyway. At least it will be warmer inside."

We walked back down to the museum and knocked on the big glass doors, but no one came to let us in. We retreated to the van and waited in its warmth for fifteen minutes before we tried again. This time a member of the night security staff stood waiting for us. Young, a little on the chubby side with sandy hair and freckles, he looked more like everyone's kid brother than a security guard. He checked our identification.

"It's not that I don't know who you are." He smiled shyly at Candi, completely captivated, her ID card forgotten in his hand. "I watch your program every week. I think you're the best interviewer on TV."

"Thanks, Mike." Candi read his name off the tag on his uniform. "It's really nice of you to say so." She gently prised her ID from his fingers.

"Do you think maybe I could get your autograph?" he asked. "For my mom, I mean. My mom thinks you're great." He took a pen and a small, spiralbound notebook from his shirt pocket and handed them to Candi. She signed her name and gave them back. He continued to stand and gaze at her.

"Mike, it's time to let us in," Candi reminded him gently. "We've got to go to work."

"Oh geez, I'm sorry." He blushed so deeply that even his freckles looked red. "Here, let me help you with that." He took the tripod from Candi and led the way to Maxwell's exhibit. We stopped outside the door.

"I'm sorry, ladies, but I'm afraid I can't unlock the door for you. My instructions are that you're supposed to wait for Dr. Maxwell to let you in."

"That's okay, Mike," Candi said. "I'm sure he'll be along any minute. And thanks for your help."

"You're welcome, Candi." He held out his hand to her. She shook it and thanked him again. Mike floated back down the corridor, a grin like the Cheshire cat's lighting his plump face.

We waited outside the door for ten minutes, but Dr. Maxwell didn't show.

"This is getting annoying," I said.

"Too bad we can't get in there and set up."

"We need the lights before we can do anything and they're still upstairs. Are you sure Dr. Maxwell wanted us to meet him here? Maybe he's waiting for us in his office."

"Ella was very clear," Candi stated. "We're supposed to meet him here, at the exit door to the exhibit, at quarter to six."

"Then he must have slept in."

"Maybe Gillian locked him in his room."

"I don't care if she tied him to the bed. I just wish she'd let him out long enough to finish this interview." I leaned my back against the door and promptly fell into the room. I landed, left elbow first, on the concrete floor. A rectangle of light from the corridor spilled in through the door, illuminating the first few feet of the space. The rest lay in darkness.

"Phoebe, are you okay?" Candi hurried over.

"I'm fine," I sat up and rubbed my elbow. It hurt, but all my fingers still wiggled. "Nothing injured but my dignity."

"How'd you get the door to open?"

"I didn't. All I did was lean back and it opened. It mustn't have been latched properly."

"Then let's get started. I wonder where Gillian keeps the switches for those work lights. Somewhere out in the corridor, I think."

"Maybe we shouldn't," I said. "We might get Mike into trouble."

"Why? He didn't let us in. The door was already open."

Something small and hard that I had fallen on was busy digging its way into my thigh. I brushed it out from under me.

"Hey, what's that?" Candi picked it up and held it to the light. "It's a rock. There's some bits of plaster or something on it."

I took it from her and looked at it closely. "I think it's part of the exhibit," I said, not quite willing to believe my eyes. "Look, it's a piece of backbone, a chunk off one of the vertebrae."

"I don't like this," Candi said. "I don't like this at all. Maybe you'd better get the flashlight."

I got up off the floor and fetched the small flashlight that I keep in my workbag. We followed its narrow beam back into the darkness and up to the exhibit. The light reflected off the Plexiglas barrier and bounced back in our eyes until I held the lens directly against a panel and managed to illuminate a few feet of Dr. Maxwell's African gully.

"They're gone," Candi said. "Someone's pulled them out of the hill."

Instead of fossils we saw nothing but blank spaces, empty holes lined with padding and shaped like the bones they had been made to cradle. We walked the flashlight along the length of the barrier. Not a single bone remained. The skeletons had vanished, leaving only their ghostly outlines in the fibreglass rock.

"Do you think maybe Gillian takes them out of the exhibit and puts them in their packing cases at night?" Candi asked, but I could tell she really didn't believe it.

"Not a chance," I said. "Besides, Gillian wouldn't toss vertebrae on the floor."

"My God, will you look at that. They even stole the baby." It was obvious that Candi thought this was about as low as a fossil thief could go. "Well, at least they didn't separate it from its mother. That's something, I guess." She said this without the slightest suggestion of irony.

"Look, the last panel in the line is down." We came to the end of the barrier. "That's how they got them out."

"Why would anyone steal fossils?" Candi asked. "Is there a black market in prehistoric bones or something?"

"I don't think whoever did this did it for money." I shone the flashlight on a piece of white computer paper taped to a panel.

"*So God created man in his own image, in the image of God created he him; male and female created he them,*" Candi read the laser-printed text.

"We'd better call the police." I led the way out of the room. "You go find Mike and make the call."

"What are you going to do?" she asked.

"I'm going to get my lights. I figure we've got at least twenty minutes before the police get here. That's enough time to tape this mess for News, but I need some light."

"I'm sure Gillian's switches are somewhere out here," Candi said.

"Then look for them if you get back before I do," I said, starting down the corridor. "But if you haven't found them we won't have to waste any more time. We already know where the plugs are."

I ran down the corridor and took the stairs up to the mezzanine two at a time. This morning snoring, not singing,

71

rocked the staff lounge. Stan and Professor Woodward slept, one at either end of the couch, in exactly the same places I'd left them the night before. They lay with their bow ties off, the top studs of their shirts unfastened, and the Scotch bottle, now down to its bottom third, resting next to their feet on the coffee table. Both emitted loud, whisky-laced snores. They didn't even break rhythm as I ran past them and up the next set of stairs to the offices.

The door to the anthropologists' office stood open. I remember being a little annoyed that they would be so careless with the station's equipment, but that was the last ordinary thought I managed until the police arrived. For me, thought and movement and time all became distorted the moment I stepped into that office.

Dr. Maxwell lay on the floor next to the lab bench staring up at me with sightless eyes. His head, tilted a little to one side, rested in a pool of blood. I saw some slimy-looking grey stuff mixed with the blood and wondered what it was. Then I realized it was his brain. I remember thinking that the back of his head looked like a smashed egg, its shell crushed and its insides oozing out. Maybe it was seeing the dinosaur egg near his skull that made me think this. One of the big ones from the top shelf lay a couple of feet from Dr. Maxwell's head, partly covered in hair and blood. I looked back at his face. It took a while for me to realize that there was something sticking out of his mouth. Perhaps my mind simply didn't want to acknowledge what my eyes saw. It was the worst. The little bone flute protruded from between Dr. Maxwell's teeth as if someone had rammed it down his throat.

I turned away and leaned against the door jamb. My

knees buckled and I slid down to the floor just as Simon, still dressed in evening clothes, appeared at the door of the inner office. He looked at me, then looked over and saw Dr. Maxwell. He stumbled over me and on out the door. I heard him retching in the hall.

I don't remember getting up or going back downstairs to the exhibit. My memory kicks in again with an image that seems frozen in time, almost like a photograph. Mike is sitting slumped on the floor in front of the empty display. His shoulders are hunched, his head is in his hands, he is weeping. Candi sits beside him, her arm around his shoulders.

"Phoebe, what's the matter?" At the sound of Candi's voice the world began to move again. She rose and walked toward me. "You're white as a sheet. What's wrong?"

I opened my mouth to tell her but no words would come out.

"Sit down. Right now," Candi ordered. She took my arm and helped me to the floor. "Put your head between your knees." I did as I was told until the wave of nausea and giddiness passed.

"Phoebe, you're freezing cold. Your hands feel like blocks of ice." She took off her jacket and draped it over my shoulders. "Now tell me what's wrong." I looked up. This time the words came.

"You're sure he's dead?"

"Oh, Candi, the whole back of his head is mush. He's dead. I'm sure." Then I started to cry.

By this time, Mike had recovered enough to crawl over and sit beside me but seeing my tears set him off again. We both wept while Candi did her best to comfort us.

"You found the light switches," I sobbed, although I can't think why this interested me unless obsessing on some manageable trivia is the mind's way of distancing itself from shock.

"Mike knew where they were," Candi said.

"It happened on my watch," he snuffled. "There are two of us, you know, but I'm the senior man and it happened on my watch."

"It's okay, Mike," Candi said gently. "No one's going to blame you."

"Maybe I should load the camera and get some shots." I wiped my eyes on the sleeve of Candi's jacket, but the tears flowed on. "There's enough light."

"Phoebe, I don't think you need to bother with that just now," she said gently. "You look like hell so stay put until you get some colour back. Okay?"

Sometime during all this, I noticed Mike's hand holding mine. Candi knelt behind us patting our shoulders and making soft comforting sounds that may have been words, or maybe not. And that's how the police found us.

5

BY THE TIME THE MOUNTIES FINISHED WITH ME, they knew more about the past eighteen hours of my life than I did. They asked me about everything I'd seen and heard from the protest march to the present. Their questions came from so many angles and in such number that when my session with them ended around eleven, I'd probably told it all three or four times. I guess that's their way of checking the consistency of what you say – if you tell the same story no matter how many ways they come at you, then maybe you're telling the truth. They were still questioning Candi when they called it quits with me. I was told I could wait for her in the cafeteria.

The museum was closed for the day by police order, both to the public and to most of the staff, including the people who worked in the cafeteria. However, someone had managed to get an urn of coffee going and set out a big basket of individually wrapped oatmeal cookies. A tray of metal teapots, each armed with a tea bag, sat next to a much smaller urn full of hot water. I filled one and put it and a cup and a cookie on a cafeteria tray, which I carried over to a table next to one of the windows that looked out over the terrace and the pond.

The place was back to being a cafeteria. The table linen and wild rose china were gone and so was Lillian the *Albertosaurus*. I missed her. The red-and-white banners stirring gently in the faint current of the air-conditioning system were the only reminder of last night's celebration. There were a half-dozen people in the big room, two policemen drinking coffee and four lost-looking museum employees, whom I recognized from last night, sitting over empty cups. I slid into a chair beside the window and looked out to where Gillian sat at the table nearest the pond. Her jeans and rumpled pink turtleneck looked like they were the first things she'd grabbed out of the laundry basket that morning. The white lab coat, her uniform of office, hung over the back of her chair. She stared straight ahead across the pond. I'd never seen anyone look so alone.

I picked up my tray and went through the big glass door out to the terrace. Gillian did not look up as I approached.

"Hello. Would you like a cup of tea?" I put the tray in front of her.

She pushed a lank strand of hair out of her eyes and stared at me, as if I had called her from a million miles away.

"Phoebe?" she said tentatively. Her face, minus makeup, was very pale. Only the circles under her eyes had any colour. They were so dark the skin looked bruised.

"Here, let me pour some for you." I poured tea into the cup and sat down in the chair across from her.

"You're very kind," she said in an almost puzzled voice, as if she were commenting on some unusual natural phenomenon.

The redwing blackbirds that made their home in the rushes growing near the edge of the water busied themselves around the terrace, searching under the tables and chairs for crumbs. One flew up and perched on the back of the empty chair beside Gillian. It cast a beadily expectant eye on the cookie. She tore open the wrapper, broke off a chunk, and crumbled it onto the edge of the table. The bird hopped over and began to eat. Its beak made tiny tapping sounds on the metal surface.

"I'm very sorry about Dr. Maxwell." Why is it that I'm reduced to the inane, or at least the inadequate, when dealing with grief? Candi isn't. She'd have known what to say.

"Thank you." Gillian nodded an acknowledgement as stiff and formal as my expression of sympathy.

"You should drink your tea while it's still hot," I reminded her, retreating to the practical world of eating and drinking. Maybe that's why people bring food to the bereaved – it's a simple, tangible representation of their desire to comfort. "Would you like some milk or sugar in it?"

"No thanks," she sipped some of the tea. "This is good." She ate a little of the cookie before she scattered the rest to the birds. As she did, I could see her making an effort to pull herself together, her very British upper lip stiffening before my eyes. Gillian sat straighter, her eyes were no longer vacant, and when she spoke her voice was almost steady. "Have the police questioned you?"

"They just finished," I said.

"I have to go back again this afternoon. They want me there when they go through the office. Do you think he'll still be . . ."

"No, his body won't be there," I assured her. Earlier in the morning while I was waiting to be questioned, I had seen two ambulance attendants wheel a loaded stretcher toward the elevator.

She seemed relieved. "Not that I don't want to see him," she added quickly. "I'm not afraid of seeing Graham's body. I'm not afraid to look at him again. But I don't want to see him like that."

We sat quietly for a few minutes. The blackbird watched us from his perch on the chair.

"You were the one who found him, weren't you?" she said.

"I went to your office to get some camera equipment Simon let me leave there last night. We needed it for our interview."

"No interviews now," Gillian said softly, almost to herself. "I loved him, you know. And he loved me. I know he did. He loved me." She leaned forward and looked straight at me.

"I could see last night that you thought I was jealous of your friend Candi. But that was nothing." Her voice began to rise with emotion. "Graham loved to flirt with pretty women and that's all it was, flirting. I couldn't be jealous of something that trivial. He loved me," she repeated it like some personal mantra. "He loved me. You could tell that he loved me, couldn't you?" This was not a rhetorical question, it was a plea. I realized Gillian had suffered the kind of emotional shock that can make normally reserved people lose their self-possession and say things they regret later but, still, her intensity startled me.

So much for the stiff upper lip. The blackbird flew away, back to the safety of the reeds. I wished I could join him.

"How did you come to work for him?" It was a pretty lame question, but at least it might steer the conversation back to a course that Gillian would not regret and that I could handle now.

"We met at a conference in London. My old tutor from Cambridge introduced us at the opening-night cocktail party." Gillian sat back in her chair and even smiled a little at the memory. Much to my amazement, my feeble effort at conversation steering actually seemed to be working. "Graham's personal assistant had just resigned and he offered me the job."

"I thought Simon was his personal assistant." Obviously, keeping her talking about her work was the answer.

"Simon's the field manager. I look after everything else." She finished the last of the tea and put her empty cup back on the tray. "You heard Graham and Simon arguing last night, didn't you?"

"How do you know that?" I'd only told Candi and the police about what I'd heard.

"I saw you walking away from the office."

"Where were you?"

"I'd just come through the door at the other end of the corridor."

"Have you told this to the police?"

"Of course I have," she said. "And I told them that they shouldn't make too much of what you heard. Neither should you. It wasn't important and it certainly wasn't unusual. Poor Simon's a belligerent drunk and he's drunk most of the time these days. He picked fights with Graham and me constantly."

"It sounded like they hated each other."

"No, no, absolutely not. You're quite mistaken." She underscored the words with an emphatic shake of her head. "Irritation maybe, but not hate."

If what I'd heard last night was irritation, then I shuddered to think what Gillian considered hate.

"You see," she continued when she saw I wasn't convinced, "Graham was very good to Simon. If it weren't for Graham, Simon wouldn't have a job. His career in anthropology would have been over before it started because no one else would hire him. But as things turned out, Simon's had a very nice ride on Graham's coattails."

"Why wouldn't anyone else hire him?"

"Because Simon faked data for his doctoral dissertation and he got caught. Don't look so shocked. I'm not telling tales out of school. It was common knowledge. Graham told me all about it. He and Simon were both working on a big project in Ethiopia at the time. They became friends. Graham had worked on all sorts of important digs by then, but Simon had only worked as a student. The Ethiopia dig was his first time out as a fully qualified professional, but, even so, he'd already made a bit of a splash in the field. Apparently his dissertation impressed a lot of people. It's hard to believe when you meet him now, but back then Simon was one of the rising young stars in paleoanthropology. At least that's what my tutor told me."

"So what happened?"

"Someone at his university found out that he'd faked part of the data for his dissertation. As it turned out, what he'd fudged later proved to be absolutely correct, but it didn't matter by then. Simon had cheated and that made his work a fraud. Science depends on the honesty of its practitioners. He was finished."

"Why would he do something that stupid?"

"Who knows? Perhaps he was young and full of himself and in a hurry and so confident of the accuracy of his phony figures that he thought he was invulnerable, that he'd never get caught. Or maybe he just couldn't wait to get out and start impressing the world. But he did get caught and the university stripped him of his degree. Paleoanthropology is a very small world and everybody knew about Simon and his dodgy data. Graham was the only one who would give him the time of day."

"Wasn't he afraid Simon's reputation would taint his own work?"

"Graham was above all that," she dismissed my remark with an airy wave of her hand. "His own reputation for integrity was beyond question."

I didn't think it would be tactful to point out that, at the time of Simon's scandal, Graham Maxwell would have been an obscure paleontologist who didn't have a reputation for much of anything. "Did you meet Simon at the London conference too?" I asked instead.

"I guess I must have, but I don't remember. All I really remember about that conference is Graham." The emotional edge began to creep back into her voice. I could hear her starting to lose control again. "We slept together that first night after the party. He was a wonderful lover. And, you know, even after three years together, he only had to look at me and I could feel my whole body wanting him, needing him inside me, knowing how it felt when –"

"Gillian," I interrupted sharply, "I'm going to get you some more tea." So much for the well-steered conversation. Gillian might not regret what she'd told me, but any more reminiscing about her sex life and I sure as hell would.

I went inside the cafeteria and filled another pot with hot water. Candi caught up with me just as I was about to head back to the terrace.

"They're done with me," she said. "Let's get out of here."

"I'm going to take this to Gillian first," I said. "She's sitting outside near the pond. She looks terrible."

"I'll let you do that alone, I think," Candi said. "I'm probably not the person she most wants to see right now."

I went back out to Gillian. She was still staring at the pond.

"I have to leave now," I said. "I have to go back to Calgary. Will you be all right?" The question was pointless. Gillian was obviously anything but all right. "Do you know anyone here?"

"I know Simon," she said.

"I mean someone you can talk to. Someone who can help."

Gillian needed someone to stay with her and hold her hand and make her a bowl of soup. Simon seemed an unlikely candidate.

"Here, this is my business card." I wrote my home number on the back of one of the cards the station issues us and put it on the table in front of her. "Call me if you want to. If there's anything I can do for you." But I knew Gillian would not call and a shameful little voice inside me whispered its relief.

The museum's forecourt was cordoned off with yellow crime-scene tape, and news vehicles lined the drive. Their crews had come from Calgary and Edmonton to cover what would undoubtedly be the hottest story of the day. The dead Dr. Maxwell and his missing fossils would give them a chance to make headlines all over the world. It could be a career-maker. The police let Candi and me out a side door so, as we drove past them in our station's van, the reporters assumed we were simply another television crew and not part of the story. I stopped and took a shot of them and their photographers strung out along the yellow tape – carrion birds of woe, feeding on every conveniently accessible occasion of human misery. I had been one of them myself, many times, but the sight still sickened me.

"We have to eat something before we drive back," Candi said as we drove into Drumheller. "It's nearly two and I'm starving." We hadn't had anything since our pre-dawn mug of coffee on the way to the museum, but even so I wasn't sure I trusted my stomach to cope with food. I had intended to try it out on the oatmeal cookie, but Gillian and the birds scotched that. I still felt pretty queasy but Candi was adamant.

We found a sidewalk table at the Dino Diner, a cappuccino and sandwich joint on the sunny side of the town's main street. Drumheller was once a mining town, but the mines have been closed for years. Now tourism, much of it a result of the Royal Tyrrell, has replaced coal as a source of income. Sleek new hotels, a flourishing bed and break-fast trade, gift shops and trendy cafés have given the little place an air of tourist gentility that would astonish the men who worked the coal face down the Western Commercial. I read over the list of designer coffees and herbal teas tucked into a little Plexiglas stand on our table. The miners couldn't have imagined a place like the Dino Diner.

"Just coffee, thanks," I said to the waiter. I gave him back the menu. A cartoon tyrannosaur grinned toothily from its cover. The dinosaur motif pervades Drumheller's commercial displays.

Candi peered at me over her menu.

"But I'm not hungry," I protested.

"It doesn't matter whether you're hungry or not. That's not the point." She turned to the waiter. "We'll each have a tuna salad on whole wheat and a double latte, please."

When Candi gets in one of her take-charge moods, there's not much to be gained by arguing.

I leaned back in my chair and stretched my legs under the table. The afternoon sun shone warm on my back. I could feel the muscles begin to relax. We sat in silence. Neither of us felt much like talking about our morning at the museum. We were talked out. The police had seen to that. I assumed they had asked the same questions of everyone who had been at the museum that morning, although I hadn't had a chance to talk to anybody but Candi and Gillian. I did see Stan, Professor Woodward, and their colossal hangovers being escorted down the hall near the library by a police constable. Professor Woodward walked very gingerly as if he were trying to prevent the shock of his shoes hitting the carpet from transmitting up to his aching head. But he was nothing compared to Stan. Pasty-faced, trembling, and sweaty, the poor little fellow looked like he'd regard death as a welcome release. Simon was nowhere to be seen.

"What do you think they'll do to Mike?" Candi asked.

"What will who do?"

"The museum," Candi said. "Do you think they'll fire him?"

"Probably not. What could he have done? I doubt that Mike or anyone else could have helped Dr. Maxwell."

"I didn't mean about Dr. Maxwell. I was thinking about the fossils."

"Mike probably couldn't have done much about that either. Whoever stole the bones must have planned it out to the last detail. They'd know exactly where he and the other guard would be when they made their move."

The waiter brought our lattes. Tiny versions of the menu's cartoon tyrannosaur danced around the rims of the cups. I took a drink and felt the hot, milky liquid warm my insides.

"I think that Mike's job probably has more to do with keeping an eye on the building systems and preventing vandalism and fires than it does with murder and major theft. Besides, fossils weigh a ton. They're not exactly the smash-and-grab special. You'd need a crane and a semi to steal the big dinosaur stuff at the Royal Tyrrell. Maxwell's exhibit was an exception – small, relatively light, and very valuable."

"You really think he was murdered?" Candi said.

"Of course he was murdered. That egg didn't jump off the shelf by itself."

"Could it have fallen off? You said the eggs didn't look too safe up there." Candi was in high speculative gear. How she manages to lure me into being her straight man for these theorizing binges I'll never know. You'd think that after all this time I'd be able to resist answering, but I never learn.

"Right. The rock fell off its shelf and bashed out his brains. Then he shoved the flute down his own throat."

"Yeah, I guess not. You have a point there," she conceded.

I shuddered slightly. The grisly image of Maxwell lying on the floor with the gazelle bone protruding from his mouth haunted my mind. It would for weeks.

"I'm sorry, Phoebe," Candi said. "I should have gone with you. You shouldn't have had to do that on your own."

"Don't be dumb," I said. "We didn't know I'd find him dead."

"Poor old Dr. Maxwell," Candi said. "I mean, he may have been a total egomaniac jerk, but he was a really alive one. He had a kind of vitality that you don't meet all that often. And you know, I think he may have loved his work almost as much as he loved himself."

"Yeah," I agreed. "Maybe that's one of the reasons Gillian fell for him. You know, we shouldn't have left her there all alone. She's a mess."

"What else could you have done? The police obviously weren't going to let us stay and there's no way they'd let her come with us even if she wanted to," Candi said sensibly. "Besides, I doubt there's much anybody can do for the poor woman right now, especially strangers. Kind of makes you wonder how many Gillians Maxwell had in his career. I mean, it's classic – the great man and his faithful female assistant."

"I'd say he had quite a few. He obviously liked them young and good-looking, so a certain turnover would be inevitable."

"He and Simon have sure been together a long time. No turnover there. Maybe being middle-aged and male gave him some sort of job security."

"Simon wasn't middle-aged when he went to work for Maxwell," I pointed out. "He started with him more than twenty years ago, before Maxwell made his first big discovery. Gillian told me about how Simon came to work for him." I repeated the story of the faked data. "Maxwell was the only one who would give him a job."

"That sure explains some of what you heard last night when they were fighting. You don't think Simon could have killed him, do you?"

"Candi, I don't know who killed him. And I don't see much point in our sitting here guessing. There were a whole slew of people at the museum last night who had good reason to despise Graham Maxwell. But despising is one thing, murdering is another."

"You're probably right," she agreed. "I mean, Simon was angry enough about the fossils' name to fight about it and I know Gillian was really mad at Dr. Maxwell for leching after me. And Stan is a card-carrying creationist so that gives him a reason too. But none of it seems enough to kill somebody over, does it?"

"You forgot Professor Woodward," I said, thinking of his Maxwell lookalike son. "And Mrs. Woodward and Trevor."

"Now you're just being silly, Phoebe. You might as well add Mike's name to the list."

"Why not? He might enjoy being one of the gang."

"Of course, the same people who stole the fossils could have killed Dr. Maxwell while they were at it," Candi added another possibility to her list. "But they didn't look like murderers to me."

"Who's they?" This time Candi had leapt ahead without me.

"The Geologists for Jesus, of course. They stole the bones, but I don't think they murdered Dr. Maxwell to get them."

"How do you know the Geologists for Jesus stole the fossils? There must have been three or four different protest groups out at the airport to meet Maxwell's plane. And there's probably lots more where they came from. And how do you know it was protesters at all? It could have been a plain old robbery for profit."

"What about that quote from the Bible taped to the Plexiglas?"

"Anybody could have done that. What if professional fossil thieves stole the bones and wanted to throw everyone off the scent. They might just write a note with a religious . . ." Oh no! Candi had me doing it now.

I was saved by the waiter and our food. Crazy as her theories about crime were, I had to admit that Candi was spot on about eating. By the time I'd finished half my sandwich, the queasy jitters I'd felt for most of the morning were pretty much gone.

"You're looking better now, Phoebe," she said. "You've got some colour back."

88

"I feel a lot better."

"It's getting late. I guess we'd better phone Ella."

"I don't think I feel that much better," I said.

"She'll already know about Dr. Maxwell and the robbery. It'll have been on the news." Candi took the cellphone out of her briefcase, switched it on, and punched in the station's number.

I left her to it and carried our cups into the restaurant for refills. By the time I returned to the table, the conversation was over and the phone back in Candi's briefcase.

"Well, what did she say?" I asked.

"Not much. She's pretty upset about Dr. Maxwell. She says she's never known anybody who got murdered before. And she asked if you were okay."

"She asked about me?" I was stunned. "Didn't she yell about the program?"

Candi shook her head. "She didn't yell at all."

"You're telling me Ella didn't say one word about her program?"

"Well, she did mention that she has some ideas on how we can save the hour," Candi admitted. "But she didn't shout about it. She wants to talk to us when we get back to the station."

"Well that'll be a real treat, won't it?"

"You know, Phoebe, you really are unfair to Ella sometimes. She isn't so unreasonable."

"Are we talking about the woman who wanted me to run over that protestor yesterday so we could get to the museum on time?"

"Ella didn't really want you to run her over and you know it. She was just feeling frustrated and angry and I don't blame her. You know, we've got the easy parts of this job. All I do is stand in front of the camera and talk while you hide behind it and take pictures. Ella's the one who has to take the flak when things go wrong, not us. Ella's the one who has to scramble to put something together to fill the time slot, not us. So I think we should cut her a little slack now and again." It's really irritating when Candi's right. "Besides, even you have to admit that she's been much better since Maggie was born. She seems to care about other people's feelings."

"I'll grant you that maybe we should cut her some slack," I agreed. "But I think you're pushing it with the caring and feeling stuff."

"Maybe," Candi conceded. "But at least now she notices that other people have feelings. Well, some of the time anyway." She collected the bill and got up from the table. "Come on, put your eyebrows back down where they live and let's go home."

6

CANDI DROVE US BACK TO CALGARY. The warm sun shining through the glass and the soothing hum of the tires lulled me to sleep before we'd reached Horseshoe Canyon. I woke with a start and a crick in my neck as we pulled off the Deerfoot onto Glenmore Trail and hit our first red light. It was after four-thirty by the time Candi parked the van in its regular place next to the station's loading bay.

Despite Candi's assurances, I was in no rush to discuss my day with our kinder, gentler producer so I stayed behind to unload the van while she went ahead to check with Ella and fill her in on what had happened at the museum. I did my best not to hurry with the equipment, but, since the police still had half of it sealed in Dr. Maxwell's office, it only took five minutes to stow the remainder back in the photography department. I put the batteries on the charger and then cleaned the camera's lens very carefully. I polished the viewfinder too. I even tidied my workbag. Ten minutes. I went back to the van, opened the side door, and stood toying with the idea of vacuuming the floor. I contemplated the layer of detritus that looked like it had been accumulating since Dr. Maxwell's fossils were children and decided that even Ella in a temper wasn't worth tackling that. At least I knew what to expect from Ella – God knows what I'd turn up under the back seats of the van. Fifteen minutes. The worst should be over. I took our overnight bags, put mine in the trunk of my car, and carried Candi's into the building.

Ella's office was empty when I got there. And peaceful. I sat in one of the two easy chairs she keeps for guests. A television set tuned to our station sat on top of a filing cabinet mouthing a silent soap. Her computer hummed quietly in the background while screen-saver tropical fish swam lazily across its monitor. A single yellow rose sat in a bud vase on the desk. Ella's husband sends a rose to her office every Monday morning. How such an incurable romantic as Marty ended up married to our producer is beyond me. Candi says that Ella is basically a romantic too, but that she sometimes comes across a little hard-nosed because she's insecure.

"Well, if it isn't Calamity Phoebe," the basic romantic said as she and Candi came into the office carrying mugs of coffee. "You really are a magnet for trouble, aren't you?" she added, although not altogether unkindly. "Candi told me what happened this morning. Finding Dr. Maxwell's body must have been horrible. Are you okay?" She placed one of the mugs on the table in front of me. Behind her, Candi gave me a very pointed I-told-you-so look.

"Thanks," I said. "I'm fine now." And oddly enough I was. My early morning in the anthropologists' office seemed far away, almost unreal, like it had happened to someone else.

"So what do you think of changing the program to a memorial tribute to Dr. Maxwell?" Ella offered me a digestive biscuit from the stash she keeps in the bottom drawer of the filing cabinet.

"It's a good idea, but we don't have nearly enough material to fill an hour." I accepted the digestive. It felt like we'd signed a little peace pact. At least I think the digestive was a peace offering. Could be Ella just thought I might like a biscuit.

"Then we'll have to tape more, won't we?" She sat behind her desk, picked up her clipboard, and began drumming on it with a pencil. At last, a little normal Ella behaviour. "I've been doing some checking but nobody knows where Dr. Maxwell's funeral will be, or when, or if there will even be one. But if there's any sort of memorial service for him here in Alberta, we could arrange to go and then set up some interviews later with the people who attend. You know, tributes from friends and colleagues, that kind of thing."

"He's lived in Africa for years. He owned a house in Nairobi," Candi said. "I'll bet you his funeral will be in Africa."

"And while you're at it you can bet your back teeth that the station won't spring for three plane tickets to a funeral in Kenya," Ella said. "We'll have to make do with whatever happens in Alberta. So it's here or nothing with maybe – and this is a big maybe – a little trip to Lethbridge if we're lucky. One of his ex-wives lives there. I'm trying to set up an interview with her."

"One of? How many ex-wives did he have?" I asked.

"Four if you like round numbers, or three-point-something if you want to be picky," Ella said. "He had three that were definitely ex and a fourth who's currently in the process of becoming an ex."

"Guess today speeded that up some," Candi said.

"You think Gillian was hoping to be Mrs. Maxwell number five?" I asked.

"Well, numbers two and four were both his personal assistants." Ella looked at the notes on her clipboard. "Two was a geologist and four was an anthropologist. I'd say Gillian had to think she was at least in the running." She resumed her drumming. "Did you get any of the shots on my list?"

"For God's sake, Ella, the whole place was cordoned off by the police." This was more like it. "I'm lucky they let me keep the camera. They took all the tapes I had with me."

"The tape with the sunrise shots? They've got my sunrise shots?" She was nearly back to normal.

"Your sunrise is right here." I fished the tape out of my workbag and placed it on her desk. "I put it in the van before we went to meet Dr. Maxwell. They only got the blank ones I had with me in the museum."

"Well, that's something, I suppose. When do you think you'll be able to go back and get the rest of the shots on the list? Did the police tell you when they'd be finished?"

"I asked the officer who questioned me," Candi said. "She said the museum will be open again tomorrow. At least the public parts will. The research offices will still be closed. But I think you better check with the people at the Royal Tyrrell to make sure."

"We don't need the research offices. The labs and the public part will do fine," said Ella. "Phoebe, you can go out there tomorrow and finish the list."

"Tomorrow's Saturday. I've got things planned. Can't it wait until Monday?"

"Saturday, Monday, whatever – I guess it doesn't matter much now, does it?" she answered with a resignation I'd never heard from her before. Really, this new calm and kindly Ella had me off balance. "Too bad we didn't get there early enough yesterday to take some close-up shots of Maxwell's fossils, but there's no point in worrying about that either." She swung her chair to face the computer, tapped a key, and the bright fish disappeared, replaced by the station's equipment log. "Rats. News has booked two cameras and the extra van." The news department's needs are a lot higher on the station priority list than *A Day in the Lifestyle*'s. "The premier's in Calgary on Monday, spouting off about something or other."

"Probably going to announce he's privatizing the weather," Candi said.

"That'll stick it to those freeloading ski resorts," I said. "They can kiss all that nice public snow goodbye."

Ella ignored us, which, given the turn the conversation had taken, was probably a sound strategy. She continued tapping. "There's a camera and a van free on Tuesday. That do?" She asked over her shoulder. I nodded an affirmative. "Then I'll check with the museum to make sure it's okay and call you before you go. I'll have to revise that shot list."

By the time Ella decided our meeting was over, rush hour was at its peak and, to add to the vexation, I had to

drive across town to pick up the dog at Cyrrie's. I put a
Mozart disc in the CD player, cranked the volume up and
the car windows down. The Queen of the Night's aria
soared over the din of the traffic on Elbow Drive. I think
it's probably a nice change for people if the car stereo they
hear boom boom booming toward them from three blocks
away is amplifying Mozart instead of the usual junk. So, if
it's a warm day and I'm in the mood, Wolfgang and I do
our best. Really, when you stop to think about it, playing
Mozart with the windows down is a form of public service.
Cyrrie doesn't agree. He says that noise pollution is noise
pollution whether it's rock, rap, or *The Magic Flute*. I say
if that's the way he feels, then he shouldn't have given me
a new car CD player for my birthday.

It's hard to define my relationship with Cyrrie. Probably
uncle is the best description, but technically we're really not
related. Cyrrie is originally from England, although he's
now such a staunch Bluenose and beaver-tail Canadian
that if he cut his finger he'd probably bleed maple syrup.
He and my Uncle Andrew met and fell in love during the
Second World War. Andrew was stationed in England with
the RCAF and when he came back to Canada, Cyrrie came
with him. They lived together for more than forty years
until Andrew's death. So whether it's official or not, Cyrrie
is as much a part of our family as any of the more conventional aunts and uncles.

Whenever I have to be away overnight, I leave my dog
with him. Both of them enjoy these visits, the dog especially
since Cyrrie is a very good cook and persists in feeding Bertie
samples despite my strict dog food–only instructions. It's all

very well for Cyrrie to be so cavalier. He doesn't have to spend an hour driving home trapped in a small space with the after-effects of these gourmet extravaganzas.

Cyrrie still lives in the big house on the brow of the North Hill that he and Andrew shared. It's on Crescent Road, just above the city's centre, and the view from the living-room window over the office towers and out to the Rocky Mountains is quintessential Calgary. Today the air was clear, free of the hazy yellow layer of pollution that sometimes collects in the Bow Valley. On days like this the mountains seem much closer than their actual distance. The jagged line of white peaks shone in the afternoon sun, a bright contrast to the muted blue of the slopes.

When I pulled up in front of the house, Cyrrie and the dog were sitting on the front steps, Cyrrie enjoying the view and Bertie beside him keeping an eye on the passersby. Cyrrie didn't run toward me, fling himself at my feet, and burst into hysterical yelps, but I think he was pleased to see me too.

"It's Miss Phoebe and her Mozartmobile." He followed Bertie down the path at a leisurely pace. "We heard you coming over the Centre Street bridge. Hello, my dear." He gave me a hug while the dog continued to wriggle and run in circles around us. "For heaven's sake, Bert, do calm down. Remember, you're a dignified German shepherd. You'll be pleased to know, Phoebe, that Bertie's been doing a little work on his dignity while you've been away." He put his arm around my shoulders and we started toward the house.

"I can see that," I said as the dog flopped down on the sidewalk in front of us, rolled over on his back, and stuck all four legs in the air. Even upside down, he still managed to keep wagging his tail. "Might need just a touch more polish, I think."

"Well, you can't expect perfection this soon. After all, the poor fellow's just started. And besides, we don't want him to get too stuffy, do we?" We sidestepped the flailing paws and went up the stairs into the house. Bertie collected himself and charged ahead. He made it to the kitchen before we did and sat beside his empty dish, looking up at us in an eager, yet dignified, manner.

Cyrrie poured me a glass of wine from a bottle of Italian red that stood open on the counter. We sat on high-backed stools on opposite sides of the T-shaped island that serves as a kitchen table on the downstroke and a work surface on the cross. Stainless-steel colanders, copper-bottomed pots, and other tools of a serious cook hung from hooks over the working end of the island. The savoury smell of a daube simmering in the oven filled the room. The dog lay on the floor with his head on my foot, drooling decorously on my shoe.

"I'm glad you're back," Cyrrie said. "I've been worried about you ever since I listened to the news this morning and heard about that scientist who was killed at the Royal Tyrrell."

"Graham Maxwell," I said. "We did an interview with him last night."

"Were you at the museum when they found his body?"

"I was the one who found him." I knew this would horrify Cyrrie, but he'd be even more horrified if he read it in tomorrow morning's *Herald*.

"Oh no, my poor girl." The colour drained from his face.

"It's okay, Cyrrie. I'm fine. It was pretty horrible but I'm all right now."

"Dear God in heaven," he shook his head. "Why did it have to be you?"

"Because I was there and it had to be someone."

"You're right, of course." He paused. "That was a very foolish thing for me to say. But I still wish it hadn't been you."

"Me too."

"Tell me what happened," he said. And I did.

I told him the whole thing from meeting the protesters to discovering the fossils missing and finding Dr. Maxwell's body, with the flute shoved down his throat. I told him about Stan and the Woodwards and Simon and Gillian and about my hours with the police. He sat quietly and listened to me stumble along. I tried to explain how full of life and energy Dr. Maxwell had been the night before and how it made what I'd found in the morning even more grim. I don't think I succeeded.

"He was so alive last night. How could he be so still and so absent when I found him this morning? How could he be so there and then suddenly so not there. I'm not making sense, am I? But there was nothing left of what made him himself. Nothing."

"My dearest Phoebe, that is death," Cyrrie said gently. "And it doesn't come in degrees."

"I know that," I said. "But it still seems impossible for someone as alive as Graham Maxwell."

"Probably he thought so too, the poor man."

"Maybe his being murdered makes it worse. If it had been an accident or a heart attack or something it might seem different, more natural. But someone killed him."

"They didn't say anything about that on the CBC. Is that what the police think?"

"I don't know what the police are saying officially, but it's obvious that they're running a murder investigation. At first Candi thought there might be a possibility that it could have been an accident, but I know it wasn't. That flute was no accident. Graham Maxwell was murdered."

"Which makes his death something for the police to worry about, not you. It's all over for you now, isn't it?" It was more a statement than a question.

"The police said they'll want to talk to me again but that's it." I finished the last of my wine. "You know, Cyrrie, I liked him. Graham Maxwell was a pompous, lecherous old egomaniac, but he truly loved his science and he did his best to make other people love it too."

Cyrrie smiled. "A little backhanded maybe but, all in all, not too shabby an epitaph."

"You should have heard his speech last night. He had me sold. I was ready to buy a plane ticket to Africa and go to work."

"Why doesn't that surprise me?" Cyrrie laughed. "You've always wanted to go to Africa. Remember when you were a little girl and watched those films by the Roots? They're what got you hooked on wildlife photography in the first place. That one about the big tree, what was it called?

"*Baobab: Portrait of a Tree.*" I supplied the title of one of the classics of wildlife filmmaking.

"That's the one. You were ten when we watched it. You didn't talk about anything else for weeks."

"I'll go there someday," I said. "But it won't be to work for Graham Maxwell. Did I tell you *A Day in the Lifestyle* is doing a memorial program on him?" Cyrrie look alarmed. "It's a tribute and nothing more," I reassured him. "We're not investigating anything. Besides, Ella and Candi are doing most of the work on it. Remember, I just take the pictures."

"And make sure you remember it too. You have a dreadful tendency to get involved in things, Phoebe. But stay away from this one. And that goes for Ella and Candida too. All three of you. Whoever rammed that flute down Dr. Maxwell's throat is a very nasty piece of work."

"I do not get involved in things," I protested indignantly. "I'm the most uninvolved person I know. Candi's the one who gets involved, not me."

"Calm down, calm down. Perhaps 'involved' is the wrong word. Maybe I should have said that things tend to happen around you."

"That's because I work for a television station and I get paid to be around to take pictures when things are happening. Really, Cyrrie, you're starting to sound like Ella. She called me Calamity Phoebe this afternoon."

"Well, Calamity," he laughed, "I assume you're staying for dinner. You need some proper food after what you've been through today and I know that if you're on your own all you'll do is open a can of soup, if that." Fussing is one of Cyrrie's ways of comforting me. It drives me nuts but, at the same time, being irritated takes my mind off whatever is bothering me. Maybe that's why he does it. "And besides, you can't drive home after guzzling all that wine on an empty stomach."

"You don't have to convince me," I said. "I'm staying. And I did not guzzle my wine. One glass does not a guzzle make, but if there's any more in that bottle I'll let you know how many it takes."

While Cyrrie poured me another glass and put a pot of noodles on to cook, I told him about Professor Woodward and Stan and the sorry results of their guzzling. "I've never seen anyone that hungover in my life. Woodward looked bad enough, but poor Stan was really ill, all pale and sweaty."

"Whisky on top of champagne – what did the old fools expect?" Cyrrie remarked with a singular lack of sympathy. He began to tear lettuce into the big Medalta mixing bowl that he uses for salads. "Stan Darling drunk." He shook his head. "That must have been quite a sight. I'll bet Stan hasn't had more than one small glass of sherry in the last thirty years, and that was probably at someone's funeral."

"You know Stan?"

"I was his broker for thirty-five years, if we're talking about the same person. How many small, bald, elderly, anti-evolution, retired oil geologists named Stan Darling do you think there can be in Calgary? And did I mention rich? He's that too. Bags of it."

"Then you must have given him good advice."

"I never gave him any advice at all that I remember. If anything, Stan advised me and I wish I'd listened to him more often. I'd be a much wealthier man today if I had, not that I have anything to complain about as it is."

He added a little dressing to the salad and slid the bowl down the counter for me to toss. "No, Stan did it all on his own, I simply made the trades for him. He was probably the cleverest client I ever had. He had a real gift for playing the market. Today he'd be the perfect candidate for on-line trading. Wonder if he does any of that now he's retired?"

"If you don't mind my asking, what was a religious fundamentalist like Stan doing dealing with a gay stockbroker?"

"I'm sure he hadn't the slightest idea that I was gay. Probably still doesn't. The possibility would never have entered his mind. Remember, we had a professional relationship that started in the 1950s. Things were very different then."

"Did he belong to the Geologists for Jesus when you knew him?"

"That's something he's done since his retirement. And Stan doesn't simply belong to the Geologists for Jesus, my dear, Stan *is* the Geologists for Jesus. He started the organization and he's the only real geologist in it. The rest of the people you saw are members of his church."

"How do you know all this?"

"Because Stan put my name on the Geologists for Jesus' mailing list. I expect everyone he knows gets the *Rocks of Ages*. That's their monthly newsletter."

"And you actually read it?"

"Faithfully. Stan writes a financial advice column on the back page of every issue. Wouldn't miss it. I sometimes read the rest as a form of payment."

"Do you have a copy around?"

"I think the latest one is here somewhere. There's a stack of papers in the back porch waiting to go to the recycling bin. Look through it."

The *Rocks of Ages* was a very professional-looking eight pages printed on glossy paper. There were even colour photographs. The whole thing seemed quite sane and respectable until you started to read. The first two sentences of Stan's page-one editorial confirmed my suspicion that he had, indeed, been quoting himself at the protest march. I turned to the centre and there, glaring up at me from page five, was Myrna. In a head-and-shoulders shot on top of what turned out to be a guest opinion piece, Myrna Darling looked considerably cleaner if no cheerier than she had out on the highway. I didn't think I'd had enough wine to risk reading her opinions.

"Is this woman related to Stan?" I asked.

Cyrrie glanced at the paper. "She's his niece. I haven't seen her for years, but aside from growing up she doesn't look to have changed much. Was a dour little thing twenty years ago too."

"This is a pretty snazzy newsletter. It must cost a fortune to produce. I was expecting one of those dog's breakfast 'I did it on my own computer' things."

"I'm sure Stan doesn't stint when he thinks he's doing God's work."

"May I keep it?"

"Be my guest. And make sure you read Stan's financial advice."

"But, Cyrrie, I don't have any finances. I'd be like a nun reading Dr. Ruth."

Cyrrie put one of the colanders in the sink and drained the noodles. "Time to set the table. We'll eat in the dining room tonight. Bertie's already had his but he can watch. And no, I didn't give him any daube. He's had nothing but dog food since you left. Well, almost nothing."

After dinner the three of us settled in to watch *Flying Down to Rio*, an early Fred and Ginger movie Cyrrie had on loan from the public library. Bertie loves watching videos with Cyrrie because he gets to lounge on the old chesterfield in the den. I think I may have dozed a little at one point, but I was wide awake for the film's colossally silly ending with its choruses of dancing girls parading on the wings of airplanes in flight and its improbable parachute drops into the arms of love.

"Simpler days, simpler tastes." Cyrrie pressed the rewind button.

"Simpler minds and simpler airplanes," I said.

"Well, slower airplanes anyway. Can you imagine the chorus cavorting on the wings of one of Tony's jets?" My brother is a pilot with WestJet, which impresses Cyrrie no end. Me too. It would impress me more if Tony would quit trying to fix me up with his pilot buddies. He says an airline pilot would be perfect for me because they're not home all that much.

"You know," Cyrrie continued, "I think I'll give Tony a copy of this for his birthday. After all, it's almost a piece of his professional heritage. What do you think?"

"I think I have to go home now," I said.

"Why not stay the night and drive home in the morning?" Cyrrie resumed his fussing. "You slept through half the movie and you still look weary."

"It's tempting but I can't," I said. "Tim and his daughter are coming tomorrow to spend the weekend so I have to go home and get ready. Get some food organized."

"Well, yes, houseguests do like to eat now and again," he agreed.

"Sometimes it feels like that's all they do," I said. "Get yourself a houseguest and it's one damn meal after another."

"You can take some tomato soup home with you," he offered. "Those Manitobas down by the raspberries were perfect yesterday so I made up a big batch and froze it." Cyrrie's garden tomato soup is famous throughout the family. "That will get you through one lunch."

"And they use a lot of toilet paper too," I said. Cyrrie looked puzzled. "Houseguests. They use tons of the stuff. I sometimes wonder what they do with it."

"I can see you're really looking forward to this visit, aren't you?"

"It won't be so bad. Tim's daughter is horse-mad so she can ride Pete. Tim's bringing his violin and Brooke's bringing her clarinet so we can play some music. We'll have a barbecue and maybe a bonfire. If all else fails I've got a video lined up. It won't be that bad. I'm sure it won't. Really."

7

IT WAS THAT BAD. IT WAS WORSE THAN THAT BAD.
The visit was a fiasco from every point of view including
the dog's and he's an incurable optimist.

Tim arrived at my place late Saturday morning but
without his daughter. I didn't tell him what had happened
to me at the museum. He didn't give me a chance. He was
very agitated, wound too tight to sit and drink the coffee I'd
offered him. He paced back and forth across my living room
delivering a complicated set of reasons for Brooke's absence.
They seemed to involve working late, a pony club meeting,
and cars at the garage, but they all boiled down to the fact
that Marilyn, Tim's ex-wife, would be dropping Brooke off
at my door shortly before noon. As usual when he has had
an argument with Marilyn, which seems to be every time he
speaks to her, Tim could talk about nothing else.

"So then I said, 'If you think for one minute that I'm
bringing her back at three, then you can think again. I get
her for the whole weekend, not just the parts of it that you
decide I can have.' And then she said . . ." He suddenly
stopped talking and ran an anxious hand over the close-
cropped black curls that covered his head. I'd fallen for

those curls, soft and crimped as a new lamb's fleece, the moment we met. The fact that what's under them is an athletic six-foot-two with a smile that made me smile too hadn't exactly hurt either.

"I guess you're not very interested in this, are you? I don't blame you. God, I can be a bore sometimes. Come on, Bert," he called to the dog. "Let's go for a walk and cool down. Sorry, Phoebe." This was the first time Tim had ever noticed himself obsessing on his rows with Marilyn. It was probably a good sign. However, my own restless night, filled with dreams of dinosaurs and dead bodies and small bone flutes, had pretty much stifled any inclination I might have had to sympathize with his domestic difficulties. To be honest, I had to admit that inclination was slight at the best of times. There's nothing more boring than listening to people gripe about their former spouses.

I stood on the deck and watched as Tim and the dog set off across the pasture toward the stream that flows through my land. Beyond the stream, the hills rise to the Rockies. The mountains seemed so close they looked as if you could stroll over to them before lunch, a fifty-kilometre illusion. It was a perfect foothills day, this Saturday on the last weekend before Labour Day, warm and still and burnished by the honeyed light of summer's end.

I glanced at my watch. Time to go inside and put Cyrrie's soup on to thaw. I'd no sooner put the pot on the stove and begun to scrub some carrots for carrot sticks than Tim ran into the house, slamming the screen door behind him. Bertie stood on the outside looking in indignantly. If he'd been human, he'd have been rubbing his nose.

"Phoebe, there's a flasher in your pasture." Tim glared at me accusingly.

"There's a what?"

"Right out there." He jabbed an exasperated thumb over his shoulder. "Down by the stream. A flasher."

"You mean a flicker?" I asked, thinking he might be trying to tell me about a bird he had seen. But why would he be so upset about a woodpecker?

"No, I do not mean a flicker," he replied with exaggerated emphasis. "I saw a flasher. As in indecent exposure." I still must have looked blank. "For God's sake, Phoebe," he shouted, "there's some old wienie-wagger prancing around your pasture stark naked."

"Oh, you must have seen Professor Woodward," I said as the dawn finally broke. "He's out here working on a research project."

"And just what is he researching down by the stream with nothing on but a big grey beard when my eleven-year-old daughter is due to arrive here for lunch in exactly ten minutes?"

I realized that Professor Woodward was going to need some explanation, but I wasn't sure ten minutes would do it. Professor Woodward is a fairly complex phenomenon. I put down the soup spoon and prepared to give it my best.

"He probably came here to have a bath in the stream," I said. "That's the only time you ever see him naked. And he only bathes in the stream on my land. He's very careful about that."

"Well, that is a comfort." Sarcasm does not come naturally to Tim, but the sight of Professor Woodward *au naturel* seemed to have tapped a hidden vein. "When the old goat drops his pants in front of Brooke I'll tell her not to worry. He only does this at Phoebe's place."

I decided that this was not the time to tell Tim about Professor Woodward's last encounter with eleven-year-old girls. It had ended in disaster. Professor Woodward had been in the midst of his weekly bath in what he thought was a secluded section of the provincial forest reserve that borders on my land. Unfortunately, the eddy in the stream he had chosen was also the favoured picnic spot of a troop of Calgary Girl Guides out on a Saturday hike. The guides themselves managed their brief view of professorial nudity with remarkable sang-froid. Professor Woodward told me later that some of them had actually pointed and laughed, which I think rather hurt his feelings. However, their adult leaders did not regard the incident so lightly and he was arrested on charges of indecent exposure. Thanks to the intervention of the president of the university and Professor Woodward's promise never to appear on public land again without his clothes, the charges were dropped. That's why he was at my place. After the Girl Guides incident, I made him agree that in future he would use the stream that runs through my pasture for his Saturday scrub. On my land he would be safe from the prying eyes of eleven-year-old girls. Or so I thought. I hadn't reckoned with Brooke.

"Look, the man's a university professor." I tried to sound reasonable. "And he's a friend of mine. I took a geology class from him once. He's a paleontologist. He does his fieldwork in the foothills and occasionally he likes to take a bath, so he comes to my land where he can have a little privacy."

I was spared having to explain the finer points of Professor Woodward's theory of de-evolution by the dog. Bertie woofed his single, discreet bark that lets me know I have visitors and bounded ahead as Tim and I went out to meet Brooke and her mother. I noticed Tim looking anxiously over his shoulder toward the stream, scanning the terrain for any stray nudes, but Professor Woodward seemed to have beat a prudent retreat. I swung open the big wooden gate at the entrance to my land and Tim's ex-wife inched her bright red BMW through. It stalled to a jerky stop ten feet down the drive-way. The sloppy clutch work was the only indication that Marilyn might feel as uncomfortable as I do about our occasional unavoidable meetings. This was her first time on my turf. The dog looked up at the car and wagged his tail when he caught sight of Brooke. Marilyn lowered her window a few inches and peered out nervously. "Does that thing bite?"

Bertie is so gentle that I forget how intimidating a very large German shepherd can look. Brooke answered her mother's question by bounding out of the car and throwing her arms around the dog's neck. He reciprocated by licking her face. Brooke and Bertie had met on a couple of previous occasions at Tim's apartment in Calgary and had taken quite a shine to one another. Truth be told, the dog liked the child a lot better than I did, but maybe that's because he wasn't having a relationship with her father that seemed to be getting more difficult by the day.

"Brooke, don't let him do that," Marilyn snapped. "You'll catch something. You never know where these guard dogs have been."

Poor Bert didn't know whether to be offended at this slur to his personal hygiene or thrilled that someone actually thought he was a guard dog. I called him and he came and sat next to me.

Marilyn opened the car door a crack and stuck out a cautious Italian-shod foot. When Bertie didn't rush over and bite it off, the rest of her followed. It lived up to the shoes. She was a small woman, not conventionally pretty but very sleek and striking. Everything about her from the tailored linen slacks to the smoothly-styled dark hair said good and expensive. Marilyn looks like what she is, the vice-president of a highly successful public-relations firm. She made me feel like a slob in my jeans and runners. She tossed a perfunctory hello in my direction and then proceeded to forget my existence while she rattled off a list of instructions to Tim about exactly when and where he was to deliver Brooke back to her the next afternoon.

"Three's too early," Tim protested. "It's after twelve now. That's more than eighteen hours later than she's supposed to start her weekend with me. Friday at six is what the agreement says. That means I can bring her back on Sunday whenever I want." For both Tim and Marilyn, every second that Brooke spends with the other is a second spent with the enemy. Her time is tracked with stopwatch precision.

"It was Brooke's own choice to stay in town and go to the pony club meeting. You could have taken her there yourself . . ." Marilyn glanced at me, adding a clear although unspoken *if you hadn't been out here with her*.

"You know I had to work last night," Tim countered. "I didn't leave the office until after nine." Like Marilyn, Tim is in the career fast lane. He is a lawyer, a rising star in the Crown prosecutor's office.

A cellphone rang inside the car, but Marilyn didn't bother to answer. Instead, she slammed the door shut on the noise. The phone's muffled bleats continued to punctuate the conversation.

Tim and Marilyn were at the stage where they didn't even try to be civil to one another. Who knows, maybe they'd never get beyond it. And poor Brooke was caught in the middle. This competition for her time was only one aspect of the battle. Her parents competed just as shamelessly for her love with gifts and treats and trips. I wished I could paint Marilyn as the villain of the piece, but Tim was as much to blame. Their argument continued as if Brooke and I did not exist. Brooke returned the compliment by turning her attention back to Bertie and simply tuning her parents out. I wanted to do the same but I hadn't nearly as much practice. Instead, I turned and walked toward the house. Brooke and the dog followed me.

"We drove past Spruce Meadows on our way here." Brooke spoke the name of the internationally renowned equestrian centre in the reverent tone of a devout pilgrim who has glimpsed the holy place. "You're really lucky to live here. It's so close."

Brooke was right. I am lucky to live where I do although proximity to Spruce Meadows is not the draw. For me I suppose it's the solitude and the sheer beauty of the hills. Most of my neighbours would probably say the same. My land is about a half-hour's drive southwest of Spruce Meadows, right in the heart of Alberta's horse country. The whole area is a gentleman ranchers' paradise, a quick commute from Calgary that boasts some of the best scenery and the priciest land in Alberta. I'd never be able to afford to live here if I hadn't inherited my forty-acre parcel and the small house on it from Uncle Andrew.

"Someday I'm going to ride at Spruce Meadows in The Master's," Brooke confided earnestly. "My instructor at the pony club says that if I work hard enough, there's no reason I can't make it, maybe even all the way to the Olympics. Except I have to start working for it now and I need a new horse. Corky was okay when I was a kid, but she's not good enough for me any more." I'd heard this song before. Brooke had been campaigning vigorously for a new horse all summer. She had just the jumper in mind. It would cost a little less than Marilyn's BMW. So far both her parents had managed to resist.

"Want to go see the horses before we have lunch?" I asked.

"Sure."

We stopped at the house and put some carrots in a bag. Brooke continued to detail the shortcomings of her present pony as we walked down the path to the pasture. The horses dozed about a hundred yards from the fence, the two adults in a standing snooze, the foal flat out on the grass. Behind them, the pasture swept down to the stream. The grass had lost its summer lushness and patches of brown hinted at the rapidly approaching autumn.

A movement near the trees on the west side of the stream caught my eye and I looked over in time to see a fully clothed Professor Woodward disappear into a poplar grove. Truth be told, the sight of Professor Woodward dressed in his primitive man gear is far more startling than a glimpse of him in the nude. While he's at work on his research he wears only the skins of animals that he's caught and cured himself. God knows what little creatures or how many of them he snared, bludgeoned, skinned, and then smoked over a wood fire to create his present ensemble. The result is both gruesome and smelly. On chilly days he wears the tunic with the fur facing in so you get the full effect of the crudely stitched raw skin on the outside. On hot summer days he wears nothing but a few strategically placed field mice but somehow the reek of old smoke still lingers. He claims the mosquitoes don't trouble him and I believe it. Even mosquitoes have standards.

The horses hadn't noticed our approach. I whistled and held up the bag of carrots. It galvanized them into instant action. They came at a run, Pete with his roly-poly pony's gait, the foal pumping his long legs, desperate to keep up, and Elvira, his racehorse mother, with the long, easy lope that was just a promise of what she could do if she really decided to turn on the speed. That day, with the sun dappling her dark bay coat and her movements as fluid as the mountain water that flowed over the rocks in the stream, Elvira looked beautiful enough to bring a lump to my throat. The sight of her devastated the horse-obsessed Brooke. She could hardly talk.

"She's yours?" Brooke looked at me with new respect.

I shook my head. "Elvira belongs to my friend Cyrrie. She lives out here with me. She's a racehorse. At least she was. She won the Alberta Derby before she retired. She's a brood mare now and that's her first foal. The pinto is her friend Pete. He was her lead pony at the track. Because I'm away from home so much, my next-door neighbours' son looks after them. He does a great job."

Pete stood quietly at the fence, staring pointedly at the carrot bag, a portrait of rotund optimism. I offered the bag to Brooke, but she had eyes only for Elvira, who stood a few feet away looking every inch the tempestuous Thoroughbred, snorting and tossing her head and pawing the ground with a front hoof. I gave Pete a carrot myself.

"Can I ride her?" Brooke asked.

"Nobody rides Elvira now," I said. "Besides, I don't think she'd be much fun. All she knows how to do is run."

"But I could teach her." Brooke offered a carrot to Elvira, who momentarily forgot she was a prima donna and came to take it out of her hand. "I could train her to be a jumper." She leaned over the fence and stroked the mare's neck.

Like many cossetted, middle-class children, Brooke had greatly exaggerated ideas of her own abilities. I'm an expert on cossetted, middle-class children, having been one myself. I'd also seen Brooke ride. With luck, she might manage a trot around the pasture on the good-natured Pete. I tried to think of a tactful way to tell her that she had no more hope of riding and schooling Elvira than she did of leaping tall buildings at a single bound. Not that Elvira is a mean or stupid animal, she is simply a very determined one, firm in her decision not to allow alien creatures to sit on her back. In her days at the track she was hell on exercise riders and had managed to throw every jockey who'd ridden her at least once. It wasn't until the starting gate opened that Elvira was all business. No one had even considered riding her for pleasure until today.

"I think you'd better steer clear of Elvira. We don't want you to get hurt," I said. "But you're more than welcome to ride Pete. We could saddle him up after lunch." Pete nuzzled my hand in search of more carrots. Brooke looked at me as if I had just offered her the keys to the old Chevy when there was a Ferrari parked in the drive. "Pete's a dear and he loves taking people for rides."

Brooke didn't bother to answer. Refusing her request to ride Elvira had consigned me to the same limbo as her arguing parents. She continued to feed carrots to Elvira and talk to her as if I weren't there. My suggestion that it was time to go back to the house for lunch met with a sullen shrug. She followed me back up the path in silence.

Tim was waiting for us when we arrived. "Well, what did you think of Phoebe's horses?" he asked in a far too enthusiastic voice. "Isn't that Elvira something?" Brooke answered with another shrug, this one indicating indifference, and flopped down on the couch. "Time to go wash your hands for lunch," he ordered heartily. "The bathroom is right over there." She scooped herself up and slouched off to the bathroom.

"What's the matter with Brooke?" Tim asked anxiously.

"She's probably hungry," I suggested, unwilling to tell him that his child was in a sulk because I wouldn't let her ride Elvira. Not that he'd have believed me. Tim doesn't recognize sulking in his daughter. He prefers to think she's not feeling well.

"I'll bet Marilyn didn't bother to give her breakfast," he said. "I know she isn't feeding Brooke properly. No wonder the poor kid feels sick so often. You know, you've got to be very careful when you're dealing with young girls and food. Marilyn keeps this up and before you know it Brooke will be anorexic."

He droned on about eating disorders while I set the table. He didn't change the topic until Brooke came back from the bathroom. When it comes to his daughter, Tim's responses are not exactly grounded in reality. Then again, reality wasn't intruding much on our own relationship these days. I'd known almost from the beginning that Tim and I had no future. Unfortunately, I didn't know how to tell him without hurting him and right now he didn't need to be hurt any more.

Brooke actually spoke a couple of times during lunch. All things considered, I think I'd have preferred her to continue the silent treatment.

"What kind of soup is this?" She looked suspiciously at the bowl in front of her.

"Tomato," I said. "Your Dad told me that it's your favourite. Cyrrie, my friend who owns the horses, made it with tomatoes he grew in his own garden."

"Come on, Brooke, taste it," her father encouraged. "Cyrrie's a great cook."

He watched anxiously as Brooke dipped a reluctant spoon into the bowl and took a sip. She grimaced in disgust.

"This is gross."

"I bet you'd like a peanut-butter sandwich, wouldn't you?" Tim said quickly. He got up and began to slice bread.

Brooke sat with elbows on the table staring into her bowl. One hand propped up her head, the other held a spoon that she paddled listlessly in the soup. I had just decided to drown her in it when Tim whisked the bowl away and replaced it with the sandwich. He and I did our best to make conversation about our plans for the afternoon while Brooke tore the crusts off the bread, peeled the slices apart, and scraped the jam off the peanut butter. Finally, when she had finished reducing her food to its component elements, she asked to be excused. I gave her permission and she and the dog were out the door before Tim could protest her lack of proper nourishment.

Brooke's absence didn't improve the conversation much. Maybe we were each too preoccupied with our own concerns. Tim found still more to say about eleven-year-old girls and the psychology of food. While he worried aloud and at length, my thoughts returned to the Royal Tyrrell. I hadn't told him about my involvement in the now much-publicized death and fossil theft. I didn't really feel like talking about it, but I supposed I should at least mention that I had been at the museum. I wondered if he would eventually be involved in the case professionally.

"If a person is murdered in Drumheller, would they have the murderer's trial there or in Calgary?" I asked.

"Drumheller, probably," he said, looking a little startled at this interruption to his monologue on the perils of bulimia. "Unless it was deemed that the accused couldn't get a fair trial there. Then they'd shift it somewhere else. Are you thinking of that anthropologist who was killed at the Royal Tyrrell?"

"I was working out there the night of the murder."

"How do you know it was a murder? The police haven't made that public yet. All they've released is that the death is under investigation. At least that's what I heard at the office."

"I'm the one who found him and from what I saw it was murder."

"No!" The news sat Tim back in his chair. "You actually discovered the body?"

"We were at the museum to do an early-morning interview. I'd gone to collect some equipment from an office when I found him. It was pretty horrible." I took our empty soup dishes and put them in the dishwasher. Then I told him what I'd seen. I had to stop for a moment before I could manage the part about the flute.

"Jesus, Phoebe," he said when I had finished. He got up and came over to where I stood. He put his arms around me. "Hang on to me. I won't let go." And so I did. I clung to him while he held me and stroked my head. "Why didn't you call me?" he murmured. "You shouldn't have been alone last night. You should have called me. I would have come."

Before I could say anything, we heard a loud scream. It came from the direction of the pasture. Tim pushed me away and was out the door before the scream stopped. I followed at a run. We arrived at the pasture in time to see Professor Woodward walking toward the house, carrying a sobbing Brooke in his arms. The dog trotted behind them.

"What have you done to my daughter, you pervert?" Tim shouted. "Put her down!"

"She's hurt," Professor Woodward said. "I think she may have broken her arm."

"If you've hurt her, I'll kill you," Tim roared, totally lost to reason.

"I didn't do anything to her," the professor protested, confused and distressed that his good Samaritan efforts should be met with such rage. "She fell off that big brown horse of Phoebe's."

"I did not fall off." Brooke managed to stop crying long enough to denounce this insult to her horsemanship. "Elvira threw me." Oblivious to the reek, she buried her face in the shoulder of Professor Woodward's tunic and resumed wailing louder than ever. The dog contributed to the confusion by barking at top volume. Bertie seldom barks, but the sight or, more probably, the smell of Professor Woodward's coat of many creatures makes him uneasy at the best of times, and this was far from the best for any of us except, perhaps, the author of the drama. She stood a few yards away calmly cropping grass, her foal at her side nursing. I finally got the dog to shut up by calling him to me in my sternest obedience-school voice and ordering him to sit. Professor Woodward continued to hold Brooke, clutching her so stiffly she might have been a bundle of sticks. He looked like he'd sell his soul for five minutes solitude.

"Get your filthy hands off her." Tim tried to pull his child out of the professor's arms. She screamed in pain. "Now look what you've done, you son of a bitch. You've hurt her again." He drew back his right fist and took direct aim at Professor Woodward's nose.

"Dad, don't hit him," Brooke shouted at her father. "He helped me. It was all my fault. Phoebe told me not to ride Elvira, but I did and she threw me and he came running out of the woods to help me. Please don't hit him."

You had to give Brooke full marks for honesty. Upset and in pain as she was, it was pretty decent of her to come to Professor Woodward's defence and admit to riding Elvira.

For an eleven-year-old, that took some courage. Maybe she'd survive her parents after all.

Tim slowly lowered his fist, still not totally convinced. He stood glowering while a relieved Professor Woodward relinquished Brooke to him. Her sobs subsided but the tears still ran down her cheeks as she settled into her father's arms. Tim took a step back to balance himself. His foot came down heavily on the dog's tail. Bertie leaped into the air with a heart-stopping shriek that spooked the horses. They wheeled and ran for the stream, passing so close to us I felt the ground shake with the pounding of their hooves. Even Pete managed an impressive turn of speed.

"For God's sake, would someone help me get this child to a hospital," Tim bellowed. "Am I the only one here who knows how to act in an emergency?"

8

IT TOOK TWO HOURS FOR THE DOCTOR at the Oilfields Hospital to decide that Brooke would live. I spent the time in the emergency waiting room, along with four anxious-looking strangers, flipping through back issues of *Maclean's* and an antique *Saturday Night*. The available reading material was in perfect harmony with the rest of the afternoon. At last Brooke and Tim reappeared. Brook's arm was in a sling, but she walked down the corridor on her own steam.

"The arm's not broken, just bruised," Tim reported with obvious relief.

"Badly bruised," Brooke amended. "And swollen."

"The doctor says she should be fine in a few days."

"That's good news," I said. "You had us all pretty worried, Brooke. I'm glad you're okay. Professor Woodward will be too."

Brooke did not reply. She was feeling well enough to sulk again. Instead she gave me one of her shrugs. The movement made her wince.

It was obvious our weekend was over. Tim drove me home on his way back to Calgary. Soon after we left the hospital parking lot, Brooke fell asleep covered with a blanket in a corner of the big Jeep's back seat.

"Must be the painkillers," Tim said. "The doctor gave us enough for a couple of days. Said they'd make her sleepy and get her through the worst."

"I'm very sorry she got hurt," I said.

"These kinds of things happen to active kids. It's frightening as hell but it's all part of being a parent," Tim replied reasonably, which, considering his earlier behaviour, came as a surprise. He'd calmed down during his two hours in emergency. "But God knows what I'm going to tell Marilyn. She's really going to lose it when she hears about this."

We drove in silence for the next few kilometres. Near Turner Valley we passed a grove of scrub poplar already showing a few yellow leaves. A flock of robins busied themselves in the short grass at the side of the road. Both were sure signs of autumn.

"I'm sorry about all this, Phoebe," Tim said. I understood "all this" to mean the domestic dramas of the day. "You didn't need it. Especially after yesterday."

"I'm okay," I said.

"Want to talk about it some more? It might help."

I didn't and it wouldn't, but I'd told the story of finding Dr. Maxwell's body so many times that I'd managed to detach myself from it, as if I were seeing the events through the lens of my camera. I wished I could convince my subconscious to do the same, but images of the dead man and his little flute continued to flash into my mind, unbidden, unexpected, and startling in their intensity. Most of all, I hoped the dreams would stop. So instead of rehashing what I knew about the murder, I told him about the protestors and about some of the people I'd seen at the Royal Tyrrell later that evening.

"Do you think the police know who killed him?" Tim asked.

"I don't know. Maybe they do but I sure don't. It seems impossible that any one at the museum could have rammed that bone down his throat."

"We all assume people we know couldn't possibly be murderers," he said. "But that's one of the things I've learned in my time with the Crown prosecutor – the nicest, most unlikely people can do the most godawful things. Makes you take a second look at your neighbours some days."

"But none of them had enough of a reason for murder. Maybe they were jealous of Dr. Maxwell or had some scientific disagreements or thought he was a pompous ass or whatever, but none of that's enough to murder someone over, is it?"

"Maybe not for you, Phoebe. You're pretty good at detaching yourself from what goes on around you. Sometimes it's like you look at the whole world through that camera of yours. But other people aren't like that. Maybe for them those things are enough. They were for someone."

Brooke didn't wake up when Tim pulled over and stopped in front of my gate. "Sorry about Bertie," he said. "I hope his tail is okay."

"He seemed to be wagging it pretty vigorously when we left. I think he was more startled than hurt. Professor Woodward promised to keep an eye on him."

"Please tell Woodward thanks for his help, will you?" I knew this was as close to an apology as the professor was going to get. "And thanks a lot for putting up with us.

You're a good lady, you know that?" He leaned over and kissed me softly on the cheek. I opened the door and climbed down from the high front seat. "Hey, Phoebe," Tim called after me as I opened the gate. "Why does Woodward wear those smelly animal skins?"

"I'll tell you sometime when you've got a day or two."

"Take care. I'll call you tonight and let you know how Brooke's doing." He waved and drove off down the gravel road in a swirl of dust.

Professor Woodward and Bertie were snoozing on the deck. They both woke up when I climbed the steps. Bertie trotted over to greet me. He seemed a little subdued but the tail in question wagged briskly.

"Just bruised, not broken, eh, Bert?" I stroked the thick fur on his back and ran my hand over his tail. Everything seemed to be in the right place.

"How's the little girl?" Professor Woodward asked. He yawned and stretched but didn't get up from the big Adirondack chair. He looked worn out. Really, he was getting far too old for this primitive man stuff, especially so late in the summer. The foothills nights were already very cool.

"Her arm is bruised but there's nothing broken." I said. "She's fine."

"So she's your friend's daughter. At first I thought she was another of those peeping Thomasinas from the forest reserve." The Girl Guides incident still rankled.

"He asked me to say thanks for your help," I reported faithfully. "He really appreciated what you did for Brooke." I added a small embellishment of my own.

"Such a very, um . . ." Professor Woodward hesitated, searching for the most tactful word. "Such a very, ah, volatile fellow. Does he often do things like that?"

"Behave like a total jerk, you mean?"

"Now really, Phoebe, I think that's a little strong, don't you? After all, he was very upset about his daughter. I remember how I felt the day Trevor fell off the garage roof." Professor Woodward was a lot nicer than I would have been about someone who'd tried to flatten my nose. "And I suppose that to some people I do look a little unusual in my working clothes."

"Did you see what happened?"

"I was at the edge of the pasture gathering some dried grass when I saw the girl climb onto the fence. She sat there for a minute and the horses came right over to her. Probably looking for carrots. Next time I glanced over she was climbing from the fence onto Elvira's back. Then Elvira turned and trotted toward the stream and the child simply bounced off. That's when she screamed."

"So she wasn't bucked off." I was amazed that Elvira hadn't let rip the moment she felt weight on her back. Maybe motherhood was having the same mellowing effect on the mare as it was on Ella. Still, it was probably a blessing that Brooke had fallen off before Elvira had lapsed back to her old racetrack ways and launched her into low-earth orbit.

"I ran over to make certain she was all right – a little tumble like that shouldn't have done much damage but you never know. And that's when you and . . ."

"Tim," I supplied the name. "Tim Roberts."

"That's when you and Tim came to the rescue." He reached into the depths of his tunic, drew out a handful of dried grass, and wiped his nose on it. "That cold of mine is coming back."

"Then you probably shouldn't be sleeping out tonight." I said, sounding like Cyrrie at his fussiest. "And if you've got a cold, why were you having a bath in that freezing stream this morning?"

"I guess I still felt a little thick-headed from Thursday night," he mumbled sheepishly. "Thought a wash in cold water might snap me out of it. Stupid to drink that much. A person should know better at my age. You don't get over it like you do when you're young. I still don't feel quite right."

"You should at least take a sleeping bag with you tonight. I've got one you can have. I heard on the CBC that there's a danger of frost in Millarville."

"Don't worry. It's pretty warm in my nest and I can always light a fire if it gets too cold. I'll be fine." He sneezed wetly into the grass, propelling particles of foliage and I prefer not to think what else into his great mess of a beard. I did my best to repress a shudder.

"Want to go for a walk with me and Bert?" I asked.

"Just to the top of the hill and back. I'm not up to one of your forced marches this afternoon."

We strolled through the pasture, the dog running ahead of us and the horses ambling behind. Elvira and the foal stopped at the stream but Pete carried on. He let me hang over his back going across the water so I didn't get my feet wet. The dog splashed through, impervious to the cold, while Professor Woodward brought up the rear, stepping carefully from rock to rock, following the crude crossing Uncle Andrew had laid across the stream bed many years ago. He slipped on the last one and soaked his right moccasin, but he didn't seem to take much notice.

Beyond the pasture, the path to the top of the hill starts into the trees. It was much cooler in the shade of the forest. Sunlight filtered through the poplar leaves and mushrooms dotted the damp leaf mould underfoot.

"Look, there's a patch of puffballs," said Professor Woodward. "They're supposed to be delicious fried in a little butter. We should pick some for your dinner on our way back."

"Actually, they're Fly Amanita and if we did it might be my last supper."

Professor Woodward's knowledge of edible plants is so shaky that I often wonder how he has managed to survive this long as a primitive man. However, I find it's best not to think too much about what he eats or where he finds it. His food is like his clothes – you really don't want the details. Still, I fervently hoped that wild fungi were not a large part of his diet.

"I don't eat mushrooms myself," he admitted, much to my relief. "I'm allergic to them." That allergy had probably saved his life. "But are you certain these aren't puffballs?"

"Positive. They're very young *Amanita muscaria* and even though they might not actually kill you they'd make you so sick you'd probably wish they had. If you like we can look them up in a mushroom guide when we get back to the house. I've got a copy of Schalkwijk-Barendsen's book. She has some good stuff on the amanitas. Beautiful watercolour illustrations too. You'd enjoy reading it."

"Oh, I couldn't do that, Phoebe." Professor Woodward was shocked. "I'm thousands and thousands of years away from written language."

This was not strictly true. Although it's something we never talk about, I know that the professor reads a fair bit over the summer. Early on, when he'd first begun to use my stream for his baths, I'd agreed to take telephone messages from his wife and pass them on to him. At first I'd delivered the messages in person, riding Pete into the forest reserve to his latest campsite, but this was so impossibly time-consuming that, after the first couple of times, I made him a mailbox. I emptied a big metal box I'd once bought at an army surplus store to keep film in and dragged it out to the base of a tall spruce tree on the south side of the pasture. The box's waterproof interior made a perfect place for written copies of Mrs. Woodward's bulletins.

However, Professor Woodward's reading isn't limited to personal messages. He told me once that he thought the most difficult aspect of de-evolving was the sheer boredom of the process. That and loneliness. After he'd seen to the basic essentials of life there was very little Professor Woodward needed to do and, worse still, no one to do it with. So I took to leaving him library books that I thought might interest him. The books always disappeared and then reappeared back in the box a few days later. Except for mystery novels. They reappeared overnight. I'd also post a note in the box if I were going to watch a video, telling him what and when. Then I'd leave the big sliding door to the deck open so he could watch through the screen. I could tell, or rather smell, when Professor Woodward was part of the audience and had observed over the course of two summers that primitive man had a taste for romantic comedies. However, we never discussed any of this. Probably it violated just about every rule of research he'd dreamed up for his project. So, although books were read and movies watched, we never said a word about them. It was our own version of don't ask, don't tell.

We emerged from the trees at the top of the hill into a meadow that swept down the slope of the valley in front of us and halfway up the next hill. Beyond that the foothills grew steadily more rugged until it became impossible to tell where they ended and the mountains began. Dusty purple asters bloomed in the meadow grass and the hum of bees working the flowers filled the air. We sat down next to a clump of wild roses, their spindly branches weighed down with big red rosehips. The lengthening rays of the afternoon sun intensified the colours. Bertie chased chipmunks. Pete browsed a patch of fireweed. Professor Woodward sneezed again.

"Bad business at the museum." He absentmindedly uprooted another handkerchief. "You'd never think something so terrible could happen at a peaceful place like the Tyrrell."

"Why not?" I said. "It's a place full of people, and people do terrible things to each other sometimes."

"You're right, of course," he said. "I guess I find it hard to believe because I know the museum so well myself – a lot of those people are colleagues of mine, they're friends. I've been working on a research project with one of the museum paleontologists for the past five years. As a matter of fact, I'm supposed to deliver a cabinet full of Foraminifera to her sometime next week. I know it's irrational, but Graham's death still doesn't seem real to me. I guess we think murder always happens somewhere else and to people we don't know."

He dabbed at his nose. A tiny aster remained clinging to his beard. "I heard you were the one who found him, poor old Graham. He had the world by the tail and then it ended. Just like that." He snapped his fingers. "Dead as those fossils of his."

"How well did you know him?" I asked.

"I knew him very well back in our university days. But after that I didn't see much of him. Met him once at a conference in San Francisco when we were both in graduate school but that was it until this last time in Drumheller. We went such different ways, Graham and I, that there wasn't much chance of meeting, at least not professionally. I stuck with geology, but he really left that behind when he threw in his lot with the anthropologists. I followed his career, of course. All of us did." Professor Woodward picked a rosehip and popped it in his mouth. "Lots of vitamin C in these things. Good for colds."

"Could you have guessed he'd become so famous?" I asked. "He must have shown some signs at university that he was going to be a major player."

"You know, Phoebe, that's an odd thing. Graham wasn't particularly talented. Rather the opposite. I'd have called him an average student at best. I remember he had a hell of a time finding a graduate school that would take him. You could have knocked me over with a feather when he started making all those fancy finds." He chewed thoughtfully on another rosehip. "But Graham did have one very big talent. He could talk. He had the gift of the gab and no doubt about it. Could get you believing anything. Well, you heard that speech on Thursday night. Practically made you want to buy yourself a ticket to Africa and go sifting dirt for him on his next dig, didn't it? Graham would have made a great confidence man. Or a politician," he added as an afterthought.

"So how did he parlay a mediocre geology degree into a career as the world's leading paleoanthropologist?"

"Now that's the million-dollar question, isn't it? And I don't have the answer. After graduate school Graham managed to wangle himself a job as a junior paleontologist with one of the big guns in the field. He was a minion on some important digs – you know, chief assistant to the assistant fossil duster, that kind of thing. But even back then he must have known that he'd managed to get a toe in the door of the glamour end of paleontology. Dinosaurs and hominids – that's where the glory is," the professor said wistfully. "And Graham knew it. He bided his time and worked for other people for a lot of years. Never really made much of a splash except by association. The next I heard of him, he'd gone out on his own. All very modest at first. He couldn't afford to hire any staff except for that odd South African fellow who still works for him. Pretty soon he started making the big finds and after that, well, I'm sure you know the rest as well as anyone else who reads a newspaper. So that's what Graham did. As to how he did it, I can't tell you."

"But he loved paleontology. You could tell by the way he talked about it that science was the most important thing in his life."

"And maybe it was. But, Phoebe, just because you love something doesn't mean you're any good at it. No matter how much I love to play golf, I'll never be a Tiger Woods."

"But Dr. Maxwell was the Tiger Woods of paleoanthropology," I pointed out. "So wouldn't someone who accomplished all that he did have shown some sign of talent early on?"

"If that were the case then Stanley would be the famous one. If any of the three of us was going to make a big splash in science, I'd have put my money on him."

"The Geologist for Jesus?"

"One and the same. A brilliant student and absolutely the best field geologist I ever met. I've never known anyone who could hold a candle to him. It was like he had X-ray eyes and could see under the ground. Stan had a real gift. Astounding to watch him at it. Then he went to work for the oil boys and that was the end of him as a scientist."

"Surely you can't blame it all on the oil business? What about Stan's religious beliefs? Not believing in evolution has to be a bit of a hindrance to a paleontologist."

"Well, his brand of religion didn't do much for his science and that's for sure," the professor admitted. "But it didn't stop him finding oil. Stan was very good at that. It must have broken his bosses' hearts when he took early retirement."

"Did you keep in touch with him over the years?"

"Not really. I'd bump into him every so often. Occasionally he'd turn up at a class reunion or some such get-together. That's about it. Except for the time he called me at the university and asked me to give a talk on evolution to his church group. Like a fool I agreed. They all listened very politely and at the end of it some woman got up and asked me the meaning of life. Can you believe it?

How on earth should I know what your life means, I said. I'm not a fortune teller – I'm here to talk about science. What an evening. Diana went with me. Of course, she thought it was all hugely funny. She still laughs about it. Stan spent the whole time mooning over her. He was in love with her at university, you know. Everybody was. Most beautiful woman you could imagine, Diana. As lovely as your friend Candi. Still is as far as I'm concerned." He smiled and his whole face lit with pleasure. Professor Woodward was a man still very much in love with his wife.

"Say, we should pick you some of these." He got to his feet and began to gather the rosehips. "They make delicious tea. Here, we can put them in my hat." He produced a hairy little beanie from a pouch hidden in the folds of his tunic and tossed a handful of rosehips into it. I joined him in the picking. Having come down so heavily on the mushrooms, it was the least I could do. "You can make jelly out of them too, you know. I think Diana has an old recipe of her grandmother's for rosehip jelly. I'll get her to give it to you." I chose not to regard this as a threat.

When we got back to the house I fed the dog and put the kettle on for tea, real tea, two bags' worth of English Breakfast. Professor Woodward sat at the table out on the deck sorting rosehips. The keepers went into a jar and the rejects over the railing. I poured him a mug of tea. This was the first time he had ever eaten or drunk anything at my house while wearing his working clothes. Another blow to his research rules.

Drinking the tea made me realize how hungry I was. "Would you like something to eat?" I asked. "I was planning on a barbecue tonight – hamburgers and all the trimmings."

"An outdoor cookup would be excellent. We'll have to eat it out here, of course. I can't sit in your house in these clothes. They're a bit smelly for inside, you know," he added confidentially.

Crusty buns and a tossed salad completed the dinner I'd organized for Tim and Brooke. The professor seemed to enjoy it so much that I put a second burger on the grill for him. Bertie lay beside my chair, dozily full of his own food but ever hopeful that some happy accident might cause a little of ours to fall his way. I offered the professor a glass of wine but he refused.

"I don't think I can face alcohol just yet," he said. "Bet Diana's still mad at me. Can't say as I blame her."

"Did Trevor catch up with her at the museum? I saw him just before we left. He was looking for both of you."

"So he told me. Said he couldn't find Diana anywhere. He looked for her for ages. She finally turned up at the car and they drove back to Calgary. They didn't get home until after one. Can't imagine what they were doing all that time." He finished the last of his food and sat looking at me.

"You know about Trevor, don't you?" he said at last. "I could tell by the way you looked at him when you were taking our pictures."

"The resemblance is pretty striking," I said, amazed that he had noticed my reaction. Maybe the professor saw more of the real world than I gave him credit for.

"It's never made any difference. Trevor's my son in every other way. In all the important ways. The ways that count."

"Does Trevor know that Maxwell was his father?"

"He might, but if he does it wasn't me who told him. Even Diana doesn't know that I know. At least I don't think she does. Besides, it was all so long ago. We've been married for forty-four years – it'll be forty-five next May. We were married a week after we graduated. The week Graham left for graduate school in the States."

"And all those years you've never once talked about it with her?"

"I wanted to at first but I couldn't. I didn't know what to say, how to start. And then that December Trevor was born. I took one look at him and it didn't seem to matter any more. When Nora and Sean came along it mattered even less. They were all three my children. I guess I simply stopped thinking about it."

"Even when you read about Dr. Maxwell in the news?"

"It crossed my mind then, I suppose, but after all that time what did it matter?"

"What about when you saw him again at the museum?"

"Yes, well, that did hurt a little," he admitted. "When I saw them standing together, him and Trevor, looking so much alike. But I think what really got me was remembering what he'd done to Diana. Got her pregnant and dumped her. Took himself off to graduate school and didn't look back. Just left her. Oh, I know no one bats an eye about unwed mothers these days, but this was more than forty years ago. Attitudes were a lot different then. I knew that Graham had got her pregnant. He told me. I think he was afraid Diana's father was going to come after him with a shotgun. He knew I was in love with her. He wanted me to bail him out, to tell everyone the baby was mine. I told him to go to hell, but he went off to graduate school instead. The next day I asked Diana to marry me and she did. So I guess Graham got his way after all because for the last forty-four years everyone has assumed that Trevor is my son."

"And you never told Mrs. Woodward that you knew she was pregnant?"

He shook his head. "Trevor arrived a little prematurely, that's all. And after he was born, what did it matter who his actual biological father was? It was me who was there when he fell off that roof, not Graham Maxwell." He stretched, settled back in his chair, and smiled at me. "This must sound like ancient history to you. Nothing more boring than an old fart blathering on about the past."

"Why do you think Dr. Maxwell invited you to the opening of his exhibit?"

"Probably for the same reason Diana and I went – curiosity. And maybe we helped to back up his old Alberta boy image. He couldn't have predicted Trevor's being there. That was a bonus. And Stan was invited because he's rich and because Graham could never resist taking the religious mickey out of him. Mostly the latter, I'd guess, because I can't see old Stan giving a dime to Graham's godless research. I do wish he'd come to the staff lounge and had that drink with us – it would have been really something to hear the two of them at it again. Stan and I waited for him but he never showed up. And if he came later I was, um, asleep." A pained expression, indicative of a hangover recollected in tranquility, crossed the professor's face. "You know, Phoebe, this is the first time I've felt like eating since Thursday. Delicious food. I think I could manage that second burger." He polished off the last of the salad too.

"How did you get home from the museum?"

"Trevor came back the next day when the police had finished with us and drove Stan and me back to Calgary. Said the police had been at the house that morning asking him and Diana a lot of questions too. Such a bad business. Must have been a pretty grim thing for you, finding his body. Shocking."

The sun dropped behind the hills and the temperature dropped with it. I made coffee while Professor Woodward lit a bonfire in the firepit a few yards away from the deck. He used a little bow that he produced from the same pouch as the hat. He was very skilled with it and had the fire crackling along in less time than it would have taken me if I'd used a match. We sat on a log bench drinking our coffee and watching the flames.

"How's that film of yours coming?" The professor had taken off his still-damp moccasin and placed it to dry on the warm bricks at the back of the firepit where it steamed nicely, looking and smelling like a large fuzzy kipper.

"Fine," I said. "I've pretty much shot all the film I need except for some autumn sequences. And it's going to pay for the hour on the otter colony that I was telling you about. I'll be able to start work on that next spring."

My part-time job for *A Day in the Lifestyle* finances my other work as a maker of nature films. I'm producing such film records as I can of the wildlife of the Alberta foothills while there's still some left to record. Although my films win the occasional obscure award, they rarely make any money. I'm lucky if they pay for themselves. The one I was working on now was an exception. It was a job Candi had set up for me with a company that specializes in the educational market. *Right in Your Own Backyard* was aimed at elementary schoolchildren and documented a year in the life of an urban prairie garden. I'd used Cyrrie's garden and the project had been fun, but I was beginning to miss my wilderness work.

"Mind you don't spend too much time doing things just for the money," Professor Woodward said. "Too long away and you'll forget what your real job is. You do important work, Phoebe, and you're very good at it. Don't neglect it for something as meaningless as money." Thus spoke a full professor with a regular salary, dental coverage, and a pension plan. Still, it's difficult to be annoyed by someone who thinks what you do is good and important. "And you never know how long you're going to get to do these things." Dr. Maxwell's death was much on his mind too.

Although it had been almost ten years since I'd sat in Professor Woodward's geology class, our friendship still had elements of the student and teacher in it, a certain formality. However, that relationship seemed to have shifted over the past couple of days. Before, he'd never have told me about his personal life or lectured me on work and money, and I'd never have questioned his reasons for taking up his own strange research. But tonight was different.

"Why are you doing this, this . . ." I didn't really know what to call his de-evolving project. "Why are you doing this kind of research?"

"Experimental paleoanthropology?" The professor supplied the label. "I suppose I wanted a change. I'm a micropaleontologist by training. I've spent my entire working life looking down a microscope at fossils smaller than a speck of dust. Sneeze and a year's research is out the window before you can say godblessyou. It's interesting stuff and it's been very good to me over the years. All things considered, I think I've managed to do some pretty respectable work. Not splashy stuff like Graham's discoveries, just honest, everyday science. But I got to the point where I knew I'd done about as much as I could with it. I needed a change." He took his moccasin off the bricks and felt the inside.

"But why paleoanthropology? Isn't that a little far from your field?"

"Well maybe," he conceded with the casual air of someone who obviously didn't think that mattered much. "But it's a subject that has always fascinated me and I've done a lot of reading over the years. Besides, I wanted to do something totally different with the last few years of my career. I know that thinking about my grandchildren and what kind of future they can expect had a big influence. And maybe the teacher in me had something to do with it too. But whatever the reasons, I wanted to work on something that might set people to thinking more about the world and how we could try to live with it instead of against it. That's one thing studying geology teaches you, Phoebe – you can't fight something as mighty as Mother Nature. She'll beat you every time. She did for the dinosaurs and she can do for us too. No mistake about it." He fluffed up the moccasin and put it back on his foot. "I know that most of my colleagues think I'm the original mad professor, that I'm cracked and what I'm doing is a joke. Maybe they're right. But even if they are and nothing comes of my research, I can tell you it's a hell of a lot more fun to be out here for the summer than it is to be stuck in a lab looking down a microscope at dust specks. Got any more of this excellent coffee?"

I fetched the coffee while Professor Woodward added another log to our bonfire.

"I was surprised to see you out here this weekend," I said when we were settled back on the bench. "I thought you'd be home with Trevor."

"He and his mother have gone to Medicine Hat to visit Nora and George and the grandchildren. Somehow I couldn't see myself surviving a weekend whoop-up with the grands just now. Besides," he added with a sheepish smile, "it'll take a day or two for Diana to forget she's mad at me."

"How long is Trevor here?"

"He has some business in Calgary early next week and then he's back to Halifax on Thursday. He's driving out here to pick me up after his meeting on Monday. Around five. If you're going to be home, maybe we could drop in for a visit before we head back to Calgary?"

"I'd like that."

We finished our second cups of coffee and watched the flames die down to embers. The mosquitoes came to watch too.

"Time to go inside," I said as I swatted a blood-filled bug and felt the histamine itch begin. "Want to come and watch a video? I'm afraid all I've got is a golden oldie I rented for Brooke – *Roman Holiday*.

"One of my all-time favourites," said the professor. "The scene on the barge is the best."

"Shall we go watch it then?"

"I'd love to but I mustn't smell up your furniture. I'm really pretty ripe and Diana says I linger."

"We'll throw a sleeping bag over a chair for you. They're easy to wash so you don't have to worry about lingering."

I doused the remains of the fire before we went inside. Bertie chose to stay out with the mosquitoes. Professor Woodward helped me spread a sleeping bag over an easy chair.

"You're sure this will work?" he said. "Remember, you have to spend the night in this room." Except for the bathroom and a tiny guest room, my small bungalow is one very large space in which I work, eat, and sleep.

"Don't worry. It'll be fine," I assured him as he settled onto the chair. I popped the cassette in the VCR and started the movie. Just after the opening titles, the gentle snores of a weary elderly gentleman with a head cold began to rise from the chair. The professor was asleep, so soundly that he didn't wake when the telephone rang.

"How's the weekend going?" Candi asked. "Everyone fed, bonfired, and videoed?"

"Not exactly," I said.

"What's up? Or can't you talk right now?"

"No, it's okay, I can talk. I'm here alone except for Professor Woodward and he's asleep."

"Why is Professor Woodward sleeping at your place?"

"We're supposed to be watching *Roman Holiday*, but he fell asleep. I think he still hasn't quite got over Thursday night."

"Where's Tim?"

I gave her a brief account of my day.

"Well, that doesn't sound too good." Candi has a flair for understatement. "Did you get a chance to talk to him?"

"Talk?"

"To Tim. Weren't you going to tell him you think you should stop seeing each other?"

"Come on, Candi. His kid was in the emergency ward because of my horse. It was hardly the time to discuss our relationship."

"So what are you going to do?"

"I don't know. I'll find some way to tell him soon. It's not that easy, you know. I really don't want to hurt him."

"What you really don't want is a big emotional scene," Candi said. "You're not just afraid he'll be hurt, you're afraid he'll carry on about it. You've got to admit it, Phoebe, you don't like dealing with emotions, your own or anybody else's. So why don't you invite him out for lunch?" She did one of her rapid conversational shifts. "Somewhere really nice. But conservative, even a bit formal. Maybe the Palliser. Yeah, the Palliser would be perfect. Lunch at the Rimrock. Your treat."

"You've lost me," I said.

"Well, no one would make a big scene in the Palliser dining room, would they? At least no one who's a lawyer with a career to make in the Crown prosecutor's office. You can tell him there and it will all be very civilized."

"You mean dump him over lunch?"

"If you're going to break his heart anyway, then what's wrong with doing it over a bowl of railway hotel clam chowder?" Candi said.

"So, should I do it before or after dessert?"

"Now you're being silly, Phoebe," she said. "But you know I'm right."

"While we're at it, any advice on what I should say?"

"Well, it's all your fault, of course. That gives him a chance to be gallant and take some of the blame. But first you have to think of a good reason why it's your fault like maybe you're not ready for this kind of emotional involvement so soon after your divorce."

"For God's sake, Candi. It's been five years since Gavin and I split up. How long can it take?"

"You tell me."

After Candi hung up I let Bertie in and then went back to *Roman Holiday* and the sleeping professor. The princess was just about to get her hair cut when the phone rang again. It was Tim with a progress report on Brooke. She was sleeping very bravely. He hadn't told Marilyn about her accident yet. I interrupted before he could launch another Marilyn rant.

"Want to have lunch on Monday?" I asked. "At the Palliser. My treat."

"The Palliser? What's the occasion?"

"I got a cheque from the film company and I want to celebrate." It wasn't really a lie. I had got a cheque. "Twelve okay?"

"Can you make it twelve-thirty? I'm in court that morning."

"See you there." I hung up before he could reintroduce his domestic difficulties into the conversation.

Professor Woodward's snores continued long past the end of the movie. He didn't wake when I pulled the sides of the sleeping bag over him and turned out the lights. I went to bed in my little guest room. I lay there reading, reluctant to surrender to a sleep haunted by dinosaurs and the dead. I woke in the middle of the night overcome by a nameless grief, my face wet with tears and the book still clutched in my hands. I must have been dreaming but, if so, I didn't remember the dream. Half-awake, I sat on the edge of the bed and listened for Professor Woodward's snores but the house was quiet. I supposed he had left to go back to his burrow. I felt an overwhelming sense of loss and loneliness. Then the snores started again, this time even louder and more moistly reverberant than before. I crawled back into bed oddly comforted by the racket. Lulled by the rhythmic nasal dysfunctions of primitive man suffering from a virus older than mankind, I turned out the light and slept a gentle sleep.

9

I SLEPT UNTIL AFTER NINE ON SUNDAY. Professor Woodward had left by the time I got up. The sleeping bag lay neatly folded on the chair. There was a note on top of it written in his precise, spiky handwriting.

"Dear Phoebe,

Thank you for the food and the company. Impromptu occasions are often the best.

I took the liberty of helping myself to a box of tissues which I shall, of course, replace.

Again, many thanks for your hospitality.

Yours,
Adam Woodward

P.S. I let Bertie out."

Mrs. Woodward was right. The professor did linger. I tossed the sleeping bag in the washing machine and then went to the kitchen corner and made some coffee. Thanks to my ex-husband who loves to cook, I have the best-equipped small kitchen that he could imagine and we could almost afford. I'm not what I'd describe as a keen cook myself and, at first, all Gavin's fancy appliances intimidated me. However, I've come to realize that grilled-cheese sandwiches taste the same whether you make them on a tin hot plate or built-in, stainless-steel burners.

I took my coffee out to the deck. In the shade of the house, the air was cool enough to make me shiver in my wool dressing gown. Bertie trotted over from where he had been sleeping in the sun and we retreated back inside to the warmth, me for a second cup of coffee and him for the other half of his nap. Perhaps later I'd go for a walk, or play the piano, or maybe do a little work on my film – a whole Sunday stretched ahead of me, hours of it and all of them unexpectedly free from people and commitments, a day to savour.

My gloat lasted all the way through showering, dressing, and a bowl of cereal. It ended as I settled in with yesterday's *Globe and Mail*. The dog woke up and barked once. I listened for a car in the drive but didn't hear the sound of an engine.

"You must have been dreaming, Bertie." I turned back to the *Globe* to see what poor wretch Jan Wong had sliced, diced, and served up for lunch this week.

Bertie began to bark in earnest, which is so unlike him that I put down the paper and went to investigate. We walked up the drive together and this time I did hear a car. A grey sedan pulled away from my gate in a hurry. I hoped it wasn't more kittens. People from the city have a nasty habit of driving out to the country to abandon their unwanted animals. Last spring I found a box of kittens that someone had tossed into the ditch by our road. They had drowned. Bertie gave the place where the car had stopped a thorough sniff-over while I looked around, but neither of us turned up any deserted creatures.

Later in the morning we collected Pete and went for a walk. On our walks the advantage is always with the quadrupeds. Unlike me, the animals never seem to tire although they cover far more ground than I do, Bert in his relentless persecution of small rodents and Pete in his endless quest for the perfect mouthful of greenery. However, they are both amiable creatures and far too polite to suggest that I may be deficient either in the number or strength of my legs. Sometimes Pete lets me ride partway home on his back. We walked a few hours west until the climbs got so steep and long that my legs told me it was time to turn for home.

Pete dropped me off at the pasture fence. The dog ran ahead to the house. By the time I caught up to him he was standing in the middle of the driveway happily terrorizing a short, middle-aged woman. He stared at her as she stood clutching a purse and a handful of leaflets to the lapels of her bright yellow blazer. The trembling hem of her calf-length skirt telegraphed the quaking of her knees.

"Please don't let him hurt me," she begged in a shaky voice. "Please. We've come in peace."

"Don't worry. So has he." I called the dog to my side. "What can I do for you?"

"We've come to bring you the message of joy." She held the leaflets out to me with hands no steadier than her legs. My heart sank. Usually we don't get religious visitors out where I live – not enough souls in the district to make the off chance of saving them worth the gas from Calgary. It's another perk of rural living.

"Could we have a little of your time to share the Lord's word with you?" she continued, looking and sounding somewhat firmer now that Bert had stopped staring at her and fixed his attention on something down by the barn.

"We? There's more of you?"

"Just one. He's over there." She pointed in the direction Bert was looking. "He'll be right back."

As if on cue, the friend came around the corner of the barn and walked up the path toward us. He was much younger than his partner but equally well turned out in a dark suit and red silk tie. I would have taken him for a campaigning Liberal candidate, but they're even scarcer in rural Alberta than religious visitors.

"What were you doing in my barn?"

"Sorry," he said with an attempt at an ingratiating smile that missed the mark by a mile. "I wasn't in the barn. I was looking for your outhouse. Doris warned me not to drink so much coffee right before we left Calgary." He added a self-deprecating little chuckle to the smile.

"You should have asked," I said. "I know it's hard to believe, but I do have indoor plumbing."

"You'll have to forgive Bill. He's from Ontario," the woman said. She glanced at him. He shook his head, a movement so slight and quick it was almost imperceptible.

"Well, I guess you do seem to be a little busy to talk with us just now." She turned her attention back to me. "So we'll leave you to get on with whatever it was you were doing when we knocked at your gate. I hope we haven't disrupted your whole afternoon and stopped you from taking that doggy for a walk or whatever it is you like to do on Sundays. We know time is a real precious thing, especially on week-ends, and we won't take up any more of yours." So much for my soul.

The woman kept up her one-sided prattle as she hustled her partner to the gate. He hurried to start the car they'd left parked on the road while she latched the gate behind them.

"Well, bye now and you have a really, really great day," she called over her shoulder as she jumped into the car and slammed the door. The man spun gravel in a sharp U-turn and aimed them back to the city.

That night, the dog discovered more uninvited company. It was past two in the morning and I lay in bed reading, once again reluctant to face my dreams. Bertie was sound asleep in his basket by the door and, judging by the twitching feet and thumping tail, his dreams were happy ones. I put down my book, turned out the lamp, and lay staring out the big windows at the moonlit pasture, listening to the quiet of the foothills night. I was beginning to drift off when a car moving at good speed on the gravel road broke the silence. As it neared the entrance to my place, the sound of its engine stopped. This puzzled me but not enough to get me out of my warm bed to look. I'd have turned over and fallen asleep if it hadn't been for Bertie. He got up from his basket and began to pace back and forth in front of the windows, whining and whimpering in the same worried way he had the night a black bear appeared on the deck. I got up, turned on the deck lights, and looked out the window. This time, no large furry face stared back at me.

"See, no bears. It was only a car. Now go back to bed."

I obeyed my own command, but Bertie continued to pace and fret. I gave up. This time I pulled on my runners and an old sweatsuit and grabbed the big flashlight from its bracket in the kitchen. I hooked Bertie's leash onto his collar just in case it wasn't a car that had disturbed him and there really was a large carnivore waiting for us at the back door.

My precautions were for nothing. I heard an owl hoot from the grove of trees down by the barn but that was it for predators. I didn't bother to switch on the flashlight. My eyes had adjusted to the night and open spaces like the driveway were well lit by the moon. We walked to the gate. Bertie tugged anxiously at the leash. I stopped and looked out at the road. There, twenty yards away, parked over by the far ditch, was a big black pickup truck, the kind with high bumpers and a bar of floodlights on the roof. At the moment the truck was dark, but I could see someone sitting in the driver's seat. At least I could see the back of a head with a hand pressed to one ear. The driver had stopped to use a cellphone.

"See, what did I tell you? It was just a car. Well, okay, a truck if you're going to be picky." Bertie looked up at the sound of my voice. I could tell he wasn't convinced. We started back to the house, but at the path to the barn he veered off, dragging me behind him.

"Bert, heel!" I shouted as he pulled me along. "Heel!" He stopped so quickly I nearly pitched over his back but not because of any orders from me. He stood very still, his ears pointed forward, his whole body quivering with excitement. I heard a loud scuffling in the trees near the barn. A large, black shape crashed through the underbrush.

I stood as still as Bertie, my heart pounding. I quivered too but for an entirely different reason. Bears scare the hell out of me. I heard it running toward the road. Then it yelled out something unintelligible to its companion in the truck. The engine roared to life, a door slammed, and the bear and his accomplice sped off toward Calgary.

When my heartrate had returned to something near normal, I let Bert off the leash. He dashed ahead to the barn and stood waiting for me. I caught up to him and reached out to open the door. That's when something rushed toward me from behind the barn. Suddenly a bright light shone in my eyes, nearly blinding me. I heard two shrieks. One of them was mine.

"Good heavens, Phoebe, it's you!" Professor Woodward turned off his flashlight.

"Of course it's me," I squeaked. "I live here."

"My dear girl, I'm so sorry. I had no idea you'd be out at this time of night. I do apologize if I frightened you." He carried a long stick. A stone spearhead bound to its end glinted evilly in the moonlight.

"What's that?" I asked.

"A spear, of course," he said. "I made it myself." The professor seemed distracted, almost flustered. "I always carry a spear at night. There are bears around, you know. I saw one last week."

"Why aren't you in your burrow?"

"I couldn't sleep because of this wretched head cold, so I thought I'd go for a walk and do a little stargazing."

"Did you hear that truck take off?"

"Was that a truck? I heard some shouts. That's why I came running."

"You probably heard me yelling at Bertie," I said. "But there was someone else down here by the barn. He ran through the brush out to a truck. Maybe I'd better give the police a call."

"Don't you think that's a bit of an overreaction? My guess, it was only a couple of neighbour kids out for a joyride. Nothing to worry about. Certainly nothing to bother the police over."

"Maybe you're right," I agreed half-heartedly.

"Of course I am. You mustn't let a little thing like this worry you." The professor was at his reassuring best. "Besides, whoever it was is long gone. Not much the police could do now."

"Well, whoever it was really scared me. I thought he was a bear."

"And he could have been. That's why you should always carry a spear when you go walking at night." He seemed to have recovered his equanimity. "I'll make one for you if you like."

"Thanks for the offer, but I don't think I'm ready for hand-to-paw combat."

"What time is it?" Timekeeping at night is difficult for primitive man, even one with a flashlight.

I turned on my own light and looked at my watch. "Two-thirty."

"My goodness, I had no idea it was that late. Time to get some sleep. Well, see you tomorrow." With a jaunty little wave, he stepped off the path into the trees and disappeared in the darkness.

Bertie trotted around, sniffing his way through the underbrush near the barn while I took a quick look inside.

As far as I could see nothing had been disturbed and nothing was missing. Not that I keep anything worth stealing there. We gave up on adventure for the night and went back to bed.

I suppose I should have been clever enough to put these Sunday incidents together into some sort of pattern. It was easy to fit them into place later but, at the time, they simply seemed like unrelated annoyances. Maybe if I'd told Candi she could have speculated her way to making sense of them, but, then again, she was so busy working on my love life that she really didn't have time. She phoned me from work shortly after nine on Monday morning.

"Everything's set," I said before she could start. "I asked him out for lunch. Twelve-thirty today at the Palliser."

"Good, but that's not what I'm calling about," she replied. "It's Simon."

"Dr. Maxwell's Simon?"

"That's the one."

"What about him?"

"He's sitting in my office. He was waiting for me when I got to work. He wants to talk to you."

"To me? What about?"

"He won't say."

"Why couldn't he phone me himself?"

"He wanted to but he couldn't get your number. He had no idea where you live and the station doesn't give out home phone numbers. That's why he's here waiting for you."

"Okay," I said. "Put him on."

"I can't. I'm using the phone in Ella's office."

"So go back to your office and call me from there. I'm not going anywhere."

"Well, we can try but my guess is he won't talk on the phone. If you're coming into town for lunch anyway, why not leave a little early and stop here on the way?"

"Let's try the phone first," I said.

"Did you see the *Herald* this morning?" she asked. "You were right – the police are now saying Dr. Maxwell was murdered. It's official."

"Surprise, surprise."

"You should wear that blue suit Margaret gave you," Candi pitched one of her curves.

"You've lost me."

"Wear the suit."

"To talk to Simon?"

"Not for Simon. For lunch. It's perfect for the Palliser."

I'm the grateful recipient of the occasional hand-me-down from my ultra-chic businesswoman sister-in-law. Although Margaret's and Cyrrie's contributions to my wardrobe mark me as a spiritual descendant of Second-Hand Rose, at least they put me among that lady's better dressed progeny. Thanks to my relations by marriage, I do formal evenings and power lunches with equal panache. Fortunately, neither of these crowds my engagement calendar so my wardrobe manages to keep pace.

I took Candi's advice about both Simon and the suit. When it comes to clothes and people, she's usually right and on this occasion she had certainly read Simon's reactions correctly. He did refuse to tell me what he wanted over the phone. He said he needed to talk to me in person, that it was a matter of the gravest importance. The only matter of grave importance we had in common was his boss's murder, and the prospect of an emotionally charged heart-to-heart with him on that topic was truly depressing. Nevertheless, that evening at the museum, Simon had seemed like a decent man, at least during the brief time he was sober, and he had certainly been kind to me. So, with some reluctance and more than a few misgivings, I shut down the film editing bench, put on Margaret's Palliser power suit, and left for the city.

I got to the station at eleven and found Simon in Candi's office drinking coffee from an *A Day in the Lifestyle* mug. They were discussing the stolen fossils. I thought Simon might seem upset or nervous, but he looked fine, carefully groomed, and very spruce in a tweed jacket and tie. He actually seemed a lot brighter than he had at the Royal Tyrrell even during his sober moments, although his hands weren't entirely steady when he put down the coffee mug and rose to greet me.

"Thank you for coming, Phoebe." He shook my hand. "I've been concerned about you. That was a very shocking thing for you to see. I'm sorry it was you who found him."

"It had to be someone," I repeated what I'd said to Cyrrie with about as much conviction. "Have the police made any progress?"

"If they have, they're not telling me. All I've heard from them is questions, not answers."

"They haven't found the fossils yet, either," Candi said as she gathered up some papers from her desk. "Well, see you guys later."

"You're leaving?" I said.

"I have some work to do in editing." She paused at the door. "And make sure you keep this shut. If those jerks in News find out that Simon's here, he won't get out alive.

157

They'll be all over him wanting an exclusive. Bye for now." She smiled and then abandoned me, closing the door firmly behind her. It opened again a second later. "I nearly forgot. Ella would like to talk to you about tomorrow's shoot. She wants to know if you could stop back here on your way home from lunch. Great. I'll let her know. See you later." This time the door stayed shut.

I sat down in the chair behind the desk. Candi, her three almost as gorgeous sisters, and their parents smiled up at me from a framed photo. Mr. Sinclair had a slightly dazed look, as if he were astonished at having fathered all that feminine beauty – Candida, Nancy, Catherine, Beverly. I wished all of them were with me now.

"Coffee?" Simon pointed to the carafe on the filing cabinet.

"No thanks."

He got a refill and sat down. He put his cup on the desk and pulled a small silver flask from his pocket.

"Do you mind?"

I shook my head and he poured a generous tot of whisky into his coffee.

"Don't suppose you'd like . . ." He held up the flask.

"Thanks but it's a little early for me."

"It's a little early for most people." He replaced the cap and set the flask at the ready beside his cup. "At least it's early for anyone who isn't an out-and-out drunkard. I am, you know. A drunk. I'm an alcoholic." He said it as matter-of-factly as if he were admitting to being left-handed.

"No," I said. "I didn't know." Not officially, anyway.

"I didn't know myself until Friday. Or I didn't admit it until then. To be honest, I suppose I've known for quite some time."

"What happened Friday?"

"Now that's a very good question, Phoebe. And be damned if I know the answer," he said. "You see, I don't remember anything from after the banquet on Thursday night until I saw you in the doorway of Graham's office on Friday morning. It's a blank."

"You'd had a fair amount to drink."

"What I had was an alcoholic blackout," Simon stated flatly.

"And that's what made you realize you have an alcohol problem?"

"Well, it was rather a big hint, don't you think?" He smiled at me over his mug, but the sadness in his voice belied the wry humour of his words. "That and admitting that I've been averaging a bottle of whisky a day for the last God knows how long. But, yes, I'd say the blackout was what really did it. It's frightening to lose part of your life."

"What are you going to do?" I asked.

"I don't know. But I do know that for now I have to keep going and that there's no way I can do that without drinking. Not yet." He took a sip of the coffee. "At the moment, the tricky part is controlling how much – walking the line between feeling functional and getting blasted."

"You can't simply stop?"

"I'm not certain that I want to," he said. "And right now it's the only way I'm going to get through this. I have to see it through. Right to the end, no matter what that is."

"By this, I take it you mean Dr. Maxwell's death?"

"Graham's murder," Simon corrected.

"His murder," I agreed.

"And I need your help, Phoebe. That's why I'm here. I need your memory. I need you to tell me everything you know about what I did that night."

"I'd like to help you, but I don't know much. I left the museum a little after ten."

"Did you see me after dinner?" he asked. "Did we talk?"

"I didn't see you," I said. "But I did hear you."

"You heard me and Graham in the office, didn't you?" It was more a statement than a question.

"Yes. You were arguing with him. I overheard you when I came to pick up my equipment after dinner."

"Then they were telling the truth." His shoulders slumped and suddenly he looked drained, his face grey. "The police said they knew we'd had an argument. They told me there was a witness, that someone had heard us. If that was true, I thought it might be you. I knew you would come back for your things." He rubbed the palm of his hand slowly down the side of his face as if trying to wipe away an old and infinite weariness. "So it's true – we really did have a row that night." Something Simon hadn't wanted to believe was now an irrefutable and unhappy reality.

"Yes, you did."

"Was it bad?" He spoke so softly I could hardly hear him. "Please be honest. I need you to tell me the truth."

"What I heard was pretty unpleasant, but I didn't stick around for long."

"What did I say?"

I thought Simon should count himself lucky that he didn't remember his fight with Dr. Maxwell. I remembered every word, every detail. I could still hear the anger and hatred in their voices. Just thinking about it gave me the same sick feeling I'd had that night in the corridor. But Simon had asked and he deserved an answer.

"You called him a phony. You said that he couldn't find a fossil in the Royal Tyrrell unless you drew him a map. That this time you were going to blow the whistle on him, destroy his reputation."

"And how did Graham take that?"

"Called you a drunk and a failure and threatened to fire you if you didn't pull yourself together. Said that no one would believe you and that all you had a reputation for was being a drunk and faking data."

"Did I threaten to hurt him?"

"Only his reputation," I said. "At least that's the only threat I heard you make."

"Did I sound violent?"

"You sounded drunk. You sounded like you loathed him."

"What about Graham?"

"He was sober. He sounded arrogant, contemptuous."

"Well, we'd been there enough times before," he commented to himself. "Did I say anything else?"

"I don't know. I left. I decided to come back for the equipment in the morning."

Simon got up and poured himself another cup of coffee. This time he didn't add any whisky.

"Have you talked to Gillian?" I asked. "She saw me leave. She was at the other end of the corridor. Maybe she heard more."

"Even if she had, she wouldn't tell me," he said. "Gill wouldn't tell me if I were on fire."

"You don't get along?"

"I always get along with Graham's women." He shrugged. "They come, they go, they're all alike."

"Then why does Gillian dislike you?"

"I expect it's because Graham needed me," he said. "He needed me, but he didn't need her. I was necessary to his career. Gill was expendable and she knew it."

"You're saying she was jealous of you?"

Simon considered this for a moment. "I'd say not so much jealous as angry. Angry that I had something she wanted and would never have. She was desperate for something to bind Graham to her, something that would make her different from all the other Gillians. Poor kid. Graham had half a dozen just like her in the time I knew him. They were interchangeable – young and very pretty and naïve enough to worship him. He even married a couple of them. But he always got bored and then they were gone, replaced by the new model. I could see the pattern repeating itself with Gill. Her days were numbered and she knew it."

"He was going to leave Gillian?"

"That's not the way it worked. Graham always arranged it so that they had to leave him. Less inconvenient that way."

"But either way Gillian would be gone?"

"I'd have been surprised if she'd lasted out September, especially after she'd finished getting the exhibit set up and running. It's the old story – she loved him, he didn't love her. I knew Graham, probably better than anyone, and I can tell you for certain that the only thing he ever really loved was his work. But that was the old story too – it didn't love him, poor bastard."

"And that's why he needed you," I said. "You weren't just blowing smoke when you said he couldn't find a fossil unless you drew him a map, were you? It was true."

"Graham could understand the science we did after the fact, but he couldn't put it together before, which is when it counts, when it's still a theory and original and risky. He could explain what we'd done, but he couldn't do it himself. He could never make the big finds on his own and he knew it. Graham had everything except talent," Simon said. "That's what I supplied." It should have sounded egotistical, but Simon's statement came across as a simple declaration of fact.

"So you really did draw the maps. Literally."

"Yes, I did."

"Why couldn't Dr. Maxwell put the theory together himself? He seemed like an intelligent man to me."

"You're quite right. Graham was reasonably bright. Not as bright as he sounded but not stupid by any means. But his talents weren't for science. Besides, I don't think what I'm talking about has all that much to do with intelligence. Of course, to do this kind of science you have to be smart enough to get the training and the background and all of that so intelligence does play some role. But most of all you need, well, I don't know what you'd call it."

He sat forward in his chair as he struggled to explain. "I guess what you need is an intuitive feeling for the work. You have to be able to make sense of what, at first, seems nothing but a mass of unrelated details. You have to be able to look at a myriad of tiny bits of information and see the whole big pattern they make."

He thought for a moment, searching for an example to illustrate his theory. "Maybe you could say it's like a symphony. There must be hundreds of thousands of separate sounds in Beethoven's *Ninth*, but there's only one way to fit them together that results in the 'Ode to Joy.' That's what I do. I put the thousands of tiny pieces of data together to make that one perfect pattern. I make the details sing. And when I hear their music, it's the most wonderful feeling in the world. Graham could never hear it, no matter how hard he tried. But I can."

"If the music is so wonderful, then why do you drink?"

"Why should the two be connected? Besides, you don't get to hear the music very often. The times between are long."

"And someone else got all the credit for your discoveries," I said. "Graham Maxwell stole your work. That must have been galling."

"I guess it was sometimes. Especially lately." Simon got up from his chair and walked over to the window. He stood with his back to me looking out over the parking lot.

"At first I thought as long as I could do the science I wouldn't care. I'd do the work that counted and let Graham go off and make the speeches and guest appearances and be important to his heart's content. Graham was very good at speeches and importance. It worked for a while too. But things changed. I don't know how it started or even when, but at some point Graham began to believe his own press releases. He actually began to think of himself as a great scientist and not just a great mouth. Instead of sticking to what I told him to say, he started making up theories and explanations on his own. And as his confidence in his role of the great scientist grew, so did the theories. They got crazier by the year. I honestly think Graham went a little mad. I don't know how we managed to get this far without being laughed off the stage. *Homo musicus* was the worst. No, I take that back. *Homo musicus* was worse than the worst – it was insane." For the first time, Simon seemed truly agitated. He turned to face me. "Not only was he getting the credit for my biggest discovery, he was going to bugger it up. That ridiculous name was only the beginning. This time he'd gone too far."

"Then you meant it. You really were going to blow the whistle on him."

"I guess I was. But who knows? Perhaps Graham was right and no one would believe me."

"Do people have such long memories? Surely, that business with your doctoral dissertation was a very long time ago."

"Where did you hear about that?" he asked sharply. "No, don't bother telling me. I can guess. The nearly departed Gillian."

"It's true, though, isn't it?"

"Unfortunately. But it wasn't half as serious a sin as I've no doubt Gill has led you to believe."

"It was serious enough to cost you your degree," I said. "What made you do it?"

He shook his head. "I must have asked myself that a million times and I've never come up with an answer that made any sense. I was young. I was impatient. I was arrogant. I wanted to get out in the world and start my work, not plod along in some academic backwater filling in lists of numbers to make a lot of has-been never-was professors happy."

"How did the university discover what you'd done?"

"Someone told them," he said. "But I've never known who. Occasionally, in my more paranoid moments, I think it might have been Graham. I met him on my first real job, a big dig in Ethiopia that he was working on too. I liked him. Sometimes of an evening we'd knock back a few together. Maybe we knocked back a few too many now and then. I think I might have told him one night when we were drinking but I don't know. Besides, even Graham wouldn't have been that miserable."

"Gillian says he gave you a job when no one else would hire you."

"That's partly true. Maybe even mostly true," he admitted. "Other people might have hired me but only for scut work. They'd have kept me well down the ranks where my sullied academic reputation couldn't rub off on anything. But I knew I couldn't work at rubbish like that, not for a day. Graham knew it too. He offered me a partnership – I'd do the science, he'd do the money, and together we'd set the paleoanthropology world on fire. At least we'd do it together after he'd fronted our first few years and given me some time to redeem my reputation. I'd have to work in the background, be a silent partner for a while. Well, a while turned out to be a very long time, didn't it? Graham never did reckon that my reputation had recovered. And that's what you heard us arguing about."

"I wish I could help you, Simon." I didn't know what else to say to him. "I'm sorry."

"That's all right. I suppose I didn't really think you could, but I had to ask." He smiled. "You know, Phoebe, I wish we'd met under different circumstances. But then I wish a lot of things were different." He took my hand in his and held it against his cheek for a moment. I felt an odd pain in the back of my throat. "Anyway, thanks for coming today." He retrieved the silver flask and slipped it back into his jacket pocket. "Now maybe I'd better call a cab. I have to catch the twelve-thirty bus back to Drumheller. The police are still crawling all over the museum and I'm supposed to be helping them find my fossils."

"Any leads?"

"Not that anyone's mentioned to me."

I walked Simon to the front door of the station. Despite Candi's dire predictions, no reporters ambushed us along the way. We waited outside for the cab.

"I understand from Candi that you're going to be working at the museum tomorrow," he said.

"I have to finish the work I couldn't do on Friday." I suppose it may have seemed callous to Simon, but we still had to put a program on the air.

"I'll look forward to seeing you then. Maybe you'll be free for lunch."

His taxi pulled up to the curb. Simon opened the passenger door but, instead of getting in, he turned back and looked at me.

"Phoebe, do you think I killed him?"

"I honestly don't know."

"And that's the hell of it," he said. "Neither do I."

10

"SORRY I'M LATE. I had to go back to the office for a few minutes after court." Tim slid into the chair opposite me at our table in the Palliser dining room. He was in his lawyer uniform: dark suit, silk tie, polished black shoes. With me in Margaret's hand-me-down we looked like a matched pair. So much for appearances.

"Hey, I'm sure glad you got this table. That thing is half the fun of coming here." He gazed up at the massive, brass-hooded fireplace next to us. Carvings of strange heraldic animals, chimerical birds and goats, embellished its elaborate stonework. In the centre, a sculpted steam locomotive puffed its practical way through their midst. An imposing crest, representative of who knows what, crowned this functional monument to mercantile glory. Tim shook his head in disbelief. "Only in a Canadian railway hotel, eh?"

There are lots of good restaurants in Calgary now, but in earlier days the Palliser was the city's place to celebrate. Maybe because my family has lived here for so long – my great-grandfather immigrated from England before the First World War, which, by Calgary standards, practically makes us pioneers – we still hold to the tradition. Engagements, weddings, births, anniversaries, graduations, new jobs – from the day it opened in 1914, the Palliser was the place to toast them all. Tim's family has lived here even longer than mine so it's been a part of their celebrations too. I was sorry we didn't have much to toast today.

"I should bring Brooke here for her birthday. My grandmother used to stand me to lunch at the Palliser every year on mine. It's not trendy enough for Marilyn so we've never been, but I think Brooke would enjoy it."

"The horses would go over well," I said. "There can't be too many restaurants where you get to eat under a wall-sized painting of a herd of mustangs."

Tim craned his neck so he could see past the pillar that blocked his view of cowboys on their ponies herding wild horses across the south wall of the room. "That thing makes the fireplace look restrained."

I couldn't disagree, although I had to admit to myself that a little of the childhood love I'd felt for the mural still lingered. Well, to be honest, more than a little. That painting packs a real emotional wallop for a susceptible seven-year-old. It endures.

I ordered a bowl of clam chowder, the Palliser's specialty, and a salad.

"I'll have the clam chowder too," Tim said to the waiter, "but I'd like the big one that comes in the bread thing." He refused a glass of wine, saying he needed a clear head for an afternoon meeting although I suspect the real reason was a kindly effort to spare my purse. Tim is very aware of the difference in our incomes and, although it doesn't worry me in the least, if our positions were reversed it would bother him very much. For Tim, money is one of the markers of success, a way of keeping score. For me, it's something I need enough of in order to do what I want.

"To Phoebe, photographer and filmmaker extraordinaire, and to the company that sends her cheques." He raised his water glass to me. "May they be even bigger and better in the future. That's the cheques," he added, "not the films. You couldn't improve on them." I could but, even so, the praise was welcome. "You do great work, Ms. Fairfax, and if the world were a fair place you'd be rich and famous as well as talented and sexy." He smiled at me. This was not going to be easy.

"How's Brooke's arm?" It was time for a little dose of the real world.

"There's a pretty good-sized bruise on her shoulder, but that's it. I'd say she'll be riding Corky again by the end of the week."

"That's good. I'm glad she's doing so well."

"Plus she's as horse-crazy as ever. Being tossed off Elvira doesn't seem to have changed that."

That was all he had to say about Brooke. He didn't even mention Marilyn or her reaction to the accident but that might have been because the waiter, with impeccable timing, delivered our food. You can't work up a good rant with a mouthful of Palliser chowder.

"How are you doing?" he asked. "I mean, about that Drumheller business."

"I'm okay," I said. "The police are probably going to want to ask me some more questions but, other than that, it's over. At least for me." I didn't tell him about my talk with Simon and this made me feel vaguely guilty. However, I'd probably have felt even guiltier if I'd blabbed Simon's confidences to one of the Crown prosector's staff. Besides, the police knew all about his troubles so I wasn't keeping anything a secret from the official investigation.

"I thought you had to go back sometime this week and do more taping."

"That's all I'm doing, taping. Period. I'm going to the museum tomorrow to get some shots so Ella can finish her program," I said. "Nothing to do with Maxwell's murder."

"I really am sorry I wasn't there for you. I should have been, but I wasn't."

"There's no way you could have known. There's nothing to be sorry for." Time to change the subject. "Have you heard any rumours at work about how the investigation is going?"

"Not a thing. The police are being pretty close-mouthed about this one, probably because it's so high profile. It's not everyday that somebody world famous gets murdered on our patch. Big stuff."

"Do you think you might get to work on the case?"

"Me?" Tim laughed loudly enough to turn a few heads at nearby tables. "I'd be lucky to carry the big boys' brief-cases on this one. Believe me, Graham Maxwell will get the very biggest gun we've got and I'm a year or two away from that. Besides, the Mounties have to get their man before we have anything to do with it. Hey, how's Candi?" It was Tim's turn to change the subject. "Haven't seen her and Nick for ages."

Candi and Nick and our families and politics and movies got us through the meal although the conversation began to flag just before the waiter returned with the dessert menu. The man was a genius at timing. However, it wasn't until Tim had finished a dish of hot apple pie with brandy sauce that I was willing to admit the time had come.

"That was one great meal." Tim sat back in his chair and folded his napkin. "I'll probably have to bike to Canmore and back to work off that pie but it was worth every mile."

We sat in silence for a minute and sipped our coffee. When the minute began to feel like an hour, I knew I had to speak, but before I could say anything, he stole my opening line.

"Phoebe, I think we have to talk."

"We do?" I said, like I hadn't rehearsed the scene in my head a hundred times.

"Yeah, we do," he said very gently. "You know, things aren't going like they should. With us, I mean."

I nodded. I didn't know what to say. I hadn't written his part of the script and he'd taken over mine.

"I know that it's my fault." No! Now he was letting me down lightly. "There's still too much unresolved stuff from my marriage. I have no right to drag you into the mess between me and Marilyn, but I don't seem to be able to help myself."

"Divorce is hard," I said, which might not rate a ten on the originality scale but sure beat the hell out of sitting there nodding like an idiot.

"Yes, it is," he agreed. "And in a lot of ways I'd never have guessed. Everything gets so muddled. Right now, I can't even tell what I'm going to be feeling from one hour to the next. Sometimes I'm furious with Marilyn, sometimes I'm lonely for her. And I always miss Brooke. You know, this quality-time stuff? It's crap. I'm her father. I want to be there all the time. I want to help her with her homework. I want to hear her practising her clarinet."

I couldn't trust my voice, so I fell back on a little more nodding. Pretty soon he'd be telling me what a great person I am. At least that's what I'd have been saying about now if we'd stuck to my script.

"You know, Phoebe, you are one ace lady and I wish like hell that our timing had been better. But it's too soon for me. I'm sorry, it's just too soon."

"You've got nothing to be sorry for," I said. "It's the way you feel. Sometimes things don't work out the way you want them to." Like this conversation.

"I'm sorry if I've hurt you. Are you going to be okay?"

"Don't worry about me. I'll get along." Oh God, now I was quoting Billie Holliday songs. Next thing you know, I'd be telling him not to cling to some fading thing that used to be.

Before Tim could tell me that he hoped we'd still be friends, the waiter made another of his felicitous appearances, this time with the bill and more coffee. Tim declined a second cup and got up to go to his meeting. He held my hands in both of his and said a little more about how sorry he was and what a lovely, adorable, sexy, funny, talented, etcetera lady I was. I mumbled some appropriately regretful responses. Then he stooped, brushed my forehead with his lips, and left. And that was it. End of scene.

I slipped my credit card into the folder with the bill and finished my coffee. I'm sure I should have been feeling something significant, but all I could detect was a distinct hint of disgruntled with maybe the beginnings of a minor fit of pique. The waiter returned, refilled my cup, and took my card away with him. I wondered if it might be possible to mistake a caffeine overload for pique. I was so busy contemplating this problem in self-awareness that I didn't notice Mrs. Woodward until she sat down in the chair Tim had vacated.

"Phoebe, how nice to see you." She settled her graceful five-feet-ten in for what was obviously going to be more than a brief hello.

This was a woman who didn't mess around with understated colours. Today she wore a bright fuchsia linen dress, very tailored, with a large dark green and fuchsia scarf knotted casually at the neck. It should have been too much, but on her it was perfect. I knew Mrs. Woodward must be at least sixty-five, but even though her hair was grey and her face, under its makeup, a net of fine wrinkles, I never thought of the professor's wife as old. There was something about her, an energy, a vitality, that didn't defy age but, rather, made it seem irrelevant.

"Are you in a hurry, or do you have time for another cup of coffee?" she asked.

"Of course I have time," I said. "But I think maybe I've reached my coffee limit."

"Well, I haven't." Mrs. Woodward beckoned to the waiter and ordered a cup of coffee and a cognac. "Won't you join me in a brandy or a liqueur or something?"

What the hell. I'd just been dumped. I was probably emotionally drained, so severely wounded that I couldn't even feel the pain . . . yet. I deserved a restorative snifter of something. "Thanks, Mrs. Woodward. I'd like that. I'll have a calvados, please."

"Oh dear, 'Mrs. Woodward' – now that does make me feel older than God's sister. Please, Phoebe, my name is Diana. I may not know you as well as Adam does, but I do think we've reached the first-name stage, don't you?"

I didn't mention that I wasn't on a first-name basis with her husband and probably never would be. Actually, it surprised me that Professor Woodward had taken to calling me Phoebe instead of the Miss Fairfax of my student days. Still, I didn't think I could ever manage to call him Adam, at least not comfortably.

"I met Trevor for lunch," Mrs. Woodward continued. "We were sitting over there, under the mural. I'd have asked you to join us, but you and that very handsome man seemed so absorbed in each other that I didn't want to interrupt. All the same, I'm sorry Trevor hasn't had a chance to talk with you. I know he's interested in your films."

"I'm going to see him later this afternoon," I said. "Professor Woodward is bringing him to my house for a visit before they drive home to Calgary."

"Then make sure you stay outside. Those old skins of Adam's are really ripe these days. I didn't think they could get any smellier but I was wrong."

The waiter brought our drinks along with a folder that held my credit card but no slip for me to sign. The gentleman had already taken care of the bill, the waiter explained as he topped up Mrs. Woodward's coffee. I slipped in an appropriately generous cash tip as thanks for all his well-timed appearances and closed the folder on lunch.

"Cheers." Mrs. Woodward raised her glass and took a sip. "Hmmm. Not bad. Senior citizenship does have its rewards, you know. When I started getting the old age pension I decided I was probably old enough to have earned the occasional cognac in the afternoon."

My calvados slid down very gently.

"Phoebe, I'm glad I ran into you today. I've been meaning to call you for some time. I've wanted to thank you for being such a good friend to Adam on this project of his."

"That's very kind of you, Diana, but I really don't do much," I said.

"Maybe you don't think it's much, but I assure you I rest a lot easier knowing you're keeping an eye out for him. What if he had an accident and broke his leg? What if he got sick? If it weren't for you, he could go for days and nobody would know."

"I wouldn't worry too much. Professor Woodward's pretty tough."

"Not so tough as all that. This business with Graham Maxwell has upset him dreadfully. Me too, for that matter. We should never have gone to the museum. I told Adam that but he insisted. I don't know why. You must be pretty upset yourself. Finding his body couldn't have been a pleasant experience."

"It wasn't," I admitted. "But it would have been a lot worse if I'd known him well, if I'd known him as long as you. Professor Woodward told me that you were both at university with him."

"Yes, and Stan Darling too. The four of us took geology together at U of A. We were all in the same year."

"I didn't know you were a geologist."

"I'm not really. I have a degree but I never did much with it. Too busy raising a family and by the time they were grown up and able to manage on their own it was too late. You can't be away from a science for twenty years and then expect to take up where you left off. It doesn't work that way."

"Did you ever regret not doing anything with your degree?"

"I suppose I must have at times, but there's no point in worrying about what might have been, is there? Besides, it was all so long ago that it doesn't seem to matter much now. Some things are better left in the past." Mrs. Woodward swirled the cognac around the bottom of the balloon glass, warming it with her hands. "I think that's one of the reasons I didn't want to go to the opening of Graham's exhibit. I knew it would raise a lot of old memories we'd all be better off without."

"And did it?"

"Of course it did. All the old angers and jealousies and resentments were there like it was last week, not decades ago. And having Stan show up simply put the finishing touches on the whole mess."

"I can't understand why Dr. Maxwell would invite someone he knew to be so rabidly anti-evolution to the museum. That exhibit was all about human evolution."

"Ah, Phoebe, you'd have had to know them all way back when to understand. You see, one of Graham's favourite sports was teasing Stan and, I must say, there was nothing good-natured about it. Really, what Graham did wasn't teasing at all, it was baiting. He gave Stan a constant hard time about his religious beliefs and his Victorian attitudes to sex and whatever else he could think of that he knew would get up Stan's nose. Sometimes Graham went much too far. I remember once, after a party, he upset Stan so much that the poor man actually sat down and cried. He was humiliated."

"Then why did Stan take it? You'd think he'd have had the sense to stay away from Dr. Maxwell, especially after that. He must have hated him."

"You're right about that. Stan did hate Graham. He hated him for all the baiting and he hated him even more for making him feel that hatred. You see, good Christians like Stan aren't supposed to hate anyone, are they?"

"Then why did he stick around?"

"Because he was in love with me." Mrs. Woodward said with an unpleasant touch of self-satisfaction. "I was Graham's girlfriend back then," she explained. "So if Stan wanted to be near me he had to take Graham as part of the package."

"Did you know that Stan loved you?"

"Of course I did. He sent me flowers and wrote me poems and God knows what else. Everyone knew Stan was in love. He certainly didn't keep it a secret. As a matter of fact, it was one of Graham's favourite topics for teasing. What a miserable bastard that man was when you think about it. See what I mean about old memories?"

"Poor Stan. He must have had one monumental case of raging hormones."

Mrs. Woodward laughed. "I suppose he did. But to be fair to Graham, Stan did ask for it sometimes. He could be such a self-righteous little prig that I was tempted to have a go at him myself now and then. Really, the only one who was always kind to him was Adam. He used to stick up for Stan when Graham really got going. Adam wasn't as easy a mark. He could give as good as he got, so Graham would usually back off. Adam was pretty formidable when he was angry. He still is. I think Graham was a little afraid of him."

"And maybe a little jealous of Stan," I suggested. "Could be that's why he was so cruel to him."

"I don't think so. There was never any question of my falling for Stan Darling. Graham didn't have anything to worry about on that score." Like most of us, Mrs. Woodward was the star of her own blinkered memories.

"No, I didn't mean Dr. Maxwell was jealous over you," I said. "I meant he might have been jealous of Stan's ability as a geologist. Professor Woodward told me that he thinks Stan is the best field geologist he's ever known, that he was miles ahead of Graham Maxwell as a scientist in spite of his religious views."

"That's true," she said. "Stan was the best student in our class by far. He was exceptional. Graham couldn't hold a candle to him." She paused for a reflective sip of cognac. "You know, I've often wondered how Graham ever got as far as he did. He loved paleontology, or at least the idea of paleontology, that's certain. He just wasn't very good at it. I got better paleo marks than he did and I was no whiz kid. Graham was like the fat girl who's desperate to dance *Swan Lake*. To be honest, you'd have to tell her those thirty-two fouettés are never going to happen but then, before you know it, there she is twirling around Covent Garden on her tippytoes. It's beyond me."

"Why were they friends? Dr. Maxwell and Professor Woodward, I mean."

"Graham could be very charming when he put his mind to it," Mrs. Woodward said. "And he could talk anybody into anything, men as well as women. I should know, I fell for him. People like Graham need an audience and in a way that's what we were, I suppose, his audience. Besides, I think Adam envied him a little. After all, Graham had everything – looks, charm, money."

"Everything except talent and the girl. Stan got the talent and Professor Woodward got you."

"Well, that's one way of looking at it," Mrs. Woodward smiled. "Although I doubt that Graham would have agreed with you. In his version, he became a world-famous scientist and I'm merely one of his past conquests. Very past. Did you see that girl assistant of his? She's young enough to be his granddaughter. The man was a walking testimonial to the power of Viagra." She laughed again, this time not at all kindly. "Oh dear, do you suppose that counts as speaking ill of the dead?"

Mrs. Woodward finished the last of her cognac and placed the empty glass on the table. She looked at me and thought for a moment or two, as if she were making up her mind about something.

"You know, Phoebe," she said, "if I hadn't run into you today I'd have called you anyway and not just to say thanks. I wanted to talk about Trevor. You know about him, don't you? I saw you looking at him and Graham when you were taking those photos. I could tell you knew, that you could see the likeness. You saw that Graham was Trevor's father."

"It's really none of my business," I said, but without much hope. I could feel it coming. I was in for another heart-to-heart. God knows what I'd done to deserve this many in one day. Maybe I was becoming like those people who don't like cats – they sit down and ten minutes later they're up to their eyeballs in tabbies.

"Adam doesn't know," Mrs. Woodward said. "He thinks Trevor is his."

"I'm not going to tell him so you have no worries on that account," I said. God, I wish people would talk to each other instead of to me.

"What worries me is what it would do to Adam if he found out," she said. "It would devastate him."

Mrs. Woodward had presented me with a dilemma that had enough horns to outfit a herd of Jerseys. Should I tell her that the professor already knew her secret, or not? Not. The Woodwards could solve their own problems – they'd been married for so long they must have had some practise at it. Besides, if I could keep her secret, surely I was obliged to keep his. The fact that they were the same secret was beside the point.

"Deceiving Adam is not something I'm very proud of," Mrs. Woodward continued. "All I can say in my own defence is that I was alone and pregnant and frightened. I don't suppose that sounds like much of an excuse nowadays, but things were very different back then. I was so young and so afraid that I couldn't bring myself to tell anyone except my sister and I made her promise to keep it a secret. She has, too, all these years.

"Of course, Graham ran as soon as he found out I was pregnant. He left me. Couldn't get away to graduate school fast enough. In hindsight I know that shouldn't have come as a surprise, but at the time it really flattened me. I guess girls were a lot more naïve in those days. I know I was."

Personally, I wasn't convinced of this. In my experience, women today are just as dumb about men as they've always been and I include myself in that sweeping generalization.

I had deluded myself into thinking that Gavin and I could make a life together and it had been painful when that fantasy faded. Tim had it right about divorce – sometimes I was still angry with Gavin, sometimes I still missed him. Either way it still hurt, just not quite as much as it once had.

"And there was Adam," Mrs. Woodward said. "Somehow he always seemed to be around back then. I knew it wouldn't take much to get him to propose and it didn't. The poor man was already in love with me. All these years later here I am, still ashamed of how I manipulated him."

"So you knew Professor Woodward was in love with you," I said.

"I knew, but I don't think anyone else did. You see, Adam had the sense to keep his mouth shut about his feelings. There was no wearing his heart on his sleeve, like Stan. He was a lot more subtle than that, but I still knew he was in love."

"Then he probably wanted to marry you. So why be ashamed? You did him a favour."

"Because I wasn't in love with him back then. I only married him to get myself out of a jam."

"And now?" I asked.

"Now I love him very much. We've spent forty-four years together, that's two-thirds of our lives. We've raised a family, we have grandchildren. I can't imagine ever loving another man as much as I love him, especially not a self-absorbed specimen like Graham Maxwell. When I saw the two of them together at the museum all I could think was how lucky I was that I'd married Adam."

"Then why can't you tell him about Trevor? Do you think he'd care after all the things you've had together? He must know how much you love him."

"I think he does. But it would still hurt him very much to know I'd lied to him all these years. And it would hurt Trevor too. How would you like to find out that the man you'd been calling Dad all your life was nothing of the kind?"

I gave up. The secret the Woodwards chose to keep from one another was their business, even if it wasn't much of a secret. I'd bet money that Trevor was perfectly aware of his parentage. Probably his sister and brother knew too, even the grandchildren if they were interested, which was unlikely. Only the Woodward parents were intent on keeping a secret about which everyone knew and no one cared.

"Have you seen Adam since the museum?" Mrs. Woodward asked.

"He was at my place on Saturday."

"How did he look? He was a hungover mess on Friday."

"He was pretty much okay when I saw him. Except his cold has come back."

"Well, if that's his worst complaint, then I'd say he got off pretty lightly." Mrs. Woodward's tone was less than sympathetic. "He and Stanley drank enough to float a boat. I could see Adam reverting to his student days. Well, his mind may have turned back the clock to twenty-one, but his poor old body stayed sixty-five and he paid for it the next day."

"Not half as big a price as Stan," I said. "I saw them both on Friday morning at the museum. Stan looked like he'd have been happier dead."

"No experience, that's Stan's problem," she sniffed. "A babe in the woods when it comes to alcohol. He was a tee-totaller when I knew him. This was probably the first and only time in his entire life that he's ever been drunk."

"Well, he sure didn't do it by halves. That was one sick little Geologist for Jesus I saw."

"So you know about Stan's group," Mrs. Woodward said.

I told her about our encounter with the protestors and about reading Stan's newsletter at Cyrrie's.

"Adam once gave them a talk on evolution."

"He told me about it."

"Poor Adam." Mrs. Woodward smiled. "It really was a very funny evening, but he still can't laugh about it. He can be so naïve at times. He actually believed they were interested in hearing what he had to say about science."

Our glasses were empty and Mrs. Woodward had paid her bill. Except for us, the large room was deserted. She asked me some questions about what my family was up to and we talked for a few minutes about my parents and their travels.

"They're in Australia," I said. "Right now they're on the Great Barrier Reef so my mother can snorkel and my dad can see where Captain Cook's ship got caught on the coral. They'll be home at the end of September."

"You must be looking forward to that," Mrs. Woodward said.

She asked some more polite questions about my brothers, but I could see she was distracted, there was still something on her mind. I looked at my watch. It was after two-thirty and I had to stop at the station and talk with Ella before I drove home.

"Thank you for the drink," I said. I rummaged in my purse and found my car keys. "Next time you drop the professor off in the forest reserve, I wish you'd stop for a visit at my house on your way home."

"Just a minute, Phoebe. Don't go yet. Please." She reached out and put her hand on my arm. She seemed upset about something and suddenly looked much older than she had a moment ago. "What if Adam saw?" she asked anxiously.

"Saw what?" I seemed to have lost the thread of the conversation. Being Candi's friend I'm used to this. I've learned it's best to ask questions before I become totally bewildered.

"What if he saw how much Trevor looks like Graham? What if he realized that Trevor wasn't his son?"

Now she had me. I didn't know what to say.

"Phoebe, I think they're going to arrest Adam for Graham's murder." A single large tear ran down her cheek, leaving a glittering path in her perfect makeup. "The police kept asking me over and over about him and Graham and Stan, trying to dredge up all the old stuff. Then they wanted to know where in the museum we all were that night and who we were with and when we were with them. I know they suspect him."

"I don't think that's very likely, Diana," I said. "Remember, you're talking about a murder investigation. The police have to ask everyone they talk to those kinds of questions. They asked me and Candi too, over and over –

what was our relationship to Dr. Maxwell, where did we go, who were we with? That's their job. It's nothing to be worried about."

"But he could have done it, couldn't he? I told you, Adam can be very frightening when he's angry. Maybe he saw Trevor and Graham together and knew. Maybe that's why he got so drunk. And he was in the museum all night."

"You're obviously very upset by all this, maybe too upset to think about it clearly. Give it some time. Let the police do their job. Professor Woodward will be fine."

"I'd like to believe that," Mrs. Woodward said. "And I know what you're saying has some truth to it. It's just that all this has hit me pretty hard. Not only Graham's death, although that's been difficult enough, it's having all this misery dragged back from the past. You know, my grand-mother had a saying, 'Old sins cast long shadows.' Gran was right."

11

"COME ON, PHOEBE, ADMIT IT," Candi said. "The man beat you to the draw. He wounded your pride and you're a little miffed."

"What do you mean, a little miffed? I'd like you to know there's nothing little about it. I'm a lot miffed, goddamnit. I'm miffed as hell."

"If you're that out of control, maybe you should seek professional help. You might give serious thought to attending some classes in miff management. Of course, you realize that I'm telling you this as a friend."

Candi won. I broke up. I was still laughing when Ella came into the office.

"What's up?" she asked as she sat down at her desk and fired up her computer.

"Phoebe's boyfriend dumped her," Candi answered.

"Well, that's always good for a chuckle, isn't it?" Ella tapped the keys and the printer began to hum. "Let me know when you've finished picking up the pieces of your broken heart, Phoebe, because I'd like you to look at this shot list before you go home. There are some new things on it."

"I can see I'm not going to get any sympathy here. I'll just have to suffer in silence."

"What a good idea." She collected a stack of paper, dense with single-spaced type and still warm from the printer, and handed it to me. "Can you think of anything else that should be on this?"

I looked at the first few pages of the list. "There's an awful lot of shots around the labs and workshops."

"The exhibit is pretty much a write-off at the moment so I thought we could at least see how they constructed the background and prepared the fossils."

"There is some good news about the exhibit," Candi said. "Apparently, there are replicas of all the bones back at Dr. Maxwell's lab in Nairobi. They're shipping them to Drumheller so the show can carry on, but it won't be the same knowing they're not real."

"If we're lucky they'll have the whole thing set up again before the program airs so we can get some shots of it," Ella said. "Candi's right, it won't be the same, but it will be better than nothing."

I read down the list without comment until I came to a group of shots that were to be taped in the Royal Tyrrell's storage area.

"You know, as I remember it, the light levels in that storage room are pretty low," I said. "There aren't any windows. Even with extra lights I don't know if I can get these long shots you want, especially the ones looking down the rows of shelves."

The shots might be questionable, but I could understand why Ella wanted them. I had been in the storage area once myself, years ago when I was visiting a friend, a fellow student who had a summer job at the museum helping to prepare fossils for display. I remember wandering behind him through a cavernous space filled with rows of towering industrial shelving upon which the newly excavated bones of dinosaurs, each encased in protective plaster, lay waiting to be cleaned and processed into museum specimens. The place was vast, on a scale appropriate to the thunder lizards.

"I think I can make the first twenty feet," I said. "But you probably won't be able to see much of the shelves down the line from there. They'll all be in darkness. It would take Hollywood to light that place properly."

"Do the best you can," Ella said. "Try to give some idea of the height of the shelves. Those things must be fifteen feet tall. It would be good if you could get someone from the lab to stand on one of the big ladders. Give us some perspective."

"Besides," Candi said, "even if the shots down the rows do blur into darkness, that could be interesting too. It would at least give an impression of the room's size. And maybe how eerie it is. I mean, that place is a giant mausoleum with all those huge bones lying around in their white plaster shrouds."

Candi and Ella had both toured the museum a few weeks before the opening of Dr. Maxwell's show to prepare for the program and now considered themselves experts on its backstage workings. Obviously the storage area had impressed them both.

"Any idea when the replica fossils might get here?" I asked.

"I telephoned Gillian Collins today. She says they're being shipped from Kenya at the end of the week, but I couldn't pin her down as to how long it would take to repair the exhibit," Ella answered. "It'll have to be done by the middle of September or it's too late for us."

Ella wanted to kick off *A Day in the Lifestyle*'s new fall season with the program on Dr. Maxwell.

"What about the ex-wife in Lethbridge? Are we going to interview her?"

"Candi called her this morning. She didn't seem too keen."

"Said she'd sooner be marched stark naked through the West Edmonton Mall than talk to anyone about that son of a bitch," Candi reported. "Direct quote."

"Vivid," I said.

"Decisive," Ella added. "And no help to us. I've tried contacting a few people from Nanton who knew Dr. Maxwell when he was a child so we might get something there. And I got in touch with his sister. She lives in Vancouver and she'd be happy to do an interview although she says they didn't communicate very often. A Christmas letter every year, that sort of thing."

"I managed to track down his high-school biology teacher," Candi said. "But the guy is ninety-eight and doesn't remember Dr. Maxwell. Actually, I don't think he remembers himself all that well."

"We don't need any more people who knew him way back when," Ella said. "What we need are his current associates, people who can give us up-to-date information."

"We're not going to find them in Alberta and that's for sure," Candi said. "Dr. Maxwell left the province in 1955. Nobody here really knew him any more."

"Unfortunately, you're right," Ella said. "We could use some big-gun paleoanthropologists too. But I don't think we're going to find them anywhere we can afford to go," she added glumly.

"Our first idea was best – interview some of the people who come to his funeral," Candi said. "But that's out too. Gillian told Ella it's definitely going to be held in Kenya."

"At least we've got Gillian. And Simon Visser said he'd be willing to help too," Ella said with more relief than enthusiasm. "They're both paleoanthropologists and they both knew him as well as anyone. They can give us very personal portraits. I know it would be best if we could get some other points of view, but as long as we have those two, I think we'll be all right."

"And they've agreed to be interviewed?" I asked. Considering my conversations with both Gillian and Simon, I wondered if Ella might be putting a little too much faith in Dr. Maxwell's assistants. Those portraits she was relying on so heavily could turn out to be a touch more personal than she'd bargained for.

"Both Gillian and Simon have been very cooperative," Ella said. "And don't forget, we've got the tapes we did with Dr. Maxwell on Thursday." She began to sound almost optimistic. "The program would be much better if he hadn't been murdered, but I think we can make do."

I decided to leave my car at the station and drive the van back to my place. That meant I wouldn't have to waste time in the morning stopping to pick up the equipment. I hung my keys on their proper peg in the photographers' office. We're supposed to leave the keys to any vehicle we plan on parking at the station while we're not in the building. I once forgot to do this and returned from a shoot at two o'clock one January morning to find an enormous mound of snow in the middle of the neatly ploughed, but otherwise empty, parking lot. It was my car. I haven't forgotten to leave the keys since.

I loaded the gear I needed, including an extra light kit, made sure I had a stack of tapes, and left for home. I managed to get away from the station before the afternoon traffic got so bad it officially rated as rush hour, but even without frequent stops it was still hot and sweaty in the un-airconditioned van. I couldn't wait to get back to my place, out of Margaret's suit, and into the shower. The whole day needed a change of clothes and a change of mood. I'd get cleaned up and then play the piano for a while. I've started working on some Hoagy Carmichael songs. You can't think of anything but the music while you're playing "Star Dust."

Just over an hour later, I turned off the gravel road and into my driveway. A battered old pickup truck and a late-model Jaguar sedan were parked side by side up near the house. The truck I knew. It was primitive man's emergency backup vehicle and the professor usually left it parked in the forest reserve. The big maroon Jaguar I didn't recognize. It turned out to belong to Stan Darling. I found the owners waiting for me on the deck. Goodbye to cool showers and "Skylark."

Professor Woodward sat in the big Adirondack, while Stan paced, clasping and unclasping his hands in a nervous washing movement. Somehow I knew that this visit was not good news. The professor had changed from his working uniform back into his civilian clothes. This diminished his olfactory impact, but I still smelled trouble. The dog didn't. He lolled happily between the two men, gnawing on one of his vast collection of rawhide bones, glad of the company.

"Good lord, Phoebe, I thought you'd never get here. We've been waiting for you since three." Professor Woodward spoke as if we had an appointment. Stan stopped in midstride and mumbled a hello. He stood fidgeting and, even though he wasn't covering any ground, still managed to give the impression that he was pacing.

"For heaven's sake, Stanley, will you settle somewhere," the professor commanded in his best classroom voice. Stan dropped obediently into the nearest chair, but his hands continued their anguished movements.

"Well, this is a surprise," I said. "May I make you a cup of tea? Coffee maybe?"

"No thank you, Phoebe," Professor Woodward answered for both of them. "This isn't a social call. We're here on business, aren't we, Stan?" Stan nodded miserably. "We have something very important to tell you."

"So, what's up?" I pulled a chair over and sat facing them.

"Come on, Stan, it's your story," the professor encouraged.

Stan stared at the planking on the deck. Next he gazed up at the sky for a bit. Then his eyes met mine for a second before they slid back down to the planks. We sat some more. I heard a squirrel chattering in the trees behind the house. A whisky-jack flashed by and perched on the far railing of the deck. A car approached from the north. The sound of its engine reached full crescendo as it passed the house, then faded in a long diminuendo as it continued south.

"Well, Stanley?" said Professor Woodward. "Are we going to sit here for the rest of the afternoon?"

Stan looked at him and then at me. He straightened his spine, leaned forward in his chair, and dropped his hands to his knees. He looked like a man who had come to a decision. Even so, he opened and closed his mouth several times before any actual words came out.

"Right. As Adam says, I do have something I'd like to discuss with you, Phoebe." He reached into the inner pocket of his jacket and pulled out a white handkerchief that had been rolled into a loose cylinder. He placed it on the low wooden table that sat beside his chair and, with great care, unwrapped three small fossilized bones from its linen folds.

"Please don't tell me what those are." I jumped to my feet. "Put them back in your hanky and get them out of here."

"They're finger bones. Fossil finger bones," Stan said. "We took them from the museum. The Geologists for Jesus. We took them the night of the opening. Not just these. We took all the bones from Graham's exhibit." Chalk one up for Candi.

"Put them away. We'll pretend I never saw them."

"I'm afraid it's a little late for that, Phoebe," Professor Woodward said. "Now please, listen to what the man has to say. This isn't easy for him, you know. Go on, Stan," he encouraged.

"We planned to take the fossils from the day I got the invitation to attend the opening of Graham's exhibit. Myrna said that my invitation was a gift from God, an invitation to do His will. The rest of the group agreed. We thought that the demonstration on the road would give us a good excuse to be around the museum that night. After the protest was over, I'd go ahead to the opening while Myrna and the others waited in the camper in the parking lot. Then, just before dinner when the exhibit closed and everyone was milling around drinking champagne and talking, I'd excuse myself and get them into the building. There were three of them. One was dressed up in a tux so he could pass for a guest and the other two were dressed like members of the catering staff. They're the ones who actually took the fossils out of the museum. They put them in big plastic garbage bags. That made it look like they were doing their job, taking out the trash from the party. Anyway, the whole business went just like Myrna planned it. She only told each of us what we had to know to complete our own part of the operation. My job was to get them in the building. So I excused myself just as everyone was starting to find their places for dinner and . . ."

"Stan, I don't want to know any more of this." It was my turn to pace. "You should be telling this to the police, not me."

"Maybe you could cut to the chase, Stanley," the professor suggested. "Tell Phoebe what you were supposed to do with the fossils once the Geologists for Jesus had stolen them."

"I was supposed to destroy them," Stan stated. "That was the final part of the plan. Saturday night I loaded the bones into the trunk of the car and took them to my old lab. I still do a little consulting for the company I used to work for so I have access. I chose Saturday night because I was pretty sure nobody would be working then and I'd have the place to myself. The lab has a big rock crusher. I was supposed to grind up Graham's fossils in it, turn them into dust." Tears began to flow down his cheeks.

"Steady now, Stan," Professor Woodward said gently. "You're nearly there."

"But I couldn't." It was almost a whisper. "I turned on the crusher and then I took out one of the bones. It was the smallest skull – you know the one, the baby's head. I held that little thing in my hand for so long that the rock got warm, warm as my own flesh. I tried and I tried to put it in the crusher but my hand wouldn't move and, all of a sudden, I knew why. My hand wouldn't move because that skull was real. Right then and there, I knew that fossil was exactly what Graham said it was – the earthly remains of an ancient member of the human family. It was like God was speaking to me through that tiny bone, telling me that evolution is the only possible explanation for life on earth, that evolution is a part of His Great Plan. Life evolves. I know that now. I know it deep in my heart." Stan's voice shook as he recounted his Darwinian epiphany. His tears continued to flow.

"Before that minute, I'd never realized the true glory of life. I was so busy denying evolution that I was blind to its power, its majesty. I was blind to the sheer, overwhelming beauty of it. I can't begin to explain the feeling that came over me when I held that fossil in my hand. It was like a deep and important part of me that had been dead came to life, and I was born again, born again to paleontology."

His impassioned testimonial ended, Stan took another large white handkerchief out of his pocket, this one free of stolen property, and proceeded to dry his eyes and blow his nose. I knew I should probably say something but I couldn't think what. I was stunned. How do you respond to a born-again paleontologist who has just confessed to one of the most spectacular thefts in Alberta history? I also wondered why Stan had chosen to tell me. We'd met for the first time Thursday night, which didn't exactly make us buddies.

"Look, Stan, all that's very interesting, but don't you think it's a little beside the point?" I said at last. "Don't you realize what you've done?"

"I've stolen Graham's bones," he said.

"And those bones are priceless scientific specimens. They're the only known ones of their kind on earth – they're like the *Mona Lisa* or the Magna Carta and probably more important. There's only one thing you can do now. You have to pack the whole lot up and take them to the police."

"But he can't do that," Professor Woodward protested. "They'll arrest him for theft."

"Of course they'll arrest him for theft," I shouted in frustration. "He stole the fucking things!"

"I don't think she wants to help us, Adam." Stan looked discouraged.

"Really, Phoebe, there's no need to get hysterical." The professor was not about to give up so easily. "Let's try to approach this like rational human beings. Stan has a problem and you can help us solve it," he continued as if he were presenting a lab project to a class of none-too-bright English majors.

"Stan doesn't have a problem," I said and pointed to the finger bones. "What Stan has is a zillion dollars' worth of stolen property that every police officer in Alberta is looking for."

"Well, in my books that is a problem," Professor Woodward stated calmly. "And what's more, now it's your problem too. You see, Phoebe, we hid the fossils last night. We put them behind a stack of hay bales in your barn."

I sank down slowly onto my chair.

"Are you all right?" the professor asked. "Good. Well, I'm glad we've got that out of the way. Clears the air, doesn't it?"

"No, it doesn't," I said. "Those fossils are priceless. They belong to the people of the country where they were found. They belong to the people of the world. They do not belong in my horse barn. Stan, you have to take them to the police."

"I really can't, Phoebe," he said sadly. "It's not quite that simple. You see, Myrna and the Geologists for Jesus are involved in this too. They're after the fossils. They know I have the bones and they still want to destroy them."

"Are you saying that Myrna knows you didn't put them through the crusher?" I asked.

Stan's eyes hit the planks. "I'm afraid she does."

"How did she find out?"

"I told her," he mumbled.

"You told her! Oh, Stan, how could you?"

"She asked," he said. "And I couldn't lie, could I?" He seemed genuinely shocked at the suggestion.

"Why not? You've already committed Alberta's robbery of the decade. What's one little lie compared to that?"

"I don't think you understand, Phoebe," he said. "The Geologists for Jesus stole those fossils to prevent the perversion of God's word. We may have committed a crime according to earthly values, but we were doing heaven's work. Lying to Myrna would be different. That would have been a plain old lie and it would have been plain wrong."

There didn't seem to be any point in arguing with Stan's kind of logic. I knew I'd never win. Still, I had to try. "But what about the people at the museum, what about the police? How can you lie to them?"

"If it were only me, I'd take those fossils and march them into the nearest police station right now, even if it did mean I'd go to jail," Stan stated. "But it's not only me, is it? There are other people involved. Myrna and the others were at the museum because of their commitment to the Lord. To them, what they did wasn't a crime, it was their belief in God's word put into action. I can't betray them or their faith."

"But, Stan, you went to the museum as Graham Maxwell's friend. He was murdered. Everyone who was there that night is a suspect and that includes the Geologists for Jesus. If you don't tell the police they were there, you could be helping a murderer."

This suggestion was met with silence by both Stan and Professor Woodward. The professor spoke first.

"I think Phoebe may have a point here, Stan, one I never took into consideration. What if one of the Geologists for Jesus saw or heard something that could help the police catch Graham's murderer?"

"What if one of the Geologists for Jesus is the murderer?" I said.

"That's impossible." Stan started the Lady Macbeth stuff with his hands again. "They're all good Christian men and women. Myrna is my niece. And Jason's temper may be a little short, but that's because he's still a very new Christian. No no, it's not possible." Stan did his best to convince himself, but I heard the doubt in his voice.

"Just a minute here, Phoebe," Professor Woodward came to his friend's defence. "Stan and I were both at the museum too. You might just as well say that one of us murdered Graham."

"Can't you see that from the police's point of view that's true? Either of you could have murdered him. You both had the opportunity and I bet it wouldn't take much digging to find motives. Stan has spent a lifetime protesting the theory of evolution. Who's to say that this time the protest didn't get violent? Look at the anti-abortion fanatics who murder doctors. Why couldn't an anti-evolution fanatic be a murderer? And Professor Woodward, you could have . . ." I caught myself just in time. I had nearly blurted out The Secret. "Well, there could be something in the past that made you hate Dr. Maxwell enough to kill him."

"Phoebe, you're spouting nonsense," the professor said. "We're wasting time. Stanley and I aren't murderers and you know it."

"I do," I said. "But the police don't. From their point of view, anyone at the museum that night could have killed Graham Maxwell. You, Stan, Mrs. Woodward, Trevor – you were all wandering around the building after the party." The nonsense crack had irritated me so much that I very unkindly added his wife and son to the list of suspects.

"Diana a murderer? That's totally preposterous and, may I say, it's more than a little offensive too," Professor Woodward blustered. But I could tell that the idea had occurred to him and that it made him uneasy.

"I came out here yesterday to ask Adam for his help because I knew he could appreciate how important these fossils are and that he would understand what had happened to me back in that lab," Stan said. "You know, it was a kind of miracle – I really do feel that God's hand was on mine when I stood at the crusher that night – and I guess Adam and I were hoping that another miracle would happen here today. We thought you might be willing to help us smuggle the fossils back into the museum. We hoped you might see your way clear to helping us return them anonymously when you go to do your photography there. But I suppose that's out of the question, isn't it?"

"It is. Absolutely."

"Don't you worry, Stan," Professor Woodward reassured his friend. "We'll think of something else. Everything's going to be okay."

"Nothing's going to be okay until those fossils are safe back in their display at the Royal Tyrrell," I said. "Pack them up now, Stan. Take them back where they belong."

"You know, Adam, I think Phoebe might be right," Stan admitted. "Maybe I'd better return the fossils. They're far too precious to risk leaving them in the barn any longer."

"They're perfectly safe where they are," the professor protested. "That barn hasn't been out of my sight since you left. I was there all night and not a person came near it except Phoebe."

"What about my bear?"

"Neighbourhood kids," he countered. "Harmless hijinks."

"But there were strangers around during the day too." I told them about the religious visitors Bertie had found prowling around the barn.

"Which only proves my point," the professor said. "The fossils were in no danger from those people because we didn't hide the bags in the barn until nearly midnight. Stan left after that because we thought it would be better if he and that splashy car of his didn't hang around the hiding place. But I've been on watch ever since. I even slept with the things."

"Adam, you did go to get your truck and change your clothes this morning," Stan pointed out.

"I wasn't gone half an hour," the professor said. "More like twenty minutes."

"Are you sure the bones are still there?" I asked. "How do you know Myrna didn't come along during that twenty minutes and take them away to be pulverized. They could be fossil powder by now." I dragged my fingertip slowly over the surface of the table and then blew the accumulated dust from it with a quick puff. It was a nasty gesture. And effective.

Stan was appalled. "Did you check the bags when you got back?" he asked Professor Woodward. "Are they still there?"

"They're sitting exactly where we put them," his friend assured him.

"But did you look inside the bags?" Stan continued his questions. "You're sure the fossils are there? In the bags? Myrna could have tricked us, you know, filled the bags back up with old cow bones or something. That's just the kind of thing she'd do. She's very clever. Did you look? Did you? Did you look inside the bags?" He was nearly hysterical and I could see the professor was a little shaken too.

"If it will make you feel any better, we can go check on them right now," he said.

Stan hurried us down the path to the barn. He yanked the door open and charged into the stack of hay bales, tossing them aside with the power and speed of a man half his age and twice his size until he had uncovered the two garbage bags. He dropped to his knees and tore the first one open.

"They're here. The bones are still here." He sank back onto the hay, so pale with relief that I thought he might faint. He turned his gaze to the rafters. "Dear Merciful Father, I thank you."

"You see," Professor Woodward said as he prudently checked the other bag, "a lot of worry over nothing."

"Why are they in Halloween bags?" I asked. The men looked down at the two big orange bags, each adorned with a leering black skeleton. Cyrrie had bought some similar ones last autumn that he filled with fallen leaves to decorate the yard for Halloween. His had jack-o'-lanterns on them. "Weren't these a little conspicuous at the museum?"

"These aren't the same bags we smuggled the fossils out in," Stan explained. "I transferred the bones into new bags when I got home. I thought it would be a good idea. To disguise them, I mean. Throw Myrna and the others off the scent."

Stan Darling, financial whiz and master field geologist, could now add the title of world's dumbest thief to his list.

"Don't quit your day job, Stan," I said.

"But I don't have a job." He looked puzzled. "I'm retired."

"Don't mind Phoebe," Professor Woodward said. "Sometimes she has a very odd sense of humour."

"Oh dear, oh dear," Stan sighed to himself as he re-fastened a twist-tie around the neck of one of the bags. "What on earth am I going to do now?"

"You're going to pack these things up and take them back," I repeated yet again.

"Yes, I suppose that's about all I can do, isn't it?" he agreed.

"And if he doesn't?" the professor asked, a little belligerently.

"Then I will," I said.

"Adam, please don't be angry," Stan said. "Especially not with Phoebe. You know as well as I do that she's right." He seemed to have made a decision and this gave him a new calm. "These bones do belong to the world." He spoke with a surprising strength and authority. "They are God's gift to all mankind, given so we can better understand the glory of His works. They are blessed and I'm taking them back where they belong and that's final." This time, Dr. Woodward didn't argue.

"But, Phoebe," Stan turned to me, "I'm going to ask you to give me a few hours' grace. After I do turn the bones in, I'll be in very hot water for a very long time. It's likely that I'll go to jail. So I need a little time now, just a few more hours, to get some things in order. I have to talk to my lawyer about what's going to happen to me and to my friends. Maybe there's a way I can protect Myrna and the other Geologists for Jesus from the law. That might not be possible, but I think you can understand why I have to try. I owe them that much."

"But what if something happens to the bones before you can take them back? The longer you delay, the more risks you're running with them," I said.

Stan didn't answer. He stood patiently, never taking his eyes from mine.

I stumbled on. "And if I don't say anything and something does happen to the fossils, then you'll have made me an accessory after the fact or whatever it is they call people who are accomplices to a crime they really had nothing to do with but got mixed up in later in spite of their better judgment."

Stan smiled at me kindly. He may have lost the war, but I think he knew he was going to win this tiny battle. I finally caved. "Then you promise that these fossils will be back in the museum tomorrow morning? You'll give me your word?"

"God bless you, Phoebe." Solemnly, he took my hand in both of his and shook it as if we were sealing a pact. "You have my word as a Christian that Graham's fossils will be back in the Royal Tyrrell tomorrow. And no matter what happens to me, please be certain that I won't betray you or your trust."

Perhaps, right then, I was as naïve as Stan because I believed him absolutely.

"Come on, Adam," he said cheerily. "Let's put these things in your truck and get going. I have a lot to do tonight. And would you mind collecting the finger bones when you go for the truck? I left them in my handkerchief on Phoebe's table."

Professor Woodward fetched the truck and backed it up to the door of the barn. "We're using my truck because we thought Stan's Jag might be a little too conspicuous," he confided as they loaded the fossils into the dilapidated old vehicle. Its fenders and doors were eaten with rust. Long ago, someone, probably one of his students, had attempted a home paint job but gave up partway through. The bright yellow ended at the cab.

Stan very tenderly placed the garbage bags in the back, resting them on a bed of hay to make certain the bones wouldn't rattle around and break. Personally, I thought all this loving care was a case of too little too late. The fragile fossils, so painstakingly reconstructed by Dr. Maxwell's team, had already spent four days jumbled together, rolling around their bags like a load of loose gravel. Finally, Professor Woodward threw a large green tarpaulin over the truck bed. Stan helped him to tie it down.

"There, that ought to hold 'em until we get to town." The professor tugged the last knot tight.

They set off down the road to Calgary, a pair of pale-ontologists on the lam, with their getaway truck moulting hay and rust and flecks of yellow paint, and looking about as inconspicuous as martians in a nudist colony. If I'd been a woman of faith, I'd have lit a candle to Saint Barbara, the patron saint of geologists. As it was, I caught myself utter-ing a quiet prayer, asking her to keep her two old disciples and their precious cargo safe.

The dog and I walked back to the house. I gave him his dinner, then showered and changed into jeans and a sweat-shirt, and sat down at the piano. I started to play but not even Hoagy could take my mind off what I'd just finished aiding and abetting. And, as if that weren't enough to chew on, in the past seven hours I'd listened to more people talk about their troubles than I normally would in seven years. To think that there are whole professions that earn a living listening to other people's woes. I'd be in the bin in a week.

Bertie must have been a little preoccupied too, because he didn't bark until after I heard the knock at my back door. It was Trevor Woodward looking for his father. I had completely forgotten that they planned to visit me on their way home to Calgary.

"I was supposed to meet Dad at five," he explained. "Up the road where he leaves his truck. It's almost six and he's still not there and neither is the truck. I hope nothing's happened to him."

"I saw your father half an hour ago and he was fine." I invited Trevor in. "He's already left for town. He had to help a friend deliver something. They took the truck. I guess he must have forgotten you were coming for him."

"Typical," Trevor shook his head and smiled. "Totally typical. When they started making absentminded professors, my father was the first one off the assembly line."

"Will you come in and have a cup of coffee or a drink or something before you drive back to Calgary?"

"I'd like to, but won't I be interrupting? I heard you playing the piano when I came. It sounded so nice I hated to knock on the door and make you stop. That's a very beautiful instrument you have." He went and stood beside the black Steinway grand that occupies most of the space in front of the west windows.

"I inherited it from my uncle," I said. "I'm not half the musician he was, but I try to play it as often as I can. Do you play?"

"No talent," he said. "My wife is a cellist and my son plays the trumpet. They're the family musicians."

"How many children do you have?" I asked.

"Two. The trumpeter, he's fourteen, and his sister is eighteen. She's starting her first year in computer science at Waterloo this fall."

Trevor opted for beer. I opened a couple of Big Rock while he continued to talk about his family. He was the only one of the Woodwards' three children I had met. He was a media studies professor in Halifax.

"I don't think you know my sister, Nora, do you?" he asked. "She's a high-school math teacher in Medicine Hat. My brother, Sean, is an education prof at the University of Calgary."

"So you're a teacher, your sister's a teacher, and your brother teaches teachers how to teach." I poured the beer into mugs.

"And don't forget our father, the geology teacher," he laughed. "It must be in the blood."

Trevor seemed interested in my films. I showed him the cameras and how the editing bench worked. He was very easy to talk to. He had the teacher's gift of listening and then asking the right questions. He reminded me of his father that way. I told him so.

"Sometimes you sound just like your father."

"God, I hope not," he replied and then laughed. "Don't look so puzzled, Phoebe. You know that Dad's not my biological father. Graham Maxwell was. Your jaw dropped about a mile when you saw us standing together at the museum. Funny though, I think you were the only person there who saw the resemblance."

"I wouldn't bet on it," I disagreed. "It's pretty striking."

"You know, I don't think it is. I think maybe you could see it because you have a talent for seeing. Good photographers always do. They don't just look, they see."

We carried our beers out to the deck. The dog came too, carrying his newest, barely gnawed rawhide bone. He settled at my feet for a social chew.

"My jaw really dropped?" I said. "I was that obvious?"

"You were to me, but I guess I was looking for reactions that night. It was the first time I'd seen Maxwell in person myself."

"How long have you known he was your father?"

"I was an adult when I found out, but it was still a long time ago, maybe twenty years, around the time he started making his first big discoveries. I must have been twenty-four, twenty-five. I don't remember exactly."

"How did you find out?"

"My aunt told me," he said. "I was living in Toronto at the time. I went to grad school there, at York. Aunt April lives in Niagra-on-the-Lake and I'd gone to stay with her for the weekend to catch a couple of plays at the Shaw Festival. Saturday morning we were having breakfast and reading the *Globe and Mail*. There was a photo of Maxwell along with a big article about the first of his discoveries. It was the first time I'd ever seen a picture of him. I saw the resemblance right away, just like you. I pointed it out to my aunt – I think I might even have joked about it. Of course, the *Globe* really played up his Canadian background. The article said he had graduated in geology from U of A in 1955. That was my parents' year. I was young enough to think it was pretty cool that my mom and dad had been in the same class as someone that famous. I told Aunt April I was going to ask them about Maxwell next time I went home to Calgary. That's when she told me."

"Were you upset when you found out?"

"A little, I guess, but probably no more than the average person who finds out they're adopted would be. I'd say I was more curious than anything else, but I got over that too until I had the chance to meet him in person at the Royal Tyrrell. That sure got the curiosity going again."

"And you've never told your parents that you know he's your father?"

"No, never," he said. "I guess that must seem pretty odd to an outsider, but even in a happy family like ours, you sometimes know when you should keep your mouth shut. Aunt April didn't swear me to secrecy or anything dramatic like that, but I could see that telling me made her very uncomfortable. I guess I thought that if Mom and Dad had kept it a secret this long, maybe I shouldn't go stirring things up. Besides, I was a grown man by then and all of it happened before I was born. It was ancient history. Dad was Dad – what did the rest of it matter? I still think that. I did tell my brother and sister, though."

"What did they say?"

"Not much except we all agreed it was really weird that Mom and Dad had never told us."

I wondered if I should inform Trevor that his parents had never even told each other. I decided this was another

Woodward family issue that they could resolve or not without any contributions from me. Like Trevor, I somehow knew that this was another of those times I should keep my mouth shut.

"Did you come to visit your parents because you knew you'd get a chance to meet Dr. Maxwell?" I asked instead.

"Maybe I did do a little extra arranging," he admitted, "but part of it was coincidence. I was going to be in Calgary for some meetings, Mom and Dad had the invitation, and it all seemed to work out from there. Poor Mom, I know she really didn't want to go, but Dad insisted and she sure wasn't going to let him go without her." Or tell him the reason why, I added to myself.

"What was it like to finally meet him?" I asked.

"It was like meeting a stranger," Trevor stated. "Except for our looks. That part was weird. I could see he felt a bit odd about it too."

"Did he say anything to you?"

"Not much. He asked me to come stand beside him in that photograph you took of him with Mom and Dad. Well, you heard all that." Trevor finished the last of his beer and put the mug on the table that less than an hour ago had held three small fossilized bones. "You know," he continued, "I think the only reason he asked me to do that was to rub it in to my parents, to make sure they'd see the two of us together and have a jolly dad and lad photo to remind them of it. At least that's the impression I got. Of course, I could be all wrong. Maybe he didn't have any ulterior motives. But if I'm right, it was a cruel thing to do, don't you think?"

"So you never had a chance to talk to him?"

"Oh yeah, I had a chance but it didn't amount to anything. After dinner, we ended up in the men's washroom at the same time. It was pretty crowded. Maxwell washed his hands at the sink next to mine. I told him how much I admired his work. All he said was, 'Thanks. Catch you later.' Then he gave me a little smile and left."

"And that was it?"

"Who knows?" Trevor shrugged. "He probably had the right idea. What was the point of trying to start any kind of relationship after all these years? He'd known where to find me since the day I was born but he obviously didn't want to. Besides, I had a perfectly good father and it wasn't him. As far as I'm concerned, Maxwell was a sperm donor." Trevor's words were nonchalant, but there was a trace of bitterness in his voice. I know I'd have felt more than a trace if all my father could find to say to me after forty-four years was, "Catch you later."

"As things turned out," Trevor said, "we'd never have had a chance to get to know each other anyway. He didn't live long enough."

After Trevor left I went back inside and played the piano a little longer. Then I phoned Cyrrie to make certain he was up for a Bertie visit the next day while I was off working in Drumheller. He asked about my weekend with Tim and Brooke, so I told him. I added that Tim and I had agreed not to see each other for a while. I didn't give him an explanation and he didn't ask for one.

I spent the rest of the evening wrestling with the budget for my next film, the one about otters. I had to admit that I missed Tim. I knew that what we'd done was right, that it was best for us both, but I still wanted him to call. I'd tell him how unreasonable otters could be, that they were all demanding ACTRA rates and stars on their dressing rooms and hot and cold running fish. No matter how hokey the jokes, at least we could have laughed a little. He wasn't going to call.

It was eleven o'clock. My head still buzzed with the day. I decided to settle on the couch and watch a little television, that certain sedative for the busy brain. I picked up the TV guide but was too lazy to open it. I didn't care what was on. I was so tired I'd have watched the cooking channel. Unfortunately, what was on was the news. The lead story came from Drumheller. A wide-eyed woman stood on the steps of the Royal Tyrrell and, in the exaggerated up-and-down inflections affected by Canadian TV reporters, informed me that the RCMP had arrested South African Simon Visser for the murder of his employer, the world-renowned Canadian paleo-anthropologist Graham Maxwell.

12

THE WIND WOKE ME DURING THE NIGHT gusting sheets of rain against the windows. By the time the radio alarm went off at seven-thirty, the air was still but the rain continued, a steady, bone-chilling downpour. I lay under the duvet, looking out at the sodden pasture while the CBC nattered in my ear. The report of Simon's arrest still led the news. It made the world look even greyer. Poor Simon.

I turned the radio off and listened to the drumming of the rain on the roof. I was glad Professor Woodward had gone back to town and a warm bed – sleeping out last night would have been a formal invitation to pneumonia. I knew the horses would be fine, sheltered under their lean-to in the trees. They're a whole lot tougher than the professor and don't start spending their nights in the barn until late autumn. My neighbours' son would be over to feed them later in the morning.

A skiff of wet snow covered the trees at the top of the hill but at lower altitudes what fell was still liquid. This was some consolation, I suppose, but not nearly enough to make leaving my warm bed much of a prospect. I steeled myself, threw off the duvet, and charged. I quickly folded the bed away so there could be no retreat. It was a moral triumph. Bertie watched sleepily from the warmth of his basket. He heaved a long-suffering sigh in protest at having been disturbed, and closed his eyes again.

"I don't think so, my friend." I prodded his nether end with a slippered foot. "It's a working day. Out." He crawled slowly out of his basket and dragged himself to the door, glowering at me over his shoulder along the way, a martyr to human whim. "And don't bother threatening me with the pet-abuse hotline – just get out there and produce." I opened the door to a blast of cold air and felt some sympathy for the beast.

Bertie was back in the house in under a minute with raindrops on his back and revenge on his mind. He shook himself vigorously, spraying cold water all over me. Honour satisfied, he flopped back down in his basket.

I put the coffee on, showered, and dressed in wool slacks and a sweater. In case the sun decided to shine later in the day, I tossed a pair of khakis and a short-sleeved blouse into my workbag. Sunshine seemed an unlikely prospect today, but you never can tell in Alberta in late August. Toast and coffee and a glass of juice later, I was ready to leave for work.

I zipped the camera into its padded case, then wrapped it in Bertie's towel. I pulled on my big yellow slicker with the hood and, camera under one arm and workbag over the other, dashed through the rain with the dog at my heels. The prospect of a ride had overcome his reluctance to venture out. Nevertheless, as I fumbled to unlock the van's big side door, he stood beside me nudging my leg with his nose, the canine equivalent of shouting hurry it up. He bounded in and settled himself on the floor in front of the passenger seat while I stashed the camera in the back with the rest of the gear. I climbed behind the wheel and started the engine. Before I could shift into reverse, a big grey sedan pulled into my driveway. It was the car Bertie and I had seen take off in such a hurry Sunday morning. It stopped behind the van, blocking my exit.

I turned off the engine and went to investigate. The dog gallantly abandoned his shelter and walked beside me. We stopped a few feet in front of the big hood. The passenger door opened and out climbed Myrna. I recognized her companion behind the rain-blurred windshield too. He was one of the burly, young Geologists for Jesus who had carried her to the side of the road during their protest march. I guess Myrna didn't hold grudges. However, she did seem to be making a habit of blocking my way to work.

"It's a little early for visitors, don't you think?" I said. Bertie stood so close to my side that he managed to insinuate himself under the flap of my slicker. I suppose it did keep a little of the water off his back, but the rain still streamed off his head, pasting the fur to his skull. Myrna's hair was getting very wet too, although I can't say I felt sorry for her.

"This isn't a visit. I'm Myrna Darling. I'm looking for my uncle." She pulled the collar of her short jacket up over her head, which in turn exposed her lower back to the rain. She looked like a turtle struggling to fit a shell three sizes too small. She peered out at me through the neck of the jacket.

"Stan isn't here," I said.

"So where is he?"

"I have no idea. Now will you please back up so I can get out."

"But that's his car." She pointed to the Jaguar.

"Well, so it is," I said. "I guess he must have left it here after he didn't tell me where he was going."

"Hey, there's no call to be a smart mouth." Myrna's associate joined us. He looked much more imposing than he had on the road to the museum. He was over six feet with no neck to speak of and a mass of muscle that only hours on weight machines could produce. He would have blended right in with the crowd at a professional wrestlers' convention, the bad-guy sessions anyway. Rain dripped off his stubby ponytail down the neck of his Northern Lights Casino sweatshirt. I guess his clothes were older than his religious convictions. He looked tired, unshaven, and very cold.

"It's okay, Jason," Myrna said. The man's bulk made her look almost dainty. "Let me handle this."

"There's nothing to handle," I said. "I don't know where Stan is."

"You gotta know something," Jason said. "The old guy left his car with you. He loves that Jag. He wouldn't've left it with just anybody."

There may have been some mysterious male automotive intuition underlying this remark. Its logic escaped me completely. It seemed to have missed Myrna too. She continued as if he hadn't spoken.

"I'm sorry if we got off on the wrong foot here," she apologized, not very convincingly. "I really do have to find Uncle Stan. He could be in a lot of trouble, you know. He might even get arrested."

"What for?" I asked. "What did he do?"

"Don't play dumb," she said. "You know exactly what he did." Myrna and I were back on the wrong foot again. "We've been watching your place since Sunday. We know those bags were in your barn. We saw you on your deck talking to Uncle Stan and Professor Woodward."

"If you were watching all that carefully, you saw them take the bags away," I said.

"Did they say what they were gonna do with them?" Jason asked.

"Stan said he was going to take them back where they belong."

"He can't do that. He can't." Myrna's head popped out of her collar. "He'll destroy everything we've planned, everything we've worked for. It will all be for nothing."

"Jesus, Myrna, the old fart's going to get us all arrested." Jason's concern was infinitely more practical.

"Don't use Jesus' name like that," Myrna snapped. "I know you're new to faith, but there are some things you don't do and that's one of them. Ever."

"Maybe I haven't been saved all that long, but I know what's fair and what isn't and I'm telling you this isn't fair," Jason voiced the old self-pitying lament. "So the old man knows a lot about rocks. So what? Just because he's a real geologist doesn't give him the right to screw around with other people's lives. It's not like he's a minister or nothing."

Myrna simply ignored Jason's latest wrestle with reason and turned back to me and the main issue. "You have to tell us where Stan is," she persisted, although she must have known I was a hopeless cause. "Too much depends on him. I'm not going to let him throw it all away."

"I've told you, I don't know where he is. Now move your car and let me go to work." This time, I overcame my Canadian reflexes and didn't add a please.

"We can't stand here talking all day," Jason said. "She's gonna tell us. Right now." He looked at me. "Aren't you, sweetface?"

It was not a question, it was a threat, one my body registered much more quickly than my mind. I felt my breakfast rise, propelled by the frisson of fear that fluttered over my guts. I swallowed hard. Jason took a step toward me. He stopped as soon as he heard the growl. It came from deep within the dog's throat, low and mean and menacing. I'd never heard Bertie make a sound like it. I felt the hair on the back of my neck rise in response. Bertie's own hackles bristled in a spiky, rain-soaked line from the top of his head to the base of his tail. He growled again, louder this time, and bared his huge canines. Jason backed away. I didn't blame him.

"We shoulda shot that dog yesterday when we had the chance," he said.

"We're not in the business of killing God's creatures," Myrna retorted. "Geologists for Jesus are strictly non-violent. Besides, you left the rifle in your truck."

"Yeah, like we had the time," Jason countered. "That old professor was back way before we could have gone and gotten it."

"You were here yesterday when Professor Woodward was away?" I struggled with my voice, but I think what came out sounded almost normal.

"We saw him leave so we went to get the bags out of the barn," Myrna said. "But it was no use. The dog wouldn't let us on your land. We left the car parked on the road just in case someone came while we were inside. Then we went to hop the fence, but he started barking and rushing at us every time we tried to cross. Jason made it over once, but the dog was so quick he had to dive right back. Then we saw the professor coming down the road in his old pickup so we left."

"That animal is vicious," Jason said. "He damn near took my leg off."

As if to prove the truth of Jason's words, Bertie gave another growl, but I could tell his heart really wasn't in this one. It was more theatre than threat. Even so, it still intimidated Jason, which I found greatly comforting.

"You've been watching my place. You know Stan is in Calgary and the fossils are with him. Why are you here?"

"Because you've got to know where he is," Myrna said. "You've got to."

"How many times do I have to tell you? I don't. You know more about where he is than I do."

"Last we saw he was in Calgary at some fancy townhouse up by the university," Jason offered.

The professor and Mrs. Woodward live in a row of fashionable townhouses not far from the campus. He and Stan must have headed for home.

"We followed that old truck all the way into the city," Jason continued. "The townhouse has underground parking. Him and the professor drove the truck down into the garage and that was it. Later last night, we had a look around. The truck was still there, but they must've taken the bones up into the house with them. The whole place was locked up tighter than a drum and that goes for the garage too. But she made me do it anyway." He turned to Myrna. "Breaking into that garage could've got us both arrested so I don't see where you get off telling me how to run my life."

"Jason, we are doing God's work," Myrna said sternly. "No one promised you that life as a Christian would be easy."

"Yeah, well, you can praise the Lord all you like. You're not the one whose gonna get in shit with your parole officer."

"So why aren't you in Calgary watching the town-house?" I asked.

"Because we lost them," Myrna confessed. "Two other members of our group took over at the townhouse so Jason and I could get some rest. We'd been up since Sunday morning – two straight nights without sleep." No wonder tempers were short among the Geologists for Jesus.

"But those jerks lost them," Jason said with contempt. "They let them drive away."

"Bill phoned a little before seven," Myrna said. "He told us that Stan and the professor had left the townhouse in the truck. Bill and Doris followed them to a McDonald's, but Stan managed to give them the slip. They're out looking for him now."

"Why don't you tell her the truth?" Jason demanded angrily. "Doris was busy buying her dear Billy-boy a cup of coffee when the truck pulled out of the lot. She was stand-ing in a coffee line with her car keys in her hand. Your uncle and his friend didn't give those dorks the slip. They let them get away. Jesus Christ, what a couple of dumb fucks."

Myrna didn't contradict him. She was so demoralized she didn't even bother to protest his language. "That's why we're here," she said. "Help us. Please. I'm begging you." She looked almost as pathetic as she sounded, exhausted and beaten. By now her clothes were so wet she might as well have been swimming in them. Jason's were even worse.

"I'm telling you the truth. I can't help you," I said. "And I wouldn't even if I could." Thanks to Bertie I was feeling a little braver. "I honestly don't know where Stan is or what he plans to do." Not that I didn't want to know what Stan and the professor were up to. God knows where the pair of them had gone and what they'd done with the fossils. Myrna and Jason's story made me very uneasy, but there was nothing I could do except trust that Stan was a man of his word.

"But you're our best hope," Myrna said. "You're our only hope, I guess."

It was hard to believe this forlorn specimen was the same woman who had masterminded a spectacular robbery. But there she stood in the pouring rain, begging for help she knew it would take a miracle to get, clinging to the wreckage of her crazy plan. Right then, I almost felt a little sorry for Myrna. Because of Stan, her whole operation had come unstuck at the seams. It was a failure, total and disastrous, and one for which there was no consolation, only the threat of jail. Perhaps Stan would find some comfort in knowing that his niece and the Geologists for Jesus hadn't killed anyone to bring off their scheme. At least Myrna was not Graham Maxwell's murderer. Simon had that on his conscience.

"If I'm your best hope," I said, "then I guess you're out of luck."

A cellphone lurking somewhere in Myrna's waterlogged jacket beebled out an electronic version of "Onward

Christian Soldiers." Cold and haste made her fingers clumsy as she fumbled to answer it. She nearly dropped the tiny thing before she flipped open its case and the music stopped.

"It's Doris," she reported to Jason. "They've found the truck." As she listened, her face flushed with new energy. "It's parked at the back of the Earth Sciences building at the university. Praise the Lord! They've found it!" She flung her arms to the sky and danced, whirling and leaping in the wet grass, her whole being alight with joy. A high-pitched female voice still babbled from the cellphone, but Myrna was beyond the call of earthly voices. Her miracle had happened. "Oh praise the Lord, praise Him in all His glory!"

"Shut up and get your ass in here." Jason had the car started before Myrna's feet touched the ground. She jumped in beside him. He backed out of the drive and onto the road while she struggled to close her door. That was the last I saw of them that morning and, I hoped, ever again.

In the back of the van I unwrapped Bertie's towel from the camera and did my best to dry his fur. I felt shaky and my breakfast still hadn't settled back where it belonged. I wondered if Jason would have hurt me if the dog hadn't been there. The odds were for but maybe Myrna wouldn't have let him. Then again, maybe Myrna couldn't control him. And maybe there was no point in worrying after the fact.

The towel was sopping before Bertie was anywhere near dry. I started the engine and turned on the heater. He hunkered down in the passenger foot well, under one of the vents. It blew warm air over his back all the way to Cyrrie's. For my money, he deserved the Order of Canada and a lifetime supply of rawhide bones. A bronze statue in his honour in front of the Royal Tyrrell wouldn't be overdoing it either. At the very least, Stan and the professor owed him a roast beef dinner.

Thinking about Stan and the professor was even more unsettling than thinking about Jason. What were the two old lunatics up to, gadding around Calgary at seven in the morning? More important, what had they done with the fossils? Maybe they'd taken them up to the university and phoned the police from there. I could hope. Or maybe they'd gone to the police before they went to the university and the fossils were safe. That one sounded like fantasy time even to me, and it was my fantasy. Maybe I should give up maybes.

Cyrrie was in the kitchen reading the *Herald* when I arrived. He poured me a cup of coffee and I sat down opposite him at the island. Bertie settled at my feet to continue his morning nap.

"I see they've arrested the man who murdered Graham Maxwell," Cyrrie said. "That makes me feel much easier about you going back to work at the museum today. I must admit I was a little concerned."

"Simon Visser," I said. "Maxwell's field manager. They'd been together a long time."

"He was the one you heard arguing with Maxwell, wasn't he? The one who was in the office when you found the body? I'd say you had a close call."

"I don't think so," I said. "Simon wouldn't have hurt me."

"That's probably what Graham Maxwell thought too," Cyrrie replied sharply. "Right before Visser smashed his head in." I could tell he must have been very worried. That's the only time he ever gets angry.

"I know he wouldn't have hurt me. Simon is a good person."

"Who simply had a bad moment in which he brutally murdered his boss and rammed a bone flute down his throat. Really, Phoebe, for a grown woman you can be idiotically naïve."

"Please, don't be angry." I walked around the island and put my arm around his shoulder. "It's over now. I'm safe. There's nothing more to worry about."

He let out his breath in a long sigh and his shoulders relaxed. "I'm sorry, my dear, I didn't mean to be so abrupt. But I do worry. I can't help it. I don't know what I'd do if anything happened to you."

"You're not going to find out because nothing is going to happen to me."

"Ah, Calamity, would that it were so." He smiled and pointed to my chair. "Now sit down and finish your coffee. You know, you're looking a little peaked today."

"I'm fine," I said. I wanted to tell him about my morning visitors, but I knew how he would react to my conspiring with Stan and the professor. He would never have allowed them to take the bones away. He'd have called the police immediately. It's what I should have done.

"Have you eaten?" Cyrrie began to fuss.

"Toast and juice. I'm fine."

"Let me make you a proper breakfast, some Red River cereal. You really are looking pale," he persisted. It was time to change the subject.

"You know I think there might be some truth in what you said."

"Well, you are little naïve from time to time, but maybe not idiotically," Cyrrie relented. "I admit that was a bit harsh."

"That's not what I'm talking about," I said. "I meant that you were right about Simon. I think he did have a bad moment when he murdered Dr. Maxwell, one very bad drunken moment that he can't even remember." I told Cyrrie about my conversation with Simon in Candi's office.

"Just before he left, he asked me if I thought he could have murdered Maxwell. I told him I didn't know."

Cyrrie sat quietly for a moment. "So," he said at last, "if what he told you is true, then Graham Maxwell had built his reputation on Visser's work. That certainly gives the man a motive."

"And maybe I am naïve, but Simon seemed like a very decent man to me. At least when he was sober."

"But when he was drunk he committed a terrible crime," Cyrrie stated. "You can pity him, Phoebe, but that still doesn't change the fact that Simon Visser took another human being's life."

"I know," I said. "But it's hard to believe. He was truly horrified at the thought that he might have killed Maxwell. He's one of the last people I'd have picked for a murderer. If anything, he seemed kind of gentle."

"You sound exactly like the people they interview on television, the ones who live next door to the mass murderer. 'He seemed like such a nice man, so quiet and soft-spoken.'"

"But it's true. Simon is a nice man. I like him."

"And now you're beginning to sound like one of those strange women who line up at the prison gates to *marry* the mass murderer."

"Cyrrie, don't say things like that. You know, you can be really infuriating sometimes."

"As can you, my pet. As can you."

Cyrrie opened his newspaper to a photo of Maxwell's exhibit minus its fossils. "There's an article today about the missing fossils. According to the *Herald*, there's no sign of them and the police aren't answering questions. It doesn't sound good. How are you going to photograph the exhibit without them?"

"With difficulty," I said and told him about Ella's shot list and the new direction she had planned for the program. "She was counting on help from Simon and Gillian Collins, Maxwell's other assistant. Guess that won't be happening now. Simon's interview anyway."

"So what will you do?"

"Go to the museum, get the shots on the list, and let Ella worry about the rest. She'll think of something."

"Maybe Candi could interview Stan Darling," Cyrrie suggested slyly. "Get a little controversy going."

"Too late for that. Stan has switched sides," I told him. "He's been born again, all over again."

"He's been what?"

"Stan is now a born-again paleontologist," I said. "Professor Woodward brought him to my place yesterday afternoon. They stopped in for a visit on their way back to town. Apparently Stan converted over the weekend. Seems he now believes in evolution."

"That's amazing. The man has spent years fighting the good fight, not to mention a great deal of money. What on earth could have made him change his mind?"

"Who knows?" I lied.

"Well, well, well," Cyrrie shook his head in wonder. "This is one for the books, isn't it? Who could ever have predicted that Stanley Darling would join the godless atheists?"

"He hasn't done that. Not quite," I said. "He's decided that evolution is part of God's plan. That the fossil record is God's gift to mankind."

"So, Stan's still a few steps short of total Darwinism, is he? Well, that is a relief. At least he didn't write God out of the equation completely. That would make me think he'd taken complete leave of his senses," Cyrrie said. "Dear me, there's nowt so queer as folk, and that's the truth, isn't it?"

"Do you believe in God, Cyrrie?"

"What a question for a rainy Tuesday morning," he laughed.

"I'm not joking," I said. "Do you?" Cyrrie rarely talks about religion and never about his own beliefs. I've known him all my life, but I couldn't tell you anything about his spiritual life or if he even has one.

"May I ask what brought this on?" He neatly side-stepped the question.

"Thinking about Stan, I guess."

"Rest assured that Stanley Darling will be just as fanatic an advocate for evolution as he was an opponent. For people like him, it's the believing itself that counts, not what they believe. Stan would be as cheerful an ayatollah as he would an archbishop."

The dog twitched in his sleep, happily chasing dream squirrels in the warmth of Cyrrie's kitchen. His fur was almost dry now, at least the outer coat. I finished the last of my coffee and glanced at the clock. It was past time for me to leave for Drumheller. Ella had arranged for me to begin work at the museum around noon.

"How about you, my dear?" Cyrrie asked. "Do you believe there's a God? You certainly did when you were a child."

"I don't know." I took down my slicker from where I'd hung it to dry on the back of the kitchen door. "And I'm starting to do more and more of that – not knowing things, I mean."

"How odd," he grinned. "A few years ago there was so little you didn't know."

"I figure by the time I'm thirty-five I won't know a thing."

"You may be right about that," he agreed. "Perhaps a little on the early side, though. It took me until I was forty."

The weather did not improve between Calgary and Drumheller. It may have been a little warmer in the Red Deer River valley, but the rain still pelted down. I reached the museum shortly before twelve and parked at the end of a line of tour buses disgorging their occupants as close to the building's front door as possible. The tourists dashed across the forecourt while I trudged along behind with my load of equipment. Because of the extra light kit, it took me three trips. Some days I feel more like a porter than a photographer.

The museum was very crowded. The rain seemed to have increased attendance. It was hot inside and the smell of wet clothing pervaded the lobby. An occasional child-ish wail rose above the din of voices that bounced off the granite surfaces of the walls and floor. The clerks at the information desk very kindly let me stack the gear behind their chairs. They promised to keep an eye on it while I was away parking the van.

I walked back across the forecourt. Rain bent down on the broad backs of the pachyrhinosaurs. It formed runnels as it ran down their horns and big beaky snouts. I think they found the damp dispiriting. I know I did. Candi's com-missionaire hovered nearby. He gave me a friendly wave and hunched a little farther into his slicker as I pulled away from the curb. The parking lots were so full it took me a few minutes driving up and down the rows of cars to find an empty stall. I locked the van and started down the sidewalk that followed the main road back to the museum. I did my best to avoid the puddles and not repeat my Thursday trick of slipping in the clay the rain had washed down from the hills. Maybe if I'd been looking ahead instead of concen-trating on my feet I'd have seen the van sooner.

I came to the service road that leads to the loading bays behind the museum and paused at the curb. I looked up as a van with the University of Calgary crest on its side pulled up to the Stop sign beside me. Stan Darling, dressed in his coverall, stared out the passenger window. He did an almost comic double take as he recognized me. He turned and said something to the driver. A stony-faced Professor Woodward, tidily dressed in a sports jacket and tie, stared over the steering wheel. He pretended he hadn't seen me.

I waved and started toward them, but before my foot left the curb, the professor hit the gas and the van leapt forward, its tires squealing a protest. It roared past me, through a puddle, and on down the main drive. So much for gentlemen of science. The two old poops left me standing in the road, dripping muddy water and breathing their exhaust fumes.

13

I PHONED THE PROFESSOR'S HOUSE from the museum. I was certain Mrs. Woodward could tell me what her husband and Stan were up to and what they'd done with the fossils. If they'd stayed at the professor's place overnight and brought the bones into the house with them, then she must know – they couldn't sneak in and out carrying those two big orange garbage bags without her noticing. I didn't want to consider the possibility that Diana was as much in the dark as I was. I needed to hear that the bones were safe. I let the phone ring a dozen times but no one answered, not even a machine. I cursed myself for the idiot I was in ever letting the fossils out of my sight. I should have phoned the police as soon as Stan pulled that hanky out of his pocket. If only I'd . . . the opening phrase of the fool's lament played itself in my head. I went to work.

One of the clerks at the information desk called the administration office, and a few minutes later, a round-faced woman about my mother's age appeared in the lobby with an identification badge that would allow me access to the non-public parts of the building. I'd met Carla Ainsworth before. *A Day in the Lifestyle* had done a half-hour on her husband, a jewellery designer and goldsmith with a studio in the nearby town of Rosebud, and she'd been there with him when I went with Candi to shoot his interview. I didn't know her official job title, but she seemed to be the person who kept track of what everyone in the museum was doing and where they were doing it. Her tidy white blouse and navy slacks gave her a no-nonsense look that the reading glasses dangling from a chain around her neck did nothing to dispel.

"It's so nice to see you again, Phoebe. I only wish it could be under happier circumstances." Carla took my hand in her firm grip. "My goodness, someone certainly got you," she said, noticing my filthy slicker and the muddy water that still dripped off it onto the polished granite. "I think we'd better have that slicker hosed down." She helped me out of the offending garment and presented it to one of the information clerks, who hurried it away. "Can I help carry some of this?" she volunteered. I could see that having a mess of cord and cases stacked behind the information desk offended Carla's sense of order, nevertheless it was a kind offer and I accepted. "Is this it?" she asked, tripod and extension cords in hand. "What about that other big case?"

"It's the extra light kit and I'll come back for it after we dump this stuff," I said. "I'll need it for some shots in the storage area."

The security man at the door to the restricted part of the museum waved us through and we started down the hall.

"It's quiet back here," I said. Compared to the noise of the crowded lobby, the corridor felt hushed as an empty church.

"The museum is always full, but somehow it seems like there's even more people when it rains," Carla said. "It's a real mob scene out there today, isn't it?"

"I think I saw one of my old professors from U of C as I was walking from the parking lot," I said as casually as I could. "Not in the crowd though. He was driving away from the back of the building."

"You must mean Adam Woodward. He's a micropale-ontologist at the university."

"I took a geology class from him in first year."

"He was here delivering a collection of fossils that he'd promised to the museum. And very inconvenient it was." Carla sounded more than a little irritated. "Things are still in such chaos around here."

"I remember when I was a student," I said, "Dr. Woodward worked pretty much to his own timetable."

"Well, he hasn't changed. He was supposed to come next week when Dr. Beatrice, our micropaleo specialist, will be back from holiday, but for some reason he couldn't wait. Simply trundled in about an hour ago, wheeling a storage cabinet and a stack of drawers on a pallet jack and that was it. Not so much as a phone call to let us know he was coming. Really, we don't need any more unscheduled surprises."

Neither did I, but I had the horrible feeling that, thanks to the professor and Stan, I was in for a big one. What can be smuggled out can be smuggled in. Still, Stan had given me his word. I clung to it like a drowning man to an anvil.

"Do you know the man who was with him?" I asked. "The one in the coverall."

"He's a technician from the university, I suppose, but I don't know his name. I didn't have time to talk. I simply pointed them to the storage area and told them to put the cabinet in Dr. Beatrice's space. Adam has spent so much time here over the years that he knows his way around as well as I do."

"Do he and Dr. Beatrice work together?"

"Have for years. They publish joint papers. And I didn't mean to be rude to him, but, really, things do have to run to some sort of order. I hope I haven't hurt his feelings. Adam's such a nice man and he's been very good to the museum over the years. That collection of his is valuable material and considering that each of the specimens in it is about the size of a dust speck, we probably doubled our holdings today. I'll bet there are as many fossils in that one cabinet as there are in the rest of the Royal Tyrrell."

"The flea circus of paleontology?" I suggested.

"Even smaller but you've got the general idea," she laughed. "Say, I wonder if dinosaurs had fleas?" She surprised me with a question worthy of Candi. "What do you think?"

"It's not something I've ever thought about," I answered with complete honesty. "They must have had parasites of some sort."

"I'll have to ask someone." I could see her making a mental note. "How long do you think it will take you to finish today? The museum is open to the public until nine, but the offices close at five."

"I should be done by five if everything goes well."

"I hope it goes smoothly. It would make a nice change," she said. "You'll have to forgive us if things seem a little muddled. The police have left, but they've still got some of the offices cordoned off with their yellow tape, which means we have research staff reduced to camping in the storage area. Part of the exhibition space is sealed off too. It's not right," she commented more to herself than me. "But I think you'll find the places on your list are clear to work. If you have any problems, let me know. Lord, I'm beginning to wonder if we'll ever be back to normal again. How are you feeling, Phoebe?" she added kindly. "Finding Graham Maxwell's body must have been a terrible shock for you."

"I'm fine," I said.

"Thank God they've made an arrest. It's given us a real sense of relief around here. Relief mixed with sadness, though. Did you ever meet Simon Visser?"

"The night of the opening. He helped me carry my gear. I liked him," I said, putting one in for Simon.

"I liked him too," Carla agreed. "Very much. Everyone at the museum did. We'd got to know him this last couple of weeks. He seemed like such a dear man. It's hard to believe he could hurt a fly, let alone commit a murder. But people do change when they drink and Simon has a terrible problem with alcohol. I can't imagine what he must be feeling now. Remorse wouldn't begin to cover it."

"Have the police made any progress finding the missing fossils?" I asked.

"Not that they've told us. Not that they would tell us even if they had. Which I'm sure they haven't." Obviously, the police were not performing up to Carla's expectations in this area, which was good news from my point of view. "If you ask me, unless someone walks into a police station and dumps them on the counter, the Mounties will never find Dr. Maxwell's fossils." I wished I could tell Carla that her imagined scenario might be playing itself out right now, but I couldn't even tell that to myself with any hope of believing. "I don't know why," she continued, "but I have a dreadful feeling those bones are gone for good." She stopped and shifted the tripod to a more comfortable position.

"Are you okay?" I asked. "That thing is awkward if you're not used to carrying it."

"One of the little metal bits was digging into my hand, but it's all right now," she said. "Besides, we're nearly at the prep lab."

"I thought I'd start work in the storage area," I said. Where I can check Professor Woodward's fossil cabinet, I didn't add.

"But it said on the list your producer faxed me that you're to photograph the preparation laboratory first."

"I don't necessarily work in the same order as Ella's list. The order doesn't matter as long as I get all the shots."

"Good. Then you won't mind starting in the lab," Carla said firmly. "I've made arrangements for one of the staff to help you out."

"That's very generous, but I really don't need help." I did my best not to make it sound like a protest. "I'm used to working by myself."

"I am sorry, Phoebe, but we can't have you wandering on your own back here. Especially not after everything that's happened this past week. I'm sure you understand it's nothing personal."

I didn't point out that she'd let Professor Woodward wander wherever he wanted. I thought it better not to press the issue. If what I suspected about the cabinet turned out to be true, then I didn't want Carla remembering me as overly eager to get to the storage area. But I was and it didn't help to focus my mind on Ella's list.

Carla stopped at the open door of the preparation lab, a large, well-lit room, equipped with all the paraphernalia needed to take fossils as they came from the field in their plaster casings and transform them into the burnished specimens on display in the museum's galleries. Drills, hammers, chisels, saws, tiny sharp-pointed picks – the place looked like a cross between a machine shop and a dentist's office with overtones of a hospital cast room. A large window allowed the public to watch the process. I wondered if the technicians found it disconcerting to have strangers constantly looking over their shoulders as they worked. I knew I would.

A man and a woman, both about my age, were busy in the lab, hunched over a bench in front of the window, absorbed in reassembling a single small bone from a dis-couragingly large array of fragments. They both frowned in concentration as they laboured over this ultimate in three-dimensional jigsaw puzzles.

"I think you've got it," the man said. "At least it looks right to me. I can't see one that would work any better."

They both looked up when Carla knocked on the door jamb. She did the introductions. The woman politely acknowledged my presence with a smile, but the blankness in her eyes made it plain that her mind was still at work on her puzzle. The man stood up and held out his hand. He was tall and lanky with sandy hair and trustworthy brown eyes, the kind of guy who'd be your brother's best friend.

"Jim has volunteered to show you around and answer any questions you might have," Carla said.

Jim didn't look like a volunteer to me, more like someone who'd drawn the short straw. I wasn't happy to be stuck with him either, so I guess we were even.

"Hi, Phoebe," he shook my hand. "As you can see, Gloria and I are up to our ears, but we've tried to get some stuff ready for you."

Carla left and Gloria went back to work, happily oblivious to everything but her bits of rock.

"Sorry to take you away from your work," I said.

"Don't worry. It's part of the job," Jim said. "I've set some things up so you can get an idea of how we handle the fossils here. We're not working on hominids, though. Gloria is busy with a small dinosaur today, but the preparation method is much the same. I hope that'll be okay."

On any other day, I'd have found the prep lab a fascinating assignment, a satisfying blend of esoteric information and photographic challenges, but today I could hardly wait to finish and get to the storage area. I was certain that the professor and Stan had used the cabinet to smuggle Graham Maxwell's fossils back into the museum. Well, almost certain. I had to know for sure.

"Don't you think we should get started?" Jim called me and my wandering mind back to the lab. He sounded impatient and I didn't blame him.

"Sorry, Jim, guess I'm getting a little ahead of myself." I could tell he wasn't impressed. Nevertheless, he did his best, answering all my questions and helping me with the setups. There were plenty of them. Taping the preparation lab was, like the work that went on there, a painstaking and picky job. I tried to hurry, but it still felt like I'd switched to geological time. By the time I finished Gloria had made some progress on the bone, and what looked like a hip socket was beginning to take shape. I switched off the camera.

"Done?" Jim asked, unable to keep the hope out of his voice.

"Done in here."

"Then let's go have some lunch." He checked his watch. "It's twenty to two and I'm starved."

"Thanks, but I think I'll work through until I'm finished," I said. "Would you show me the way to the storage area before you go? I'd like to do that next."

"Sorry, no can do. I'm supposed to help you out for the rest of the day, which means I'm supposed to stay with you. Orders from the upper floor. You coming for lunch, Gloria?"

Gloria opted to stay behind with her fossil and a sandwich. Jim collected a brown paper bag from a cupboard by the door and walked with me to the public cafeteria, where I bought myself a muffin and an apple. We carried our lunches to the staff lounge. There were no old drunks singing college songs today, only a scattering of museum employees nearing the end of late lunch breaks, a couple of them reading, the others playing a game of cards.

Gillian sat by herself in an armchair near the coffee urn reading a sheaf of papers on a clipboard. A cup of tea sat untouched on the low table next to her. She looked like she'd lost weight in the four days since we'd last met and her eyes still had their dark circles. She glanced up as we walked by. I stopped to speak to her.

"Hello, Gillian," I said. "How are you?"

She looked directly at me but didn't answer. Then she went back to her papers.

Jim and I took our coffee and sat on the same couch the professor and Stan had occupied during their drunken sing-song.

"Don't take that personally," Jim nodded in Gillian's direction. "She's been like that since Graham Maxwell died. Sometimes she'll talk to you, other times you might as well be a piece of the furniture. I think his murder hit her pretty hard."

"He was more than her boss."

"Yeah, that was pretty obvious," Jim said. "And it can't be much of a treat knowing it was your own colleague who murdered him."

"I'm surprised Gillian's still in Drumheller," I said. "I thought she might want to go home."

"The people back at Maxwell's lab in Kenya are shipping us copies of the fossils this week. Gillian has agreed to stay until they get here and help us set them up in the exhibit. She'll go home to England after that."

"I guess she'll have to come back for Simon's trial."

"That's not going to happen for months, if it happens at all," Jim said. "You know, except for the booze, Simon's a decent guy. He wouldn't hurt anyone when he was sober. My guess is he'll confess. Do they have a trial if someone admits they're guilty?"

"I'm not sure," I said. Privately, I thought it might be difficult to confess to a crime you didn't remember committing. I also thought it was odd that both Carla and Jim seemed to feel genuinely sorry for Simon, but neither had expressed any regret over Dr. Maxwell's death. I wondered if this attitude would hold for the rest of the people at the museum. It wasn't as if they were hostile to Maxwell, simply indifferent, which made his death seem even sadder. Was there anyone besides Gillian who truly mourned the man?

Gillian slid the papers back under the clip and got up from her chair. She walked past us and on down the stairs. She moved slowly, as if she had been ill for a long time. Her lab coat seemed too big for her slumped shoulders. I hoped she had family in England who would look after her. Gillian looked like she could use a lot of looking after.

Jim was a slow eater. He took the time to chew every mouthful of his ham sandwich, two cookies, and an orange at least fifty thousand times. I felt myself growing older between bites. I practically cheered every time he swallowed. It was two-fifteen by the time we went back to work.

"How much of what you're taping today will be shown on TV?" he asked as we walked back to the lab.

"About five minutes. If that."

"You mean we're doing all this work for five minutes?"

"The program isn't about the Royal Tyrrell," I pointed out. "It's about Graham Maxwell. This is really a sidebar, insurance in case the Maxwell stuff is a little thin. We'll use it as background for the exhibit. I'll probably have to come back when you get the copies of the fossils set up in the display."

"Five minutes." Jim shook his head. Good manners prevented him from actually lamenting out loud this waste of his afternoon but he came close. "Where next?" he asked. "How about the graphics department? Carla has lined up one of the artists to look after you there." The prospect of dumping me on some poor artist brightened his outlook a little.

"I think I should do the storage area now." This time I dug in my heels.

"Well, okay. I guess it is the next place on your producer's list." Jim gave in a little grudgingly but without any real protest. He wasn't made of the same stern stuff as Carla.

We collected the equipment, including the extra light kit from behind the information desk, and moved everything into the storage area. It was even bigger than I remembered, a cavernous space more like an industrial warehouse or some big-box furniture outlet than a museum. The light, however, was just like I remembered – ghastly and not enough. Bulbs hanging high overhead cast a sickly pall over the room but, short of ripping off the roof, there wasn't much I could do about it. The likelihood of getting Ella's fancy shots began to seem as dim as the light itself.

Aisles like gloomy alleys separated towering metal shelves loaded with dinosaur bones. There must have been thousands of fossils on those shelves and they came in all shapes and sizes. Many, but by no means all, were wrapped in white plaster. Some were bare rock, some were in metal cabinets or wooden crates, still others were stored in cardboard boxes. The shelves themselves were enormous, at least five feet wide and sturdily braced, which wasn't surprising when you saw what they supported.

"What's that?" I pointed to a huge white mound on a shoulder-high shelf. It may not have been quite as large as a Volkswagen Beetle but was much the same shape.

"Probably a skull," Jim said. "Maybe a triceratops. I'd have to look it up in the log to be sure. What do you want me to do with this gear?"

"We might as well leave it here. It's going to take me a while to figure out how to shoot in this place." Jim's face fell. This was not what he wanted to hear. "You know, you really don't have to stay. I always work by myself. I'm quicker on my own."

"But I'm not supposed to leave you. Carla's orders. She's really hyper about security right now."

"Yeah, like I'm going to slip a triceratops skull into my workbag and waltz out."

"Well, that bag is pretty big," he laughed. "Might do you a baby stegosaur."

"Come on, Jim. You know I'm not going to touch anything and having you hanging around holding my light meter all afternoon will be a waste of time for both of us."

"What about Carla?" I could see I almost had him convinced.

"I don't think someone as busy as Carla is going to bother with us. Do you?"

"Probably not."

"Look. Why don't you go back to your lab and when I'm finished in here I'll come get you and you can escort me to wherever it is I'm supposed to go next. I won't leave without you. I promise." That clinched the deal.

Jim left me to my work, and I was free to go searching. Not that I expected to find the fossils in the professor's cabinet. If he and Stan had used it to smuggle the bones back into the museum, it made sense that they wouldn't leave them in something that could be traced so easily. Still, the cabinet seemed the best place to start.

I set up the camera and a couple of lights. In case someone came into the storage area, I wanted to look like I was working. I grabbed one of the extension cords. It would give me a reason to be wandering the aisles. If anyone asked, I'd be checking for electrical outlets.

I began at the wall nearest the lab. I walked up one aisle and down the next. There was an office desk at the far end of the second aisle in the large space between the shelves and the wall. Another desk faced the wall at the end of the third aisle. Both had work lamps, computers, and a scattering of papers on them. A dinosaur screen saver told me that the computer on the nearest desk was running but there was no one around. I decided the desks must belong to the banished researchers that Carla had mentioned.

Professor Woodward's cabinet was still on its pallet, shoved up against the wall behind the last row of shelves. A bright yellow label with his name and university address printed in black letters dangled by a wire from one of the brass drawer pulls. I had been on the lookout for the usual beat-up metal box with drawers that seems to be standard storage in most labs I've seen, but the professors's cabinet was made of wood, walnut polished to a deep gloss, a beautiful piece of cabinetry probably custom built to his specifications. About four feet high and half again as wide, it held four vertical banks of shallow drawers, each about an inch and a half deep by two and a half feet long. I slid one open. It moved on silken rollers at the touch of a finger. Inside, five rows of grooved slots held banks of white cardboard microscope slides. I took one out for a closer look. A wafer of glass protected a small, black, circular well sunk into the cardboard. A label, handwritten in tiny meticulous lettering, told me there were five specimens of *Nodosaria* mounted in the well, but they were so small I couldn't see them. There must have been hundreds of fossils in that one drawer and over a hundred drawers in the cabinet. I knew they were far too shallow to house Maxwell's hominid bones, but I still checked every one.

I found nothing but more neatly labelled dust specks. Since I wasn't expecting anything else, that didn't surprise me. Nor did it help me to figure out how the professor and Stan had used the cabinet to get the fossils back into the museum. Then I remembered Carla's words. Professor Woodward had shown up with the cabinet and a stack of drawers on a pallet jack. I opened a top drawer and felt along its sides. I found a small metal latch halfway down on the left. I pressed it and the drawer lifted easily from its runners. It was heavy. I placed it carefully on the floor beside the cabinet and then unlatched and removed the next drawer down and the next. I saw that by removing even one bank of drawers I could create a hollow space inside the cabinet, big enough to stash the *Homo musicus* bones with space to spare. Stan and Professor Woodward had probably stacked the drawers in front of the cabinet on the pallet jack so they would hide the interior from view. Anyone seeing them would assume that the heavy hardwood cabinet with its drawers full of slides had been too much for the old guys to heft around so they'd very sensibly removed the drawers to reduce its weight. After they reached the storage area, they'd probably taken the bones from their hiding place and then slipped the drawers back on their runners. That meant Maxwell's hominids could be anywhere in the room. The professor and Stan wouldn't have had to bother hiding them, just stick them on a shelf along with the rest of the fossils. The purloined-letter principle in action.

I replaced the drawers and went back to walking the aisles. This time I didn't know exactly what I was looking for, but after studying the inside of the cabinet, I had at least an approximate idea of the size. I was also pretty sure that if the two men possessed a grain of sense between them, and I had some doubts about that, they wouldn't have left the fossils in those orange garbage bags. Anyone who'd ever watched a cop drama on TV would realize that by now the plastic sacks would be covered with fingerprints and hay dust and yellow paint flecks and who knows what other conspicuous bits of forensic evidence. I thought it was equally unlikely that they would put the bones on one of the high shelves. They'd have had to waste too much time finding a ladder. I was sure that whatever the bones were in, it would be at eye level or lower, but that still left hundreds of feet of shelves filled with fossils. The Royal Tyrrell didn't believe in wasting space.

It was like looking for a strand of hay in a haystack but with one small advantage – each piece of this stack was labelled. Every rock, every plaster cast, every wooden crate, and every cardboard box had its individual museum marking. Most of the cardboard boxes were sealed with tape. I didn't think the professor would have dumped the contents of any of them in order to hide the bones. He was too much of a scientist to ruin someone else's work. I walked the rows, examining every box I saw, searching for one without a label.

I found one in the second row. It had started life as packaging for a computer printer. It looked exactly the right size for the job and even had some orange plastic sticking out of its closed top. It was on the second shelf up, about waist level. I had enough sense not to open it with my bare hands. I'd watched those cop shows too. I pulled the cuffs of my sweater down to my fingertips and pulled open the flaps. No bones. Nothing but a pair of hip waders and a fishy-smelling wicker creel stuffed with an orange plastic bag. Probably one of the museum employees liked to go angling on his lunch break but didn't want the creel stinking up his office.

It took me thirty minutes to work my way across half the room. Besides the fishing gear, I found a battery-dead cellphone abandoned behind a metal upright and a box of doughnuts so old and hard they looked quite at home amid the fossils. But that was all. I started on the second half. I hit it lucky two rows from the end, right near the desks. *Homo musicus'* busy bones had come to rest in a couple of cardboard liquor boxes.

A Pelee Island Merlot carton sat in the centre of the lowest shelf, a couple of inches above the floor. A larger Gordon's Gin box rested right behind it. They were wedged into the small space between a wooden crate and a huge plaster-wrapped bone. No one simply walking past would have noticed them. I tried to shove the bone aside to get to the boxes, but it was too heavy for me. I walked around to the other side of the shelf. The wooden crate wouldn't budge either, but a few feet down there was a gap between a couple of two-drawer filing cabinets. I put the extension cord on top of one and crouched down to peer in. A narrow space ran through the middle of the shelf between the objects facing either aisle. I managed to push one of the cabinets aside, widening the gap enough for me to squeeze through onto the shelf. On hands and knees, I inched my way along the middle space toward the wine box. I checked its sides. No museum labels. Its top flaps were folded in against themselves. I slid my sweater cuffs back down over my hands and tugged them open. Inside, I found two plastic garbage bags, both of them black. I opened the first. A *Homo musicus* skull stared up at me. I stared back.

My first feeling was relief. The fossils were safe at home in the Royal Tyrrell. The second was anger. Why hadn't the old schemers told me what they had done? And why had I let myself get caught up in their absurd intrigues? I should have gone to the police when I had the chance. It was too late now. I had no evidence to prove that the Geologists for Jesus had stolen the fossils. The bones were safe, but so were Myrna and her pack of self-righteous vandals. So much for Stan and his word as a Christian.

I closed the bag and refolded the box's flaps. I leaned over it and tugged open the gin carton. It held the longer bones. I closed it too. I had just begun the backwards crawl to the gap between the filing cabinets when I heard the footsteps. I froze as clogs and a blue denim skirt passed by my shelf. The footsteps stopped. I raised my head and risked a peek over the wooden crate. I couldn't see the owner of the clogs, but I heard the tap of computer keys. I couldn't move. If I climbed out from my hidden space she'd see me for certain. Because Stan and the professor were no doubt intending to inform the museum of the fossils' whereabouts – anonymously, of course – the woman would also know who had been cuddled up on the same shelf as them this afternoon. I was stuck until she finished whatever she was doing on her computer and left. Just me and my boxes of hot rocks.

I stretched out as well as a five-foot-eight woman can in a four-foot long space and listened to the steady tapping of the keys for what seemed like an hour but, according to my watch, was ten minutes. With every minute it felt like the shelf got harder and my space on it smaller. I was very glad I didn't suffer from claustrophobia. I shifted position. An hour later another ten minutes had passed. I made a vow not to look at my watch again until Clogs left the room. I kept it for fifteen minutes.

"Hi, anybody here?" Jim called as he walked down the aisle toward Clogs's desk. I saw his khaki legs and the hem of his lab coat pass by my hiding place. "Have you seen a television photographer around?" he asked her.

"Nope." The tapping stopped. "Nobody in here but me."

"Her equipment's all set up, but I can't find her any-where."

"Maybe she went to the washroom," Clogs suggested.

"Maybe. Her name's Phoebe Fairfax. If she comes back, tell her I'm looking for her, will you?"

"Sure thing."

Jim's lab coat retreated. The tapping resumed. This time it went on for forever. I developed a nice case of pins and needles in my left arm. It occupied my attention for a few minutes until I managed to squirm into a half-sitting position with the wine box as a back rest and the tingling subsided. At one point, I stretched my legs out and accidentally kicked one of the metal cabinets. I thought for sure Clogs would hear the thunk, but she kept right on working. Every once in a while she'd stop for a few minutes and get my hopes up. Then the tapping would start again. As forever started into its second hour, I began to rethink my views on claustrophobia.

This time it was Gillian who interrupted Clogs's work. She must have come into the room by another door because she didn't pass by my hiding place.

"Hi, Gillian," Clogs said.

Gillian sat down at the desk facing the wall. I could see her back quite clearly if I kneeled and looked over the wooden crate. I heard her say something, but she didn't turn her head so I missed the words. Clogs went back to work. Gillian took a stack of white envelopes from her clipboard and placed them on the desk in front of her. Then she sat, staring straight ahead at her blank computer screen.

Ten minutes later I heard Clogs switch off the computer.

"Time to go," she said. "You coming?"

Gillian shook her head.

"Jim was here a little while ago looking for a photographer. Phoebe somebody. If you see her, let him know, will you?"

Gillian mumbled something as Clogs said goodbye and passed back down the aisle in front of me. She continued to stare at the blank computer screen. Then she put her head down on the desk, resting it on her arms. She remained in that position so long I thought she'd fallen asleep until I saw her shoulders begin to shudder in great long, silent sobs. It was as if Gillian's grief had taken on a life of its own and possessed her body completely. Unconscious, involuntary, her sobs were like the spasms of a seizure. My heart ached for her, but at the same time I felt like the worst kind of voyeur, spying on her private misery. I knew she would hate me for seeing her like this, but I couldn't turn away any more than I could comfort her.

The shudders stopped as suddenly as they had begun. Gillian lifted her head and leaned back in her chair. Then she opened the top left drawer of the desk and took out a very large revolver. She swivelled her chair around and looked down the aisle past my shelf. I saw her face, pale and expressionless, as she checked to make certain the big gun was loaded. That thing must have been fifteen inches long and probably packed enough fire power to make a charging rhino reconsider. She gave its cylinder an expert little whirl, cocked the hammer, and stuck the muzzle in her mouth. In less time than it takes to tell, Gillian was all set to blow her brains out.

14

I THINK MY HEART SKIPPED SOME BEATS. I know I stopped breathing. I clapped my hand over my mouth to keep from calling out and startling Gillian into jerking the trigger. The gun was so big that she had to hold it backwards, right thumb resting on the trigger, fingers curled around the back of the grip while her left hand supported the barrel. I sat and watched and willed her to take it out of her mouth. Please don't do this, Gillian, I begged silently. Please, don't do this. Please don't. She took a deep breath and held it. Then the still-cocked gun dropped to her side and we both began to breathe again.

I scrambled to get out of my hiding place, but before I could make it she stuck the gun back between her teeth. This time I swear my heart stopped. It was a toss up which of us she'd kill first. But again, Gillian couldn't bring herself to pull the trigger and again the gun fell back to her side. I managed to crawl out into the aisle before she could make it three times lucky. I got to my feet and walked toward her very slowly.

"Gillian, you don't want to do this," I said quietly.

She looked at me. I think that until I spoke she hadn't registered my presence. "Phoebe. Where did you come from?" she asked unsteadily.

"That's not important," I said. "Why don't you give me the gun."

"Because I'm using it," she said. "You know," she continued in a strangely conversational tone, "it's not as easy as you might think to kill yourself. It's actually a very difficult thing to do. I had no idea it would be this hard."

"Maybe you can't do it because you don't want to die." I continued my slow walk.

"My body doesn't seem to want to."

"Please give the gun to me, Gillian." I held out my hand.

"I don't think so." She pointed the muzzle at my chest. "And I don't think I'd come any closer if I were you, Phoebe. You see, I just need a little more time to get my courage up. I can't think why it should be so very difficult to make myself pull the trigger." She seemed puzzled.

"Then I guess we have some time to talk, don't we?"

Gillian shrugged as if it were a matter of complete indifference to her whether we talked or not, which it probably was. I'd read somewhere that it was important to keep suicidal people talking. It made sense. She couldn't shoot herself and talk to me at the same time. I hoped.

"Don't do this, Gillian" I said. "It's pointless. I know you loved Graham Maxwell, but killing yourself isn't the answer to anything."

"It is for me," she said and stuck the gun back in her mouth.

"Think how your family will feel." I took a step closer. Oh God, maybe she hated her family. I hadn't thought of that. "Think of what this will do to your friends, to everyone who loves you."

Gillian tried to talk around the gun barrel, but the words were so garbled I couldn't understand them.

"Gillian, take that thing out of your mouth. I can't understand a word you're saying."

She removed the gun from between her teeth and pointed it at my chest again. I had difficulty regarding this as a positive development, but nevertheless, I edged a little closer.

"None of that matters," she said.

"Of course it matters. It's the only thing that does matter."

"But I killed him," she said. "It wasn't Simon, it was me. I'm the one who murdered Graham."

"You killed him?" I took a step back.

"Is it that unbelievable?"

"Yes," I said. "It is."

"Well, maybe it's time to reconsider your assumptions." In other circumstances, I'd have sworn she was laughing at me.

"Look, Gillian, I'm the one who found him. Remember? I saw him lying there. You're not big enough or strong enough to have smashed that egg into his skull."

"How do you know? I may be stronger than I look."

"Unless you're taller than you look there's no way you could lift that egg off the shelf and hold it high enough to do the kind of damage I saw." I began to inch forward again.

"Don't come any closer." She waved the gun back and forth in an alarmingly casual manner. "I've already killed Graham. I have nothing to lose by killing you."

"Okay, okay." I held up my hands in the classic gesture of surrender. "I won't move until you say. But maybe you could tell me what happened that night?"

"It's all in those letters on my desk. I made sure. Simon will be safe now. It's all in the letters."

"But I'd like to hear it from you."

Gillian looked at me while she considered the idea. She shrugged.

"Why not? What difference can it make?" She never took her eyes off me as she spoke. "There's not much to tell, really. I watched you walk away from the office and go down the stairs. I waited a few minutes and then I went to the door. Graham was coming out of the inner office. Simon had passed out behind the desk. I saw him before Graham closed the door. Then he turned to me and started laughing. He told me about his fight with Simon, but he made a joke of it, like Simon wasn't worth taking seriously. It made me angry. I don't know why. It certainly wasn't for Simon's sake. I'd heard them argue dozens of times. I guess this time I knew he felt the same way about me, that I wasn't worth taking seriously either. I suppose some part of me had known for a long time, but I couldn't admit it to myself. I mattered even less to Graham than Simon did. At least he needed Simon in the field. He only needed me to warm his bed. I was a nice relaxing pair of open legs at the end of a long day."

"Surely you're being too hard on him," I said. "He was angry. He'd been fighting with Simon. I heard them. It was horrible. But it had nothing to do with you. He loved you. You told me that yourself."

"Well, I was wrong, wasn't I? The only person Graham ever loved was Graham."

"You're not making sense, Gillian." But she was and we both knew it.

"Of course, you're right about the fight," she said. "It was a bad one. This time I think Graham really was going to fire Simon. He told me he'd had it with him. Said he had no more use for a hopeless drunk, that he and Simon had come to the end of the road. I asked him if we'd come to the end of our road too. He called me his darling Gilly and asked me how I could say something so foolish. He told me he still had plenty of use for me. He laughed when he said it." Gillian's hand tightened around the gun. Its muzzle seemed to get bigger and bigger the longer I stared at it.

"Do you think you could point that somewhere else?" I asked. "At least until we finish talking. I promise I won't move."

Gillian didn't move either. The gun stayed where it was.

"Then I told him what I thought of him drooling over Candi Sinclair all night," she said. "I told him it made him look like a randy old goat. I thought he'd be angry but he wasn't. He only laughed some more and said well maybe he was a randy old goat at that. He asked me if I thought he might be the reincarnation of the great god Pan. Then he took that awful little flute out of his pocket and began to blow on it.

"He started spouting a load of nonsense about how he must be related to Pan because, after all, these were probably the god's own pipes and now they were his. If I didn't know better I'd have said Graham was the worse for drink.

Then he laughed some more and said he'd play for me. He called me his darling Gilly again and told me his Pan music would dance me to a bed of thistledown. He took off his jacket and spread it on the lab bench. He meant to make love to me right there on his coat on top of that filthy bench with Simon passed out in the other room. I was furious, but Graham thought he was being funny. That he was so charming I couldn't possibly resist him. He came prancing across the room to me, grinning his head off and telling me that his goat blood was up and his tiny hooves were dancing too. More than his blood was up all right. He held the flute in his teeth and started to unzip his fly. I shoved him away from me. I pushed him as hard as I could. He lost his balance and stumbled over an odd-looking suitcase that was sitting in front of the shelves. I don't know where it came from, but he fell over it and bumped into the shelves on his way down. He grabbed at an upright to steady himself. That's when the shelves began to wobble and Graham let go. His face hit the floor just before one of the big dinosaur eggs fell off the top shelf and smashed into the back of his head. It was all over before I knew what had happened. His brains were all over the floor and the flute was halfway down his throat. I murdered him."

"That wasn't murder, Gillian," I said. "That wasn't even self-defence. It was an accident."

"You think that's how the police will see it?"

"People have done far worse and nothing's happened to them," I said. "There was a woman in Calgary who emptied a pistol into her husband. She didn't spend a day in jail. Shot him six times."

"Did she kill him?" Gillian asked.

"No, but only because she was a lousy shot."

"I know I killed Graham. I don't care if the police think it was an accident or not. And I don't care about going to jail. I know what I did. I keep seeing it over and over in my mind and I can't make it stop. If I fall asleep, it's in my dreams. I can't live like this. I have to die too."

"No you don't. You didn't do anything. He tripped." I didn't think this was the time to add that it was over my light kit. "He fell. It was an accident."

"Did you know that people can die of remorse? It's true. They should write it on my death certificate, 'Cause of death: remorse.' It hurts so much and it's never going to stop."

Gillian started to raise the gun again. I lunged for her arm but she was too quick. The explosion of the shot numbed my ears and filled my nostrils with the acrid smell of gun powder.

"I'm a very good shot, Phoebe," she said. "The next one won't miss. Get away from me." I did as I was told.

"How did you smuggle that into Canada?" I asked when my ears had stopped ringing.

"The pistol? I didn't smuggle it. It came wrapped with the fossils," she said. "We always have it with us in the field. It's a standard part of the equipment. Now get out of my way." She motioned with the gun and I stepped aside. She walked past me and backed down the aisle toward the door. I started after her.

"Don't do this, Gillian. Give me the gun. Please."

She stopped. So did I. "You've been kind to me, Phoebe, and I don't want to hurt you but I will if I have to. Stay back. I'd suggest you don't watch. This is probably going to be very messy. Turn away." She put the gun to her temple this time. I didn't turn away. I don't know how long we stood looking at each other. Finally, her hand dropped and the muzzle pointed back at me.

"It seems I can't pull the trigger if you're with me," she said. "I need to be alone." I moved toward her. "No. Stay back." I took another step. I saw the muzzle flash at the same time as I heard the explosion. A puff of plaster drifted down from where the bullet lodged in a big wrapped fossil on the shelf above my head.

Gillian turned and ran. I followed. I heard a shout as she burst through the door to the storage area and sent Jim reeling across the corridor.

"What the hell is going on?" he shouted as I ran past him.

Gillian turned and got off another shot, this one on the run. I think the bullet hit the ceiling. I know Jim hit the floor. He curled his body into a protective ball like a human hedgehog.

"Call the police," I shouted back. "I need some help. Gillian's trying to kill herself."

I ran behind her down the deserted corridor and on into the lobby. The lobby was far less crowded than it had been earlier in the day, but there were still enough people to make it an impressive sight when Gillian fired a shot into the air above their heads and they parted like the Red Sea. She ran through them out the big front door and into the rain. Except for the commissionaire, the forecourt was empty. Gillian stopped at the curb. I ducked behind a pachyrhinosaur. A bullet pinged off the granite bench beside it. The horrified commissionaire dived to the pavement. He'd signed on for parking patrol, not armed combat.

Gillian ran for the hill. She started up the staircase to the deserted lookout. I ran behind her, slithering in the mud at the bottom of the stairs, clutching at the railing. She took the stairs three at a time. So did I.

By my count, Gillian had fired five shots. Revolvers held six bullets. I was pretty sure of that. Then again, I don't know much about guns. No, that's not true. I don't know anything about guns. All I knew was that the revolvers in the old cowboy movies I used to watch with Cyrrie and Uncle Andrew fired six shots. If Gillian was using the same gun as Wyatt Earp, she had one bullet left. She could use it on herself or on me. I didn't think she'd waste it on me. I prayed we'd watched the same movies. It would be just my luck if Gillian had some fancy new improved job with room for seven bullets. Even if I was right, I don't know what I thought I could do in the second or two before she fired that sixth bullet through her brain – knock the gun out of her hand, spoil her aim, say boo – but it was the only chance I had.

Probably the adrenalin had made me foolhardy – it certainly boosted me up those stairs. I arrived at the lookout deck on Gillian's heels. She started for the far railing but slipped and fell on a patch of clay left by some tourist's shoe. She was up in an instant with the gun pointed straight at me. I heard the sirens wailing below us in the distance and turned to see flashing lights racing through the rain, up the drive to the museum.

"It's over now, Gillian." I held out my hand. "Give me the gun and we'll go back down together. I'll stay with you. I want to help you."

"Then leave me. I only need to be alone for a minute. Please." Her voice sounded small and cold. "I know I can do it if you'll leave."

"Gillian, I can't leave you. You know I can't."

She shook her head. "No, I guess you can't." She climbed over the railing and stepped off the deck. She looked at me for a moment. Then she started to raise the gun. She opened her mouth, but before she could stick the muzzle in for one last try, the greasy ground gave way beneath her feet. Her arms flew above her head and the gun sailed out of her hand. I heard it splat into the mud somewhere behind me. Her arms flailed in an effort to grasp the rail, but thanks to gravity and the treacherous clay, Gillian's feet continued their slide. She fell, rolling over and over down the steep slope. I clambered over the barrier and tumbled after her, slipping and skidding to the bottom of the gully.

I came to rest near a big puddle. I remember noticing the raindrops making circles on the surface of its murky brown water. I tried to stand but my feet couldn't find a purchase on the slick ground. Gillian sat a few feet away coated in mud. Her hair, her face, her clothes, everything was covered in wet clay. I crawled over and put my arms around her. She sat quietly, her head resting on my shoulder. I felt a small shudder pass over her body. I stroked her hair, gently pushing its mud-slicked tendrils out of her eyes.

The commissionaire was the first one to reach us. He came stumbling around the hill, sometimes on his feet, more often on his hands and knees. He stopped when he saw us and began to back away.

"It's okay," I called to him. "She isn't armed. The gun is somewhere up on the hill. It's safe now."

"Are you okay, miss?" He sounded as shaky as I felt.

"I'm fine. We're both okay. But Gillian needs a doctor."

"Holy moly, Dr. Collins," he shouted at the clay-slathered Gillian. "Have you lost your mind or what?" His voice rose with every word. "You can't go around blasting guns off anywhere you feel like. This is Canada. We got laws here. Even in Alberta."

15

CYRRIE HEATED ME A BOWL OF SOUP. I thought this was pretty good of him since it was three o'clock in the morning. Bertie didn't seem to care that it was the middle of the night. He lapped up his little bowl of chicken broth and vegetables with as much enthusiasm as if it had been three in the afternoon. He avoided the mushrooms with the skill of long practice, leaving them in a tidy line along the rim of the dish.

I'd phoned Cyrrie from the Drumheller police station after the Mounties finished questioning me about Gillian and her shooting rampage. Finished the first round of questions, that is. The second and third rounds took until after midnight. Cyrrie had been decent enough not to ask for a lot of details over the phone. He still hadn't said much. He sat across the kitchen island from me in his old paisley dressing gown and watched me eat my soup.

"A little more?" he asked.

"No thanks. That was good. I needed some food. I'll just finish my milk and get going."

"You're not going anywhere tonight." He didn't exactly sound angry, more remote, almost like he was talking to a stranger. "Frankly, I'm amazed the police let you drive yourself from Drumheller."

"They didn't, actually," I admitted. "One of them drove me in the van." I drank the last of my glass of milk.

"You made the national news tonight. Lead story," he said. "They had some dandy shots of you and Gillian Collins being loaded into police cruisers."

"I wonder how they got pictures? There weren't any news crews at the museum."

"A tourist took them with his home video camera. They were good too. Very clear. Muddy at the museum, I gather."

"Very."

Neither of us spoke for a while. It wasn't a comfortable silence.

"You look clean enough now."

"I took a shower at the hospital and changed into some clothes I'd taken along in my workbag in case the weather got better."

This time the silence lasted even longer and felt even more uncomfortable.

"Well?" he said at last. "Are you going to tell me what happened or not, because if you're not, I'm off to bed."

"Are you angry with me, Cyrrie?"

"No, my dear, I'm not angry. I'm simply old and very tired and I almost lost the person dearest to me tonight, but I'm not angry. Numb maybe. Not angry."

"I couldn't help it. She was going to kill herself. I came back from the ladies' room and saw her sitting there with a gun stuck in her mouth. What was I supposed to do? Let her blow her brains out?"

"I don't know," he said. "Maybe you should tell me what happened."

And so I did. Of course, I didn't think it necessary to mention that I'd spent the better part of the afternoon hiding on a shelf along with Dr. Maxwell's fossil family. I hadn't told the police about that either. The revised version of my afternoon had me suffering a slight intestinal upset that resulted in my spending the afternoon in and out of the washroom. So far everyone seemed to believe me, including Cyrrie. In fact, I'd told the tale of my trots so many times I was starting to believe it myself. I definitely needed to be more careful of what I ate.

"The police wouldn't let me stay with Gillian. They took us both to the Drumheller hospital but in separate cars. They did tell me that she won't talk. She just kind of sits there like a lump. The last time Gillian said anything was when we were up on the hill, before she dropped the gun."

"How many times did she shoot at you?"

"She fired five bullets, but only four of them were at me. And I know she really wasn't trying to hit me. She only did it to frighten me off. If Gillian had really intended to shoot me, she would have done it with the first bullet. She wanted to kill herself, not me. I was pretty sure anyone who could feel that kind of remorse over an accident wasn't going to hurt me. At least not deliberately."

Cyrrie didn't comment. He simply shook his head. His face looked grey.

"You know in a way I can almost understand what she feels," I continued. "At least a little. Maxwell tripped over my light kit. I keep thinking what if I'd left them on the lab bench instead of the floor. What if I hadn't . . ."

"Phoebe, that is a useless, self-destructive way of thinking. Don't go down that path. Graham Maxwell's death was an accident. You had nothing to do with it." He went to the liquor cupboard and pulled out a bottle of cognac. He poured shots into a couple of kitchen glasses and handed one to me. He drained his own at a single gulp. A little colour crept back into his cheeks.

"Do you think Gillian will be able to prove it was an accident, that she didn't intend to murder him?" I asked. I swallowed a sip of cognac and felt its glow on my own face.

"I think it works the other way round. At least I hope it's still innocent until proven guilty," Cyrrie said. "The police have to prove that it wasn't an accident."

"What do you think is going to happen to her?" I asked.

"That's a question for the lawyers. You should ask Tim." He poured himself more cognac, then shoved the cork back in the bottle. "Even if they don't lay charges in Maxwell's death, they're not going to be too pleased about her shooting up the Royal Tyrrell."

We sipped some more cognac. This time the silence was a little less tense.

"Cyrrie, do you think if I'd left Gillian that she would have killed herself?"

"Impossible to say. It must be a very difficult thing to do. Despite what your conscious mind is willing, every animal instinct must be screaming no," he said. "I don't think you'll ever find an answer to that one. Probably Gillian won't either."

"But I couldn't leave her, could I? I couldn't take that chance."

"Finish your brandy, my dear, and go to bed. The guest room is all ready for you."

"What if I'd left her and she'd killed herself before I could get help? I don't think I could live with that."

"Go to bed, Phoebe."

"So now I'm stuck with her."

"What do you mean you're stuck with her?"

"I promised Gillian that I'd stay with her. Up on the hill. I said I wanted to help her. Now I'm stuck with her."

"Just like the old Chinese notion, eh? Save someone's life and you're responsible for them forever." For the first time that night, Cyrrie smiled a little. "I think you should ask Dr. Collins how responsible you are for her. She might have her own ideas on the subject. You may not be as stuck as you think. In the meantime, I'm going to bed and so should you."

For the next few days the aftermath of Gillian's dramatic, if involuntary, confession seemed to fill my life. Most of it was unpleasant, including the front-page photos that greeted me next morning in the copy of the *Herald* that Cyrrie brought to my room along with a cup of coffee. Another tourist, this one with a still camera and a very sharp telephoto lens, had snapped an excellent close-up of Gillian and me as the Mounties marched us to their waiting cars. I heard later that every major daily in Canada had carried the photo. In it, Gillian looked almost serene, at least the bits of her that were visible through the mud looked calm. I didn't. With my hair standing in muddy spikes all over my head, and big, round, panicky eyes staring from my clay-smeared face, I managed to look like everyone's idea of the archetypical criminal lunatic. I hardly recognized myself.

Unfortunately, no one else had that difficulty including my brothers. Both of them phoned in a panic as soon as they'd seen their morning papers. Alex's call beat Tony's because he managed to track me down at Cyrrie's house a little quicker. That meant he got in the first round of shouting. Tony made up for being second by being louder. Their shouts followed much the same themes – how could I be so stupid, what the hell did I think I was playing at, hadn't they taught me to take care of myself better than that. When Tony finally finished his rant, he promised to track down our parents in Australia and break the news to them.

I'd just stepped out of the shower when I got a call from my usually composed and rational mother, who, as soon as I'd said hello, proceeded to have fourteen thousand kilometres' worth of international hysterics. She kept calling me her baby and demanding that the Mounties throw that crazy woman in jail forever. My father didn't sound any more collected. He told me to calm down, kid, everything's fine now, calm down. Or maybe he was talking to my mother.

The rain had stopped and the morning sun had begun to dry the streets. Cyrrie made me my favourite breakfast, pancakes with maple syrup and bacon. He seemed more like his old self. He'd even started to fuss a little.

Candi and Ella rang the doorbell as I was finishing my last pancake.

"We've brought your car," Candi said. "Anything you want out of the van before Ron drives it back to the station?"

I shook my head. Ella waved and the van pulled away from the curb.

"How did you know I was here?" I asked as they came inside.

"Cyrrie called us this morning while you were still asleep to let us know you were okay," Ella said. "In case we were worried."

"Which we were," Candi added. "Very."

"Glad you're okay," Ella said. She didn't ask about the shot list, which I thought was very restrained of her.

Cyrrie whipped up more pancakes and Candi and Ella ate breakfast too.

"I'm a nursing mother," Ella stated, as if someone had asked her. "Maggie will burn off all these calories for me in no time." She buttered up her third pancake.

"We brought your car because we decided you'd better go straight home from here instead of stopping at the office," Candi said. "The place is crawling with reporters and not just ours. They're all waiting for you."

"For me?"

"Hey, you're a media darling. You're news." Candi handed me the copy of the *Sun* she'd brought with her. I had to admit those tourists were very good photographers. I looked even more deranged in this shot. "Get a load of this," Candi continued. "'FEARLESS PHOTOG SAVES SUICIDAL SCIENTIST.' How's that for a headline?"

"Worthy of a British tabloid," Cyrrie said, reading over my shoulder. "But how do they know what happened? I thought the police were keeping the details under wraps."

"Someone must have leaked it," Candi said.

"Well, they didn't leak to the CBC." Cyrrie sounded sceptical. He regards CBC Radio as Canada's touchstone of reportorial truth. Trust nothing until you hear it on *The World at Six*.

"The *Sun* says that Gillian killed Dr. Maxwell and then felt so awful about it that she wanted to die. Is that true?" Candi asked.

"She didn't kill him," I said. "It was an accident. She thinks his death was her fault, but it wasn't."

"Whatever," Ella said gloomily. "Gillian's not going to be around for a while. Maybe we should just give up on this program. Everyone's either dead or in jail."

"Cheer up, Ella," Candi encouraged. "If it was an accident, then they'll let Simon go for sure."

Ella and Candi insisted on driving me home. Ella and Bertie and I took my car. Candi followed in hers. The uniformed Mountie who had been sitting in his cruiser in front of Cyrrie's house came next. A couple of reporters had trailed Ella and Candi from the station. Their cars followed the cruiser. We made quite a convoy. I've photographed the Governor General with fewer escorts.

Ella and Candi pulled into my driveway. The Mountie stopped in front of the gate, blocking the entrance. The reporters parked their cars across the road, near the television van that had obviously been waiting for my arrival. I saw the Mountie get out of the cruiser and walk over to talk to them.

Stan's Jag was gone, but I found a note from Professor Woodward pinned to my back door. *"Everything is fine,"* it said over scrawled initials. I told Candi and Ella it was a note from my neighbour about the horses and we went inside.

They bustled around for a bit. Ella made us a pot of tea that no one drank and Candi checked the fridge to make certain I had plenty to eat on hand. Fortunately, I still had lots of supplies left over from the weekend so my nutritional future was secure. I was grateful for Candi's help, and for Ella's too, but I was glad when they each gave me a hug and left. I needed some time alone.

Except for a couple of trips to town to visit Gillian in the hospital, I spent the next few days at home working, going for walks in the hills, and avoiding reporters. The police stayed parked at the gate not to keep me in but to keep the reporters out. I switched on the answering machine and ignored any callers I didn't know. I was tempted to ignore some I did know too, like Stan and Professor Woodward. The professor called me that night.

"How are you, Phoebe? We're all very worried about you."

I assured him that I was fine.

"I know you must be a little angry with us about yesterday," he continued.

"You're right. I am. More than a little."

"I am sorry about the puddle," he said. "And about that other little matter, well, I can't say much over the phone, but Stan and I want you to know there's nothing to worry about. Everything's okay. You'll be hearing about it in a couple of days, so hang on until then."

"Do I have a choice?"

"You won't regret this, Phoebe."

"I do already," I said, but he had hung up.

The next morning a large box from a fashionable Calgary florist arrived at my door. Two dozen sprays of purple and white orchids from Stan. On a small thank-you card, he'd sketched a tiny skeleton with a big round happy face instead of a skull.

The police officer at the gate brought the box in from the delivery van. I guess the delivery man could have been a reporter in disguise. Bertie trotted importantly at his side. He'd become quite attached to Constable Dubrowski. He'd taken to spending part of the day with him in the cruiser, and not just lunch hour. I think he may have harboured secret fantasies about being a police dog. Dubrowski probably encouraged him. I know he let Bertie try on his hat.

Tim called, very worried about me and, I think, a little concerned about how I was going to bear up without his manly shoulder to lean on. He's an incurably protective man, and maybe that was one of the reasons I knew we would never make it together. He needs to take care of somebody who needs taking care of. Brooke called, too, which I found oddly touching. She sounded a little shaky at first, but once she'd determined I was fine we dropped the boring topic of my well-being and got on to the good stuff like her horse and the latest news of her pony club accomplishments. By the time we hung up, I realized that Brooke regarded me as a friend. I was going to miss her too.

By the weekend, Maxwell's fossils were back on page one and I was pretty much yesterday's news. The fossils had been found. According to our station's Friday-evening news, an anonymous tip – surprise, surprise – had led police and museum officials to the Royal Tyrrell's storage area, where the fossils were discovered, slightly damaged but all present. It was suspected that the bones had never left the building. The police denied emphatically that the aborted theft was in any way connected to the recent tragic death of world-famous . . . I switched the television off. Professor Woodward called right after the news. "Have you heard?" he asked. I told him I had. "Well? Well?"

"I'm glad it's over."

"And without a hitch. Whole thing went smooth as butter," he chortled. "Say, is it all right if Stan and I come out to your place sometime soon. Stan would like to talk to you. Me too."

"Give me a call before you come to make sure I'm home," I said.

"Then all is forgiven?"

"Don't push your luck."

Saturday morning Cyrrie phoned to tell me he'd read in the *Herald* that the police had released Simon from jail.

"Listen to this." He read from the paper, "'According to a police spokesperson, new evidence has been brought forward which clears Simon Visser of all blame in his employer's tragic death.' Can't think why the police are being so coy. New evidence, my foot. All of Calgary knows Gillian Collins's story." I heard the rustle of paper as he turned the page. "They go on to say that as soon as Simon got out of jail he checked himself into a rehab clinic."

"That's good news," I said.

"How's Gillian?" he asked. "Has she said anything yet?"

"Nope. I went to see her yesterday. She's still staring at the wall. I'm going again this afternoon."

"Why don't you drop Bertie off at my place and stay for dinner when you come to pick him up?"

"Sounds like a good idea. Thanks," I said. "Can Bertie bring Constable Dubrowski with him? I think they're partners now."

"Are the police still at your house?"

"Dubrowski says he's on this assignment until at least Monday. Maybe they'll have decided whether or not they're going to charge Gillian with something by then."

"I expect they can't do much until she can answer some questions."

The police had transferred Gillian to the psychiatric ward of the Foothills Hospital. So far, she hadn't uttered a word. She ate now and then, she slept, she dressed in the clothes that were put out for her, but for the rest she stared at the world in silence. The police had posted a guard at the door to her room and the hospital had her under a round-the-clock suicide watch. I had visited her twice, hating every minute that I spent watching her look at nothing while I babbled inane pleasantries. Keep talking to her, the medical staff had encouraged me, keep talking. Even if you don't get a response, keep trying. The breakthrough came that afternoon.

"Hi, Gillian," I called out full of false cheer as I walked into her room and settled into a chair. Gillian sat on the bed, still staring at the wall. Her minder hurried out of the room, grateful for the impromptu coffee break.

"Gosh, it's a beautiful day out there, a real feeling of autumn in the air. I went for a walk with my dog this morning. I saw a deer and her fawn. The fawn is looking big now. You know, when you're feeling better you'll have to come out to my place and go walking with us," I prattled on. "Say, maybe we could get permission to go for a walk near the hospital."

Then it happened. Gillian turned away from her wall to face me.

"Fuck off, you stupid cow, and leave me alone," she shrieked at the top of her lungs. "You're driving me mad. Fuck off! Fuck off! *Fuck off!*"

The medical staff came running. Gillian continued to scream obscenities at me. The nurses were delighted. Such progress. Gillian's doctor thanked me for my good work and then suggested that perhaps I shouldn't visit for the foreseeable future. Their patient seemed a touch hostile toward me. It was my turn to be delighted. Gillian hated my guts. Cyrrie was right. I wasn't stuck with her.

"Fuck off," Gillian wailed. "Fuck off."

And so I did. I walked to the elevators with a light heart. Her curses echoed after me down the corridor. It wasn't wishful thinking. Gillian really and truly loathed me.

I met Simon coming in the door of the hospital just as I was leaving. He seemed pleased to see me.

"Have you been to visit Gillian?" he asked.

"I've just come from her room."

"She's very lucky you were at the museum that afternoon," he said. "She gave you a bad time, didn't she? It must have been very frightening."

"She gave herself a worse one," I said.

"Graham taught her how to use that gun. I can't think why she packed the stupid thing and brought it here. Habit, most likely."

"Do you know how to shoot it?"

"Me? I've never touched a gun in my life." Simon was shocked at the suggestion. "That pistol was strictly Graham and Gillian's business. Has she said anything yet?" he asked.

"She managed a few words this afternoon," I said. "Her doctor seems encouraged."

"Poor Gill. What a price to pay for loving someone."

"How are you?" I asked. "I heard you'd checked into a rehab clinic."

"I have," he said. "All things considered, it seemed like a good idea."

"Did they give you a pass or something?"

"It's a clinic, Phoebe, not a jail. I'm allowed out," he laughed. "Are you in a hurry or may I buy you a cup of tea? They must have a restaurant somewhere in this place."

We found the hospital cafeteria and bought cups of what turned out to be excellent coffee. Simon's little silver flask was nowhere to be seen.

"You know, for a few days while I was in jail I really believed I'd killed Graham," he said. "It's an appalling thing to think that you've murdered someone. That you were so drunk you can't remember doing it only makes it worse."

"But you didn't kill him," I said.

"No, I didn't. And I can't describe how I felt when my lawyer told me Gillian had admitted what really happened that night. Like I'd been given a whole new life, I guess. That's when I decided to check into the clinic. Nothing like this is going to happen to me again. Ever."

"Why did it take until Friday for the police to let you go? I thought you'd be out much sooner."

"I don't think they're all that keen on letting a perfectly good murder suspect walk away free. I'd probably still be sitting in jail while they checked things out for the hundredth time if it hadn't been for my lawyer. She not only got them to let me go, they dropped all the charges too. Thank you, Betty Chan," he raised his eyes as he named one of Calgary's top criminal lawyers.

"You mean Betty Chan, herself, personally, came down to the pokey and got you out?" I said.

"She did," Simon said. "And she has agreed to take Gillian on too. Mrs. Chan is a gem."

In a way, Simon was right. From what I'd heard Betty Chan was a pearl with one hell of a price, a brilliant lawyer who knew what she was worth.

"Fortunately the new foundation is paying all our legal expenses," Simon continued. "The fellow who's starting it has guaranteed them."

"What foundation is this?"

"The Graham Maxwell Foundation for Research and Education in Paleoanthropology. It's being established by a very rich old college chum of Graham's. Ever heard of Stanley Darling?

"Phoebe, are you okay?" Simon thumped me on the back. "What happened? Did your coffee go down the wrong way?"

"I'll be fine in a minute," I gasped. My eyes ran and coffee dribbled out my nose.

Simon handed me a paper napkin. He waited while I mopped up the damage.

"I'd better be on my way," he said. "The police have given me permission to visit Gillian at four. Do you think she'll talk to me?"

"Who knows? You could be lucky."

I walked him to the elevators.

"Phoebe," he said. "Perhaps when I'm finished at the rehab clinic we could go out together somewhere, maybe for a meal or something. I'd like to see you again before I go back to Kenya. Very much."

"I'd like that too, Simon," I said.

Monday came and there was no police cruiser at my gate. No reporters either. My fifteen minutes had come and gone. Ella called that afternoon. She'd set up a new time for me to finish my work at the museum. She offered to send another photographer, but I told her I'd go.

This time, Carla Ainsworth stuck to me like gum in a kid's hair. She didn't let me out of her sight except when I had to use the washroom. Then she stood outside the cubicle and waited for me. I wasn't alone at the museum for a second. Actually, I was glad. I'd felt a little uneasy about going back to the Royal Tyrrell. Carla's presence was comforting. She also helped with the equipment.

I finished the afternoon with shots of *Homo musicus*. The fossil copies had arrived from Kenya and the display was ready to open again. The real bones were in a vault waiting for Simon to escort them back to Maxwell's lab in Nairobi, where they'd be repaired. They would probably be ready to rejoin the exhibit by the end of December.

In the meantime, Jim and Gloria had done an excellent reassembly job with the fakes. Simon had taken a morning away from rehab to come to the museum and check their work. It was still a wonderful exhibit, first-rate in every respect, but for me the magic had gone with the real bones.

Ella managed to put together what turned out to be an amazingly good hour. Even the sunrise shots worked, much to my surprise. The season's first *A Day in the Lifestyle* garnered the highest ratings in the program's history and our station's national network picked up the program, which pleased Ella no end. They sold it to an American network too, which delighted her even more.

"Not too shabby for a local lifestyles program," she crowed. And it wasn't.

Stan and Professor Woodward came to visit. Things were a little stiff at first. I made a pot of tea, which we took out to the deck. Bertie followed, glad of the company. He missed Constable Dubrowski.

"You're not still mad about that mud puddle, are you?" the professor asked.

"No. I'm still mad about the fossils."

"That's why we're here," Stan said. "We'd like to explain."

"Stan, you gave me your word," I said. "Your word as a Christian."

"And he kept it," the professor said. "He told you he'd have those fossils back in the museum the next morning and he did. The bones were in the Royal Tyrrell before noon."

"So he and Myrna and the rest of the Geologists for Jesus get to waltz away scot-free, like nothing ever happened."

"Exactly," Professor Woodward said. "And what harm will that do? They're not what I'd call hardened criminals."

"Adam, maybe you'd better let me explain," Stan said. "You see, Phoebe, right after we left your place we heard the news on the truck radio that the police had arrested Simon Visser for Graham's murder. We knew right then that none of the Geologists for Jesus could possibly have been involved. The police didn't need our help finding Graham's killer, they'd done it themselves. So I decided that if I could return the bones to the museum anonymously, then I'd have kept faith with you and protected my friends as well. It was the perfect solution."

"It was the only solution, Stan," the professor said.

"The Geologists for Jesus stole those fossils," I said. "They committed a serious crime. That didn't change just because the police arrested Simon. Stan's solution has simply made us all co-conspirators."

"I do think you're being very prissy about this, Phoebe," Professor Woodward said. "Who's been hurt?"

"I'm sorry you feel that way," Stan said. "And I'll always be grateful to you for helping me. I believe you have a good heart, Phoebe, and you followed it. You may think now that what you did was wrong, but I know it wasn't."

I should have learned by now that it was pointless to argue with Stan. You can't argue with belief.

"Don't you want to know how we got the fossils back into the museum?" Professor Woodward obviously longed to tell me.

"You smuggled them in hidden in your micro fossil cabinet." I was not longing to listen. He looked crestfallen. "I saw the cabinet when I was taping in the storage area." I didn't bother to add that I'd managed to find the fossils too. Or that we'd spent the afternoon together on a shelf. That one I'd take to my grave.

"But that was the easy part," the professor said, recovering his enthusiasm. "You should have seen us the night before. We were up most of the night."

"Diana helped us," Stan said.

"Helped us! Hell, we couldn't have done it without her," the professor laughed. "First she put down a big sheet of plastic on the kitchen table and made us empty the bones out of those orange garbage bags onto it. Then she gave us each a pair of rubber gloves and had us wipe every single one of the bones with a damp J-cloth. She got out a fresh package of garbage bags, never been opened, and we put the clean fossils in them. Then she rustled up a couple of old liquor cartons that someone had left in the parking garage. That's where we put the bags. We wore gloves all the time. There wasn't so much as a smudge on all that stuff, let alone a fingerprint. There was no way those fossils could be traced to us."

"Diana thought of everything," Stan added with a sigh. "She was magnificent. I can't imagine how she knew what to do."

"She watches *Law & Order*," Professor Woodward said. "Never misses an episode. She's very up on forensics."

"How did you get the bones out of your building?" I asked. It was weak of me, but I couldn't help it. It was the only part of the story I didn't know. "You must have realized that Myrna and her friends were watching you."

"They weren't exactly subtle, were they, Stan?" The professor snorted dismissively. "What a clueless lot. We lost them at a McDonald's and we weren't even trying.

We actually hoped they'd keep following us. Thought that would keep them away from Diana. You see, Diana had the fossils with her in our neighbour's SUV. We're looking after his apartment while he's on holiday in Europe. He left us a set of keys, including the one to his Blazer. I didn't think he'd mind if we borrowed it for a worthy cause."

"It was all part of Adam's plan," Stan said. "We left the parking garage early the next morning in the truck. Two of the Geologists for Jesus followed us. Doris and Bill, I think."

"Diana and the fossils left the house about a half-hour later in the SUV. She drove to the Earth Sciences building and brought the boxes up to my office. It was all child's play from there. The hardest part was manhandling the cabinet onto a pallet so we could get the jack on it. Even without the drawers the damn thing weighs a ton. But we managed."

"Diana helped with that too," Stan said.

"We hid the fossils inside it, took the whole lot down to the loading dock in back of the building, and wheeled them into the geology department's van. Then we left for Drumheller. Diana drove. Stan and I hid in back with the fossils until we were sure no one was following us. Then we dropped Diana off and carried on from there."

"She took the LRT home from the Jubilee Auditorium." No detail concerning Diana was too trivial for Stan to cherish.

"I guess there's not much more to tell," the professor said, but he told it anyway right up to when I'd seen them drive away from the museum in the van.

"We were going to contact the people at the Royal Tyrrell the next day," Stan said when Professor Woodward had finished. "But after what happened to you in that storage room with Dr. Collins, we thought we'd better give things some time to cool down."

"So you see, Phoebe, the fossils were never in any real danger." Professor Woodward was enormously pleased with himself. "Don't you feel better now that you know what happened?"

"I might if I knew the Geologists for Jesus won't ever do anything like that again."

"The Geologists for Jesus doesn't exist any longer. They've been disbanded," Stan said. I wondered what Myrna thought about that. Someone with her militant views and considerable cleverness might not be all that easy to discourage. "Myrna has formed a new group," Stan explained as if he'd read my mind. "Betting on God – they're part of a Christian anti-gambling movement. She's taking on video lottery terminals." I almost felt sorry for the gambling bureaucracy, but only for a moment. All things considered, they probably deserved Myrna.

"Stanley's moving on to new things too," the professor said. "He's establishing a foundation in Graham's name. The Graham Maxwell Foundation for Research and Education in Paleoanthropology. Stan's the CEO."

"I've asked Simon Visser to be the foundation's first director," Stan said. "He'll start work as soon as he gets out of his rehab clinic."

"This foundation is going to do wonderful things, Phoebe. And with Graham's name on the letterhead, raising money will be a piece of cake. Best thing he ever did for paleontology was stand under that egg."

"Hold on there, Adam," Stan admonished, although he didn't actually disagree. "After all, the poor fellow is dead."

"Stan reckons he can have an expedition ready for a dig next year, don't you, Stan?"

"That is Simon's estimate," Stan affirmed cautiously. "I tell you that man has some amazing ideas. *Homo musicus* is nothing compared to some of the things Simon's got up his sleeve."

"And you can bet your bottom dollar that embarrassment of a name will be a thing of the past," said Professor Woodward.

Stan agreed. "Simon says that the first thing he's going to do when he leaves the clinic is publish a scientific description of the fossils and give them a proper name."

"Well, are you going to ask her or not?" the professor said.

"Ask me what?" I said with a sinking heart.

"I don't know whether I should, Phoebe," Stan said. "I wouldn't want you to get the idea that I'm making you this offer as a bribe to keep you quiet or as a reward for helping us do something that I know you thought was wrong. All that's over now. At least it is for me and I hope it is for you too. I'm asking you this because you're an excellent photographer and I need your professional skills. But you mustn't feel that . . ."

"For God's sake, get on with it, Stan," the professor urged. "Just spit it out."

"Phoebe, the Graham Maxwell Foundation is going to need a photographer to document its digs and I wondered if you might consider taking on the job?" Stan said. "Of course, it wouldn't be full-time – a few months a year at most – but I assure you the work will be interesting and the pay will make it worth your while. I do hope you'll consider my offer."

"What do you mean consider it? She'll be delighted, won't you, Phoebe?" The professor beamed.

Before I had a chance to shout yes, Stan chimed in again. "You don't need to answer right now. Take some time to think about it," he said. "If you have questions, give me a call." He looked at his watch. "Good grief, that can't be the time. I really must be on my way. I can't afford to be late today."

"What's so important?" I asked.

"I'm meeting Rabbi Reddick and Bishop Thompson for lunch. The pastor from my church is coming too. I'm planning the memorial service and I want to get their input."

"You're planning Dr. Maxwell's memorial service?" I said, not believing my ears. "I thought his ashes had been shipped to Kenya."

"No, no, no. It isn't for Graham," Stan said. "This memorial is for the fossils, for the *Homo musicus* family. I think an ecumenical service would be most appropriate. Don't you?"

ACKNOWLEDGEMENTS

Many people helped me with this book. First, thanks to my friend Meinwen Jones, who grew up in Drumheller when it was a coal-mining town and remembers the miners and a way of life now vanished from the prairies. I am also grateful to the staff of the Royal Tyrrell Museum of Palaeontology. Dr. Phil Currie, whose professional life is an object lesson in what it means to be busy, gave very generously of his time. Likewise, Dr. Don Brinkman, Mary Greene, Marty Eberth, and Dr. Bruce Naylor did their best to initiate a total neophyte into the ways of their wonderful institution. Thanks as well to Dr. Jisuo Jin, formerly of the Royal Tyrrell Museum, now of the University of Western Ontario, who took me on my first behind-the-scenes tour of the museum during which the idea for this book was planted. I am also indebted to Linde Turner, head librarian at the Drumheller Public Library, for help with the Drumheller details. Needless to say, everything I got right is thanks to Linde, everything I didn't is mine alone. The same holds true for the geological details on which Dr. Glen Caldwell did his best to set me straight — the successes in this endeavour are all his, the failures mine.

In any case, he has my thanks, as does Marika Williams, whose valiant efforts to guide my amateur way through the complex paths of paleoanthropology are much appreciated. Getting the details accurate is always a challenge, but this work has been made a pleasure by my friends Larry Custead, classical scholar and Latin lover, and Gary Von Kuster, a photographer as talented as Phoebe Fairfax. Gary taught Phoebe everything she knows about television photography. Thanks as well to Christopher Power of the National Communications Services of the RCMP and Nancy Jackson of the Fairmont Palliser Hotel in Calgary, who both helped to smooth some rough edges. As always, I am grateful to Martha Gould, first reader of my work, whose fine eye and understanding heart are invaluable to me. A correctly spelled, properly hyphenated thanks, plus a bag full of monogrammed commas, to Heather Sangster, the eagle-eyed copy editor who knows more about the details of my work than I do myself. And finally, I owe a debt of gratitude to my editor, Dinah Forbes, for her patience and encouragement, and the pleasure of working with her once again.

SEEING IS DECEIVING

Phoebe Fairfax, photographer for the TV show *A Day in a Lifestyle*, is one of the sharpest and funniest sleuths you'll find in any mystery. In her latest adventure, Phoebe and her colleague Candi Sinclair are filming at a psychics' fair when one of the exhibitors collapses and dies. He's been poisoned in a most unusual way, and the police suspect his common-law wife of murder. She's an old friend of Candi's, who turns to Phoebe for help in proving the police wrong. The quick-witted and wry duo are soon chin deep in the world of fortune-tellers, loan sharks, and matters that seem to defy explanation.

0-7710-6806-9
$7.99

THE GLASS COFFIN:
A JOANNE KILBORN MYSTERY

"BOWEN SURPASSES HERSELF."
– TORONTO STAR

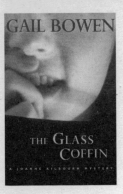

0-7710-1499-6
$34.99

This chilling tale about the power of the ties that bind – and sometimes blind – us, is Gail Bowen's best novel yet. Set in the world of television and film, *The Glass Coffin* explores the depth of tragedy that a camera's neutral eye can capture – and cause.

Canada's favourite sleuth, Joanne Kilbourn, is dismayed to learn the identity of the man her best friend, Jill Osiowy, is about to marry. Evan MacLeish may be a celebrated documentary filmmaker, but he has also exploited the lives – and deaths – of the two wives he lost to suicide by making acclaimed films about them. It's obvious to Joanne that this is stony ground on which to found a marriage. What is not obvious is that this ground is about to get bloodsoaked.

"The end . . . is chilling and unexpected."
– Globe and Mail

"[*A Glass Coffin*] takes the series into a deeper dimension."
– Times-Colonist

"Part of Bowen's magic – and her work is just that – lies not only in her richness of characters but in her knack of lacing her stories with out-of-left-field descriptives."
– Ottawa Citizen

DEADLY APPEARANCES

A JOANNE KILBOURN MYSTERY BY
GAIL BOWEN
DEADLY APPEARANCES

NOW THE MAJOR CTV MOVIE DEADLY

Andy Boychuk is a successful politician until one sweltering August afternoon when all of the key people in Boychuk's life – family, friends, enemies – gather at a picnic to celebrate his recent election as leader of his party. While he gathers his thoughts for his speech, he takes a sip of water from a glass on the lectern. Within seconds he is dead.

Joanne Kilbourn, in her first case as Canada's pre-eminent amateur detective, can't believe Boychuk was murdered by his wife, Eve, but what little evidence there is appears to implicate her. The trail Joanne follows as she tries to clear Eve's name leads to a Bible college too good to be true, long-held secrets powerful enough to die for, and a murderer who's about to strike again.

0-7710-1491-0
$9.99

MURDER AT THE MENDEL

0-7710-1492-9
$9.99

"FILTH BELONGS IN TOILETS NOT ON WALLS"

That's what one of the placards reads at a raucous demonstration marking the opening of a controversial exhibition at Saskatoon's famous Mendel Art Gallery. The protesters' target is the painting *Erotobiography*, a large, sexually explicit fresco by the beautiful, internationally acclaimed Saskatchewan painter, Sally Love.

Joanne Kilbourn is among the guests at the show's opening party, where she renews her friendship with the painter. All too soon, Joanne is ensnared in a web of intrigue, violence, and murder woven by Sally's art-world friends, her estranged family, and her former lovers.

THE WANDERING SOUL MURDERS

Joanne Kilbourn's sunny May morning is darkened when her daughter, Mieka, phones to say that she has just discovered the corpse of a young woman in an alley near her store. Just twenty-four hours later, Joanne is in for another terrible shock when her son's girlfriend drowns in a lake in Saskatchewan's Qu'Appelle Valley.

The two dead women had just one thing in common: each had spent time at the Lily Pad, a drop-in centre for Regina's street kids. By the time Joanne realizes the connection, she is deeply embroiled in a twilight world where money can buy everything – and there are always people willing to pay.

0-7710-1494-5
$9.99

A COLDER KIND
OF DEATH

A JOANNE KILBOURN MYSTERY BY
GAIL BOWEN
A COLDER KIND OF DEATH

NOW ON VIDEO
CBC MOVIE

0-7710-1495-3
$9.99

When the man convicted of killing her husband six years earlier is himself shot to death while exercising in a prison yard, Joanne Kilbourn is forced to relive the most horrible time of her life. And when the prisoner's menacing wife is found strangled by Joanne's scarf a few days later, Joanne is the prime suspect.

To clear her name, Joanne has to delve into some very murky party politics and tangled loyalties. Worse, she has to confront the most awful question – had her husband been cheating on her?

A KILLING SPRING

The fates just won't ignore Joanne Kilbourn – single mom, university professor, and Canada's favourite amateur sleuth. When the head of the School of Journalism is found dead – wearing women's lingerie – it falls to Joanne to tell his new wife. And that's only the beginning of Joanne's woes. A few days later the school is vandalized and then an unattractive and unpopular student in Joanne's class goes missing. When she sets out to investigate the student's disappearance, Joanne steps unknowingly into an on-campus world of fear, deceit – and murder.

0-7710-1486-4
$7.99

VERDICT IN BLOOD

"A seamless blend of honest emotion and artistry." – *The Chicago Tribune*

GAIL BOWEN

VERDICT IN BLOOD
A Joanne Kilbourn Mystery

0-7710-1489-5
$8.99

It's a hot Labour Day weekend in Regina, Saskatchewan, which means the annual Dragon Boat races in Wascana Park, a CFL game, family barbecues, ice cream – and tragedy. A young man is missing. And Madam Justice Justine Blackwell has been bludgeoned to death.

This is Gail Bowen's sixth novel featuring Joanne Kilbourn, one of Canada's most beloved sleuths. Teacher, friend, lover, single mother, and now grandmother, Joanne's quick intelligence and boundless compassion repeatedly get her into – and out of – trouble.